Baby Fever Promise

A Billionaire Second Chance Romance

Nicole Snow

Published in the United States of America.
First published in January, 2017.

Disclaimer: The following book is a work of fiction. Any resemblance characters in this story may have to real people is only coincidental.

Cover Design – CoverLuv.
Photo by Sara Eirew Photography.
Formatting –Polgarus Studio

Description

WE CAN'T DO THIS AGAIN. I'M FAKING OUR SECOND CHANCE...

ROBBI

Once, Lucus Shaw was my everything.

First kiss. First surrender. First man to promise me a ring, children, a life together.

I remember his rogue smirk, his soul stinging kiss, the blistering words that always made him a little dangerous.

I gave him my body for one insatiable night. He gave me secrets, heartbreak, and hatred.

Friends, to lovers, to mortal enemies. Our tragic destiny.

But I survived. Adapted. Moved on.

Fate doesn't care.

Luke's back, and I have to pretend we still have a Cinderella romance to save my career.

Hate never fades. It rages when we lie to the world, when we lust, even when I'm begging for his baby.

What if hate can't save me anymore? What if the man I swore I'd never give a second chance gives me baby fever for real?

LUKE

I was her first, and I'll damned sure be her last. I made a promise.

Robbi's an addiction I can't quit. A million of her icy looks won't make me forget what we had.

How delicious she looked when I brought her to her knees. How she ached for more. How she ripped my heart out when vicious lies ended us.

This isn't over. Love never fades. I'll make our fake kisses real.

It's not too late to have it all: my ring on her hand, my name on her lips, my baby in her.

She'll beg for me again before we're done playing pretend. Oh, how she'll *beg*.

I: Hello, Again (Robin)

Every girl knows about reckless men.

Reckless in the best ways, when they pick you up like a glass paperweight and hold you high, tilting fate just right until you're glowing in the light of their kiss.

Reckless because they always let you fall.

Always, I said. No exceptions.

Sometimes they let go, gently watching as you drift down like a feather after they've had their fun. Other times, they hurl you down as hard as a stone skipping over water, shattering everything you thought you were into a hundred vicious smithereens when you hit their world at full breakneck speed.

Reckless with hearts. Reckless with life. Reckless in the good, the bad, the ugly, and the oh-so-irresistible. Reckless because they'll never, ever be tamed.

I fell for a reckless man once.

He was my first, and deep down, I think I knew he'd be my last. He put me through hell, and he still hasn't left my side.

He taught me there's not much difference between the words *reckless* and *forever.*

* * * *

"Seven percent, Robbi, just like we agreed. Frankly, I think it's a crime my cut for making you the happiest little bird on earth is so low. Drinks are on you tonight."

Little bird. I hate when she uses that nickname because I instantly recall where I've heard it before.

Of course, she doesn't mean anything by it. She doesn't mean it like him.

Words shouldn't bother me. I'm used to Bebe Silk's antics after working with her the past six months. But nothing could've prepared me for today, when she's sitting across from me, more smug than a Cheshire cat.

I reach for the thick stack of papers she's pushed in front of me. The Berkland Studios logo gleams forest green in the header, brighter than emerald. My hands are shaking.

"Holy shit. I can't believe this."

"Believe, doll. The world's about to know you as the hottest little starlet since...well, since anything, if Mr. Pierce Rogan has anything to say about it. The film simply can't fail in his capable hands. That man could make a mouse swoon after a cat on the silver screen. This is the big break we've been waiting for." Like I don't know it. Her grin gets wider, and she clasps her hands, leaning over the desk while she beams. "Congratulations, Allison Evers."

"Allison Evers," I repeat the name, wondering how many times it'll take before it doesn't feel strange on my lips.

It's almost as incredible as hearing a legend like Pierce

Rogan is directing the film. He's made classics, works of art, and entire careers. Bebe isn't exaggerating this time, as she's often prone to do – Pierce's talent means people will be talking about Allison Evers and the woman who played her when I'm in my wheelchair.

I can't believe it's happening, but it is. The miracle I've been hoping for ever since I clawed my way up the Hollywood heights has officially arrived.

It's the sexiest, strangest kind of hocus pocus a plucky young actress could ask for. I'm playing the female lead in *Bare.*

Hundreds of millions – hell, maybe *billions* – of women worldwide are going to fill the seats for earth's biggest erotic thriller. The book only sold enough copies to rival the Bible, after all, and fan legions will line up to see how well the movie edition jives with their imaginations.

Bebe wags her finger, several thick rings on her hand jostling underneath the dull office light. "Initial in the corner of every page, please. All fifty. There's a line for a proper signature on the last one, and one for me as your very talented agent."

I run my finger down the first page, tracing legalese I can't possibly comprehend in this excitement. Bebe laughs, slaps my hand away, and guides the pen in my fingers down to the corner.

"Let's move this along, Robbi. I promised the studio I'd have it sent back by closing time. Don't you worry about the fine print, I've proofed it all myself this morning. Ran it by the lawyer I work with. No nasty surprises. Just a whole lot of fortune and fame, exactly the way mama likes."

For a second, I hesitate. My saner side says I should take my time, read through every last sentence, make sure I'm not being trapped or cheated in a lead role bigger than anything I've had before.

But if it wasn't for the shark in the red blouse and jacket across from me, I wouldn't have it at all. Someone else would be playing Allison Evers, and it would be their bare ass taking a paddling on the screen instead of mine for stardom.

Oh, God. The whole world is really going to see my ass, isn't it?

I swallow, promising I'll make peace with the sex scenes later, and start initialing.

I knew what I was getting into when I auditioned for the part. No one who hasn't been stuck in a cave has any illusions about *Bare* by Isabella Frieze.

They know about the sex, the scandal, the dirty, kinky things that are probably going to break all kinds of world records by showing up in a mainstream film for the very first time. They know how sheltered Ali loses her virginity and half her soul to the most powerful man in Chicago, how he breaks her, and how she surrenders *everything* by the end.

They know about Frieze's fanatics. Millions of adoring readers who made her book a global hit, and at least one ocean of money for her and her publishers to swim in.

They also know they're not really there to see a virgin go through losing it on her way to baby fever, or to stroke Ms. Frieze's enormous ego.

The real star is Miles Black, the tortured, broody enigma. Cold, domineering, completely covered in tattoos. I can't remember whether I melted or burst our laughing the first time I read the scene where he grabs her chin, presses his forehead to hers, and stares into her eyes for ten minutes like an obsessed maniac.

Okay, so I'm not the target demographic for sexy romance. But it still made me wet when I read the sex, rolling the paragraphs over in my mind where the billionaire finally claimed his prey, and took her night after night, flinging her body against his as they fucked like the earth itself had to be repopulated.

I'm thinking about how I had to close the book and reach for my nearest vibrator when another question grabs me.

"So, who's playing Miles? Have you heard?" I'm halfway through the papers, slurring my initials with the pen. I bite my cheek, expecting Bebe to tell me I'll be working with a household name sculpted like a Greek God.

That adds a whole new layer of anxiety, of course, but I don't care if I have to work with Zeus himself. I'm not screwing this up for anything.

"Oh, wait till you see him!" she chirps, spinning in her chair, reaching for the folder behind her. "He's a name I don't recognize. New to a major lead, but I guess the studio chose him for other qualities. Like you, he's only had a few supporting roles. He's *hot,* of course, and I saw his social media has quite a presence. I expect that's why the studio decided to take a gamble on another newcomer. Ah, here he is!"

She pulls out a photo, and pushes it over to me. It's a tall, dark, and very handsome looking young man in a leather jacket. Something about the glint in his eye causes my stomach to fold in on itself. It isn't until I hold the photo up, catching the full brilliance of his trademark blue eyes, that my heart comes to a screeching halt.

No. No fucking way.

"Jesus!" My fingers slip while I sputter a one word prayer. The picture drops from my hands and slides down to Bebe's desk.

She snatches it up with a frown on her face, giving me a concerned look. "What's this? Hey, are you okay, Robbi? Don't tell me you've worked with him before?"

If only *work* was all it had been.

If only my nightmare, my heartbreak, my reckless and stupid first crush weren't staring at me from a glossy printout, wearing the same icy blue eyes and soul destroying smirk as the day I last saw him.

"Robin!" Bebe pats my hand like she's tenderizing a piece of meat. "Do you need some water? Maybe a little fresh air?"

"It's nothing. I'm fine." Falser words were never spoken. I'm sure all the blood has left my face. I contort my lips, forcing a smile. "Sorry. It's just the excitement, that's all. I really can't believe I'm sitting here, signing a contract to play Allison freakin' Evers."

"Believe, doll! You've *earned* it." Relieved, she reaches under her desk, and comes up smiling with a water bottle. "Take a few swigs. I insist. Can't have you collapsing before

I've gotten the contract out the door."

I obey, taking a few precious extra seconds to chug the water. I'm not sure whether they're a relief or pure torture, amplifying the claustrophobic feel of the world closing in around me.

I'm putting the ink on my greatest success. I should have known these kinds of wins always come with hellish challenges.

I try to turn my eyes away from the photo I've pushed back toward my agent. *Look anywhere. Anywhere except him, damn it.*

Just get through this.

Easier said than done. I think I'll manage to finish signing my contract today without letting Lucus Shaw ruin me for a second time.

But when it comes time to actually film with him, to pretend we're professionals? When I'm supposed to act infatuated, in love, and totally not bothered by him shoving my wrists into handcuffs while he whispers how he's going to 'fuck the baby fever straight out of me?' No exaggerating, that's one of Ms. Frieze's most memorable lines from the book.

I stop, I try to breathe, and I wonder. *What sin did I commit in a past life to deserve this?*

Bebe taps her long red nails impatiently. I pull the water bottle away, realizing I've drained it. I give her an uneasy smile before I set it down, pick up my pen, and finish the signature party.

"Perfect!" She practically jumps out of her seat when I

push the documents into her hands. She bends over the scanner behind her, feeding in page after page, never giving me a second glance until the machine is done.

Plenty of time to promise myself over and over I'm not going to throw up all over her office. When Bebe turns around, her hands are on her hips. She's looking at me like a concerned mother.

"I'll have the details in the morning. Now, go home and get some rest, Robbi. Just between you and me, you look like shit. Hell, are you running a fever?"

I cringe as she presses her palm to my forehead. She lets out a low whistle. "You're freezing, dear. My God, don't tell me you're allergic to success?"

"Obviously, this much takes some getting used to," I say weakly.

She starts laughing, falling back into her seat, folding her arms in a self-embrace. "It's a joke, for heaven's sake. I'm serious about the rest, though." She sits up straight, leans forward, wagging her finger in my face. "I need you in tip-top shape when everything starts moving next week. Give me sexy, doll, and I'll give you the whole damned universe."

"I've worked too hard to get here. I won't let you down, Bebe." I shake hands with my agent, questioning her sanity for the thousandth time, and then head out the door.

The Uber ride home to my apartment is just a blur. So is crawling into bed, hugging my body pillow tight, and doing my very best not to press my face into it, screaming.

The walls here are paper thin. Plus I'm going to be a world famous actress soon, if bad memories don't kill me first. I don't need to invite any surprise recordings from nosey neighbors, happy to beam fresh weirdness into the world for nothing more than Likes and Retweets.

I'm slumped and fuming for about thirty minutes before I walk to my kitchen, grab the half-depleted vodka bottle, and slam down a couple shots so straight they make me gag.

The buzz doesn't help.

I doubt anything can. A hundred twists of hell couldn't have prepared me to face what's coming, and Luke did them all.

The bastard destroyed me once. In any just universe, that ought to be enough.

Not here. Not now. If I want to make my dreams come true, I have to give him a second chance.

How does that old saying go? Maybe I should add my own twist.

Ruin me once, shame on you.

Ruin me twice...shame on everything.

* * * *

Five Years Ago

It's the loneliest place in the world, and I'm supposed to live there.

I never thought I'd miss Chicago. I never liked the twenty-four hour lights, the constant whoosh of traffic, the three a.m. thunder of trains pounding through Union Station. When my parents first told me we'd be moving out of the city to Shaw estate almost an hour into rural Illinois, it sounded like a dream come true.

That was before we moved into the empty servants' quarters about several acres from the billionaire's sprawling palace. If I only had to hang back and look through the overgrown gardens at their sleek modern castle, it wouldn't be so bad.

But mom won't stop hounding me over working part time inside the house. She wants me dusting, cleaning toilets, washing dishes, whatever makes easy money for a girl going into her senior year of high school.

Saying no isn't an option when she acts like she's done me a massive favor. I'm expected to be on my best behavior, too, with both my parents on the Shaw payroll.

Their name is all over Chicago. They've built landmarks and soaring skyscrapers in the city and God knows how many other places for generations. By some stroke of luck, mom fit the bill for Mr. Shaw's new head of household management, and dad moved up in personal accounting.

Not corporate, but the kind that lets him oversee running the property. He moves their money to pay invoices owed to every service under the sun, ensuring no Shaw ever needs to lift a finger again. He executes the household shopping lists, processes maintenance requests, and does his best to satisfy everything at the lowest prices.

Yes, these people are so damned rich they don't even do their own shopping.

As for mom, she's taken over the head cleaner role. It's her job to make sure the Shaw's hygiene needs are met efficiently. One look at the place tells me her job is important, and at least one member of the family probably lives up to the germaphobe stereotype I've seen wealthy elites have in so many movies.

It's spotless. Pristine. Empty.

The place seems deserted the first week I'm working there after school. I never see Mr. Shaw or any of his sons.

I meet the full time maids, and take on their extra work. One of them guides me to a wing of the house that looks more like a museum than anything lived in.

"The first two rooms, you're welcome to walk through, tidy up, and wipe down," an older woman named Valerie tells me. "They belonged to the older Shaw sons, and they've both moved on. If they come home to visit, you'll have plenty of notice. It's the last room, down at the very end of the hall, that's...shall we say, off limits." She hesitates.

"Oh?" I ask, raising an eyebrow.

"Master Lucus lives there, the only Shaw boy left who still lives here full time. Don't worry, you won't be seeing much of him," she says, taking her hands off the cleaning cart she's helped me put together. "But if you do, if you're smart, you'll stay the hell out of his way."

Her face looks puckered, like simply mentioning him leaves a sour taste in her mouth. I wonder if this is a joke?

Some kind of hazing ritual the girls put new people through? This place is uber-creepy enough with everything looking picture perfect. If she's trying to make me jittery, well, it's mission accomplished.

"I'd better go," Valerie says. "The gardener needs an

extra hand today. Find me out there if you need anything, Robin. Give my best to your mom if you see her."

She takes off, leaving me alone. That's how it goes for the first week. I walk through the old bedrooms, empty except for their furniture, toiletries, and a few photographs. I call them rooms, but each one is more like its own private condo, complete with a kitchen, a balcony, and a bathroom bigger than our living room.

I'm cleaning the wing I've been assigned for the fourth time when I think I hear music. At first, I stop with my duster against the intricately carved wooden mantle in the huge library.

No, not my imagination. It's real, and it's coming from the room down the hall, the one Valerie warned me about.

Curiosity gets the better of me. I walk back through the cavernous library and stick my head around the corner, listening to an amp growling jagged electric guitar notes. I think it's the radio until I get closer, taking tentative steps down the hall.

No radio. It's too clear to be coming through any speaker. It's sad, it's loud, and it's being played by someone who clearly has some idea what they're doing. I flatten myself against the wall, just a couple feet from the door, my ears prickling when I hear a young man's voice between the wailing chords.

Go ahead, so go ahead.

Bleed for me. Bleed down there in your smoking crater.

Bleed like the day you left forever.

Bleed, bitch, bleed. Hotter than my tears.

Can't you hear me through the red wave?

Well, I still love you anyway.

This just might be the edgiest thing I've ever heard. I'd wrinkle my nose and laugh at the strange absurdity, if he didn't sound so damned serious.

There's pain in this voice. It's unmistakable. Deep, rich, and very, very real.

The amp drones on to silence. I hear a soft screech when he pulls his fingers off the strings. It seems like he's done, which means I'd better get the hell away.

I turn around so fast, I forget about the little end table with the vase outside his room. When my knee crashes into it, the thing starts to wobble. It's a huge monstrosity from Europe or Asia, black and smooth with painted gold lines crisscrossing it like veins.

There's no good reason it should go flying off the black tabletop and smashing on the ground – except for the fact that I've always had the worst luck in the world.

It happens so fast. I'm staring at the mess under my feet for no more than a few seconds before the door behind me flies open, banging against the wall.

"What the fuck are you doing out here?" He stands in front of me, fists at his sides, taller and grander than anything I imagined. "Were you eavesdropping? Listening to me?"

I don't know what I pictured in my mind. An older boy with long shaggy hair and a torn t-shirt, perhaps, a few piercings hanging from his face. One of those spoiled trust fund brats who gets his way so often he doesn't have to try to look civilized anymore.

But this is no boy.

I'm looking at a young man, angry and serious as real men can be. Strong jaw, full chest, arms thicker than my legs, his dark hair trimmed to a neat business cut. The only thing edgy about him is the pitch black bombardier jacket draped around his broad shoulders, almost a perfect fit for his tall, muscular frame.

"I was just cleaning, sir," I stammer, wincing because I realize too late I've forgotten to use his title. Not that I think hearing Master Lucus will calm him down much right now. "I'm so sorry about this mess. Um, do you have someone I should talk to about claims? I broke this. Accidentally."

"You didn't answer my fucking question, little girl." He ignores me, coming closer, pushing me up against the wall. "Were you *listening?*"

We lock eyes. Rather, his eyes lock mine down, so accusing I think I'm going to drown in his blue, stormy pools.

"No! Jeez, why would I? I'm just trying to do my job, Lucus." I forget to add the Master part. Oops. "Look, I really didn't sneak out here to spy on you or whatever. I'm not interested in any crappy music."

I'm bluffing because it was actually quite beautiful. Still, I'm not paying this huge, handsome freak any more compliments until I know he's going to let me go without tearing my head off.

"We say *shitty* where I'm from. Shitty," he repeats, his lips becoming a sinister smirk. "If you wanted to avoid it, you really shouldn't have come calling, sniffing around where you don't belong. Get used to shitty, little girl. You're going to the very top of my personal shit list."

"Please, Just let me go." He's starting to scare me now, his eyes drilling into mine.

He moves closer, pressing his chest into mine, backing me into the small corner at the end of the hall. "What are you? Fifteen, sixteen? Old enough for the stupid shit. Old enough to pay when it happens."

"Stupid, what? I don't do stupid. Clumsy, maybe." I gesture to the broken vase, trying to distract him.

"Wrong. You've fucked up, invading my privacy. That was your first mistake. The second one's lying about it."

"Then maybe you shouldn't play so loud!"

Shit! So much for denial saving my skin.

His eyes drop down, slowly working their way back up. He's taking me in, inch by inch, the way I've seen snakes eat animals twice their size on nature shows. And I'm a whole lot smaller than him.

"I have to go. If you want to bring this up with my mom, fine. Just...just let me get out of here. I swear I'll never bother you again." I don't know why it's so hard to speak.

Heat, shame, and frustration clash in my chest, constricting everything. There's something else, a weird arousal I don't want to acknowledge, especially when he's keeping me hostage.

His eyes narrow, sharpening his rich blue gaze. "You're Ericka's girl, aren't you?"

"Robin. Don't wear it out." I nod, trying to look fearless,

and failing. I tell myself it's the last of his questions I'm going to answer.

Really, I just want out of here. Almost as much as I want to force down the boulder building in my throat.

I haven't done anything evil. But he has a way of making me feel like I stepped on his kitten's tail.

A second later, Luke rips himself away, heading back to his door in a few quick, fluid steps before he pauses and turns. He fills the big frame leading into his room, arms outstretched, revealing more of his muscles and angles than I'll admit I want to see.

"Get the fuck out of my sight, Robbi. Send Valerie around to clean this shit up. Come by my room again, and make no mistake, there'll be hell to pay." His voice has softened for reasons I don't understand.

Hell, maybe he's psychotic, and whatever switch there is in his brain making him a raving monster has flipped the other way. I don't know what to say. I have zero desire to talk to this crazy asshole ever again, as a matter of fact, so I peel myself off the wall and start moving, stepping over the rubble at my feet.

I'm guessing I can kiss this job goodbye. He's going to report me. I'm sure I'll get balled out after someone screams at mom first for breaking what's probably a priceless work of art.

Asshole or not, he never did what I expected.

I wish he had.

Maybe it would've gotten us all evicted from Shaw property a whole lot sooner. Then I wouldn't have had to suffer everything this mysterious bundle of muscle and testosterone had in store for me next.

* * * *

Weeks pass, and everything is weird. My parents are barely home anymore. I guess they think because I'm about to turn eighteen, it's okay to leave me alone with my homework.

Dad's long hours are getting longer. He brings his laptop with him wherever he goes, but I'm not sure why he wants to work over it hunched at a bar, instead of at home. He stumbles in late, halfway through the night, reeking of whiskey and cheap beer.

As for mom, she's spending more time at the house. A lot more time. *Overtime,* she says, flashing me an uneasy smile whenever I ask, catching her dragging in near midnight some days.

She tells me it's the cluttered basement, a dirty pantry, or a dozen other reasons why the Shaw household needs her special cleaning expertise.

"How can their place be so dirty? I've never seen a real speck of dust in any of the corners I've cleaned." I look up from the lines I've been memorizing. The latest musical is in just a few weeks, the day before my birthday.

"Did you forget I'm a manager, honey?" She shakes her head. "You wouldn't believe the hours that go into carving out people's shifts, making sure the supply cabinets are restocked, handling complaints."

"Complaints?" I tense up, wondering if this is a subtle lead in to the broken vase I still haven't heard jack about.

"Oh, honey, not about you!" She flashes me a sympathetic look. "Frankly, I'm surprised you've taken to it so well. I know you'd much rather be spending your hours after school backstage, but look at all the extra money you're earning! You're going to put a dent in those student loans next year. Long as you decide to pick a major that's actually useful." She winks.

I bite my tongue. She doesn't approve of my plans to study acting in the city. My parents are practical people, and they expect me to follow suit.

Art is for snobs and 'people who can afford it' like the Shaws.

She always tells me things are bound to come full circle, if I don't pick a different career. What she really means is, I'll be dusting off art I could never afford for the rest of my life, instead of making it.

Surprisingly, she doesn't stop to dig into me any further. I barely have time to call out before she's heading for the door, a can of iced coffee in her hand.

"You're going out *again?*"

"Just back to the house for a little while. I have some organizing to do in the maintenance office." She stops, her face tightening, a nervous tick in the pale blue eyes we share. "Ask your father to pick something up for dinner on the way home. Hell, order pizza for all I care!" She reaches into her purse, pulls out a couple crumpled twenties, and lays them down on the counter.

"I'm sorry I've been working so much. It's for your college, honey. We're going to pay your way next year, damn it, or at least as much as we can."

She door slams shut behind her. She's gone, without even making me feel like an idiot for wanting to be an actress.

What the hell is going on here?

A couple more hours pass. Luckily, it's a Friday night, so I don't have to worry about turning in early.

I call dad around ten, but it goes straight to his voice mail. I could fend for myself and order a pizza, but I'm not very hungry. Dark curiosity pulls at my stomach, leading me to the door.

Something isn't right.

I don't know what it is, but I can't ignore the gnawing bite in the pit of my stomach. I'm heading out into the warm night. It's late April, just a few more weeks until my last big musical, and then graduation.

True, I shouldn't be worried about anything except getting away from this creepy sideshow. But before I do, I want to find out what's happening behind the curtain.

Using my key to the servant's entrance, I tip-toe into the house. It's dark as usual, a few dim light fixtures glowing on the walls, lighting the abandoned hallways.

I'm in a different wing. It's unfamiliar, so I have to listen closer, trying not to jump at every shadow. I think this is the part of the house Mr. Shaw himself uses. He never lets anyone work there except mom, plus a couple of his senior cleaners. I wonder if I'll find her there, instead of the maintenance office tucked in the basement at the end of the elevator, and what I'll say when I do.

I'm turning another imposing corner, heading deeper into the house, when I hear it.

Voices. They're faint. Strained. Two men speaking through clenched teeth and heavy breaths.

"Clearly, I'm wasting my time, and I shouldn't be," an older man says, his tone like a gun barrel echoing after the shot. "You've already decided you want to fritter away your family name chasing silly dreams. Interrupting me in my free time to ask for another handout for your madness. A fucking charter airline? Do you have any idea what that costs, Lucus? You're not even thinking! That's abundantly clear."

"What's 'abundantly clear' is that you're still an asshole, dad. You expect me to be just like them, Hayden and Grant, and I never will be. I'm not following in their fucking footsteps. It's not who I am."

"Yes, yes, how shameful that you have an older brother on Wall Street and another in real estate. I suppose asking you to get the stupid out of your system at an earlier age like Hayden would've been too much."

"Hey, I never lost six figures at the horse track. I gave you a plan. Use my pilot license and the connections I'm building in the industry to revolutionize it. We could have a stake in the luxury charter service. We could do a lot with this, if you'd open the folder I gave you, and take a goddamned look. It's amazing how blind you're being."

"Blind? You don't know the meaning of the word, Lucus. If you had any sense, you'd see you're blind, deaf, and dumb to the fact that I don't have an extra billion to piss away investing in a brutal, hyper-competitive industry just to quell your mommy issues."

My jaw drops. There's a long pause, so dark and quiet I hear my heart banging in my throat.

"That therapist I hired to pick your brain was another failed investment, I'm sorry to say. I'm done throwing good money after bad with you, boy. Better than the money I wasted on your music lessons, I suppose. They've both led you nowhere, but at least one tried to treat your childish dreams with more dignity than they deserved. I wonder what Helene would say if she could see you now."

"No! Don't you fucking *say* her name, old man. You're the real disgrace in this family." A fist comes down so hard on some hard surface I jump, holding my breath. "She deserves better than being on your tongue. You're just pissed I interrupted your latest fling. How the fuck she had the misfortune to die hitched to a man like you, I'll never understand. Who is it this time, *dad?* Another maid? Or is it just another plastic slut from the clubs down in the city? I know you like their fake tits, ten times bigger than your balls will ever be."

Mr. Shaw laughs. Deep, sardonic, and cruel. "Spare me the self-righteous bullshit, kiddo. You were too busy shitting in your diaper to shed any tears when we had your mother's memorial. You never even knew her. A mercy, perhaps, considering how much of her idealistic nonsense rubbed off on her youngest son. I'd hate to think what would've happened if she hadn't crash landed in grizzly country – that's where you'll end up, too, if you don't start using your brain."

There's another sound, a sickening crunch. Someone

screams – I think it's the older man – and I hear shoes scuffing the wooden floor.

Forget holding my breath. It won't come. It's like I have a straitjacket wrapped around my chest, constricting everything, turning me into a human pressure cooker for someone else's pain.

Where the hell is mom, anyway? Surely, she isn't hearing this crap all the time, or getting in the middle of it?

The worst part is, I'm beginning to think the spoiled asshole with the chip on his shoulder might have a good reason for it.

"Never change, you miserable fucking drunk," Luke growls. "We're done here."

The older man doesn't say anything. I hear laughter, thick and slurred. Then footsteps, coming toward me at a frightening pace.

I have about ten seconds to avoid getting caught eavesdropping like I did several weeks ago. I race down the hall, ducking into what looks like a small tea room with a fireplace. I can't tell because it's dark inside.

My nostrils flare, drinking in heavy breaths, listening as the young man's furious footsteps pound the marble floor. His silhouette passes by me for a second. I close my eyes, praying he won't see me.

He just keeps going. *Thank God.*

My heart hurts for him after overhearing the run in with his dad. It's ridiculous because it shouldn't. I'm shaking off my stupor, wondering how I'm going to get out of here. I count to sixty before I move.

I take the hallway quickly, heading straight for the nearest servant's entrance. I don't care about finding my mother anymore after the shit storm that just went down.

I'm almost to the winding staircase on the main floor when a man steps in front of me. I stall the heart attack just long enough to escape crashing into him.

"Hello." He speaks softly, eyes narrowed, straightening his tie with one hand, while the other wipes blood from his lip. "Working late, are we?"

I've only seen his portrait before. Never the man in the flesh, until now. It's Francis Shaw, larger than life, and just as merciless. He must've stepped out to the bathroom across the hall to clean up the cut his son gave him.

"Um, actually, I came to find my mom. Family emergency." I'm frozen. Nervous as hell doesn't begin to describe the adrenaline overload making me a statue.

"Ericka's daughter, of course." He steps past me, continuing down the hall, stopping next to a room adjacent to the office where I heard the arguing. Luke wasn't kidding about the drunken part – he leaves a distinct plume of fine bourbon behind him. "I know just where to find her. Wait right there, please."

He's eerily calm for a man who's just been in a fist fight with his youngest son.

Forget it. I'm out. I can't handle more weirdness. I'm running down the hall before I ever catch a glimpse of mom.

Blood racing, heart pounding, vision blurring. I hit a wall when I crash through the door leading outside. A hand reaches out, catches my wrist, and latches on like a hawk picking up a mouse.

I'm screaming before I open my eyes.

"You again?" Luke doesn't even look surprised. He's bored. "What's so interesting that you've come back here to spy on my sorry ass?"

"I'm trying to get home. I didn't hear anything, I swear!" I'm a horrible liar.

Recovering my senses, I decide to be straight, mustering up the strength to look him in the eye. Honesty hasn't done much for me in the past, but here's hoping it will. "I came looking for my mom. I thought she'd be somewhere on this side of the house, where your dad lives. I didn't mean to hear you two arguing."

He lets my wrist drop from his grip, turning his back to me. "Better that than what you heard last time. Privacy is a fucking illusion around here, anyway."

He's so…defeated. It makes me feel even worse.

"Listen, Lucus –"

"Luke. Nobody except my old man needs to be so formal," he tells me.

"Fine, Luke. I really don't mean to keep dropping in on you like this. Honest accident. Both times. If I didn't have to come here to work, or chase down my mom, you'd never see me. I'm more than happy to stay out of your way."

"Bullshit." He turns around, the smirk he wears in place of a smile returning. "Sorry, little girl. You're too young for me, and not really my type."

My jaw drops. "What?!"

"You heard me," he says coolly, beginning to walk a slow circle around me. "You're not the first girl to crush all over this, magnificent human specimen that I am. I don't have time for games and I don't fuck virgins, especially when they're offering up a sympathy lay. I can pull any pussy I want."

"Are you out of your mind?"

He stops in front of me and stares. It's a drawn out, uncomfortable, eye-fucking gaze. I hate him for making me the one who's questioning my sanity here, wondering if I'm dealing with a man or a demon who looks like an angel. But I hate him most for putting this heat in my blood, igniting a burn between my thighs I shouldn't have.

"Boo!" He throws his hands in front of my face, nearly knocking me over backward.

"Ass!" I stumble against the waist high stone wall behind me. "I'm only going to say it one more time – I'm *not* interested in you that way. I'm practically your employee. It wouldn't be right for all kinds of reasons."

He eyeballs me slow and hard, shaking his head like my reasoning wouldn't stop anything. "It's not fair."

"What? Can we please stop being so cryptic?" I want to be done so I can walk back across the overgrown path through the garden and go home.

"You know a lot of my secrets for an employee with a schoolgirl crush on me. Can't say I like it." He comes toward me again, and this time he doesn't stop until his arms are around my waist. I almost jump again, and for the first time, I see a thin smile on his face. "Your family's here until somebody quits or my father gets sick of you. Plenty of time for me to even the score. You know too much about me, Robbi Plomb. I'm evening the score. Before the summer's out, I'll know a whole lot more about you."

He's trying not to laugh when I finally wriggle out of his grasp. I check behind me several times on my way out, running down the path through the gardens.

No footsteps behind me. Zero pursuit. He's decided not to come after me tonight.

Later, I learn a man doesn't need to run to start the chase. I didn't know it at the time, but it had already begun.

* * * *

School is almost over. It's my eighteenth birthday, and becoming an adult feels…underwhelming.

I'm just weeks away from graduation, a couple acceptance letters from a local community college in my hand. They're not glamorous, but at least I'll knock out a few cheap requirements over the next year before I go somewhere better for acting or theater.

I haven't decided which direction yet. I love to sing, and I live for nights like these. I owned the musical stage and walked away, better and more tired for it. I'm still wearing my royal purple dress, fresh from playing young Queen Bearington, ruler of Sealesland, a fabulously wealthy European kingdom.

I'm sitting behind our family's bungalow with my friends, a couple dozen kids total in my class. I've got a bowl with German chocolate cake and ice cream to celebrate, just like the rest of the girls. My mother baked it before she took off for another round of overtime, handing me a card stuffed with an embarrassing amount of money for snacks and 'whatever,' in her words.

The boys among us break into a couple six packs one of their older brothers snuck from the liquor store. I haven't seen my friend, Jenny, for about an hour. I wonder if she's finally decided to get a little face time in the weeds with her longtime crush.

"Nothing except cake for the birthday gal? Typical, and disappointing." I stiffen when I hear his voice.

I look up, and there's Jenny again, standing next to someone who doesn't belong here. Luke has his arm slung over her shoulder, his hand perched dangerously close to one breast. She gives him a knowing look, melting into him.

Please, somebody tell me they didn't fuck.

Tell me he isn't here to ruin my party.

"You told me last week you were going to have fun on your birthday. Do you even know how, Robbi?" Luke doesn't let up. Jenny nuzzles into him and laughs, too tipsy not to be drunk on something. I don't know if it's beer or sex.

"I *am* having fun, jackass," I snap, stabbing my fork into the last morsel of cake. "It's called unwinding. You should try it sometime."

"Nah. Think I've done plenty of that tonight with my charity case. It's not every day I suck face with a chick who's aiming out of her league." He looks at Jenny. It takes her smiling face a few seconds to register the insult, and flatten like the melted vanilla ice cream under my fork.

"Hey!"

"Hey, what? I'm talking to Robbi now." He pushes her away, heading for me. I swear he can smell the jealousy throbbing in my veins, and he likes it.

"Walk with me, little bird," he says. I don't move. "Aw, come on. I came all the way out here to have a heart-to-heart for your eighteenth birthday. Couldn't let you step into womanhood and leave school without some brotherly wisdom."

"You're not my brother, Luke. You're a fucking joke."

He blinks, both of us surprised because I've slipped an F-bomb. It doesn't knock him off his game, whatever one he's playing, for more than a second. "Duh, princess. You don't have one, which is why you need my advice more than you think. Let's go, before I drag you inside to wash that mouth out with soap."

There's no resisting his strong hand under my shoulder. I set my bowl down reluctantly and walk with him, onto the path. There's a small pond with several soft blue lights glowing around it. My friends are down there in all kinds of compromising positions, using their phones for light in the darkness. Maybe a few are taking naughty pics they'll regret.

There's no moon tonight. Even fewer stars. A smoky early summer haze covers everything, fed by the farms beyond Shaw property lines burning brush.

"Why aren't you out there having some real fun with your friends?" He gestures to the mini-orgy going on by the pond, just as the nearest couple moans. "No use going to college with your cherry intact. Better to get it punched now, and grow up. Then you won't have to worry about the emotions getting in the way when you're locked down in your dorm, trying to study."

"I'm staying here, Mr. Authority. Taking a few community classes over the next year. I won't have a dorm."

"Typical," he says again, shaking his head, using what's becoming his favorite word with me. "I guess you won't have a boyfriend to fuck you good and proper either?"

"None of your business!" I stop in mid-step, pushing against his chest when he leans in closer. I can't stop seeing him down here by the lake with my friend, her traitor legs wrapped around him, moaning while this alpha-hole runs his tongue down her neck. "Get on something else, or this conversation is over. I don't need a sex therapist who writes bad music. Why the hell aren't you in college, anyway?"

The reference to our first meeting makes his eyes smolder like blue gas flames in the darkness. "I did the university thing downtown for about a year and a half. Business school, just like dad wanted. Didn't work out. I'm too restless to sit in a lecture hall listening to guys in shoulder patches blow smoke up everyone's asses."

"Hm, I never would've guessed. Pretty *typical,* Lucus." It's my turn now.

If he's bothered he doesn't show it. Instead, in one of his swift movements, he grabs me around the waist, pulls me close, and looks me dead in the eye. "No more games, Robbi. If you want to know the truth, I brought you out here to say congratulations. You've got a real chance to get away from the shit that goes on here. Take it, run, and live like there's no tomorrow."

He's never sounded so serious since the night we first met. "Thanks, I guess."

"Acting, right? Or is it theater?"

"Either. Both, maybe. I love the stage," I say, smoothing my hands against my dress. It helps take my mind off the huge shoulders shadowing me, the gorgeous eyes looking so protective tonight, when they're usually my biggest dread.

"It's hell getting anywhere in those fields, but try, damn it. One of these days I'm going to gas up my plane and fly as close as I can get to Hollywood. Somebody here has to make it. Whoever gets there first, we'll save the other person a seat. Promise me, Robbi."

Luke acting with me in the distant future? There's a terrifying thought.

Still, he's being nice for once. I don't have the heart to do anything except play along, staring into his eyes while I smile.

"Deal. We'll have plenty of time to talk about it since I'll be here another year, at least."

"Whenever I come home for the holidays and breaks, you mean."

"Home?"

He nods. "I'm leaving next week. Can't turn twenty-two and still be rotting away here while my older brothers leave me in the dust. I'm doing the commercial pilot thing. Landed a pilot job with a cargo company I'll try for a few months, while I get a feel for the industry. I'll wind up an actor or an airline executive someday, or I'll die."

"If you make it, so will I," I say.

He reaches for my face. The bastard makes me forget about Jenny in record time when he's touching me. His fingers are thick against my cheek, strong as the rest of him, the tips calloused from his guitar.

"Obviously. I've got plenty on you in experience, little bird. Like that sex thing we were talking about."

Not again. Just when I was starting to enjoy the asshole's touch.

My eyelids pop open. "None of your business," I tell him, ignoring my body going rebel.

"What's holding you back? Don't tell me your parents don't let you date. Can't believe you get the shy schoolgirl act from your ma."

I'm not sure what he means. Shaking my head, I stand still while he tucks my hair behind my ear, watching a heavy, suppressed growl move down his throat when he swallows.

"Like I could date here. I'm sure you've been inside these bungalows for the servants before?"

"Reed always was a minimalist. You've got his old place. He took off to the city to be my brother Hayden's valet. Sorry you've got the shitty one."

"Yeah, then you get what I'm talking about. It's too small to bring a boy home, much less do anything else."

"Anything? How about some details, Robbi? They're important in college, or so they say." Luke runs his fingers through my hair again, finesse in his touch.

Like he doesn't know what I mean. He's done this to so many girls, he has to know my panties are soaked by now. I'm too ashamed to admit it, refusing to let my guard all the way down for this freak, equal parts unpredictable and irresistible.

"Can't just be the house that's got you clinging to your panties like a stripper maxing out her tease for tips. Your parents are gone half the time. I've seen the hours they keep. Fucking awful."

"How did you know?" I press my cheek into his hand. Not thrilled where this conversation is going, but enjoying the moment too much to stop.

"I take long walks. I notice things. Half the time it's just your rusty little Toyota in the driveway. Your mom spends too much time at the house, and your old man, who the fuck knows."

"He's drinking, I'm afraid. Comes home real late with his computer and goes straight to bed. Sometimes, he passes out on the sofa watching late night junk. I have to cover him with a blanket. It wasn't like this until we moved here." I catch myself, looking away from him. "Sorry. That's family stuff, not your problem."

"I'm sorry. My old man does the same crap, ever since I was old enough to pay attention. He's always got some new bimbo in his bed. Probably goes through two or three a week when he stays downtown, before he settles on a regular fuck for a few months. They haven't lasted longer than that since mom."

"I have both my parents. I'm lucky. Can't imagine what it's like growing up without a mother." I'm flirting with fire, oozing sympathy at this tall, dark beast, poking tenderly at his obvious sore spot.

"Quit changing the subject." He taps my face with his fingertips, reminding me there are some lines better not crossed. "This isn't therapy hour. We're talking about what it's going to take to get you laid."

"Right, Dr. Jekyll." I smile, goosebumps peppering my skin. "I think we agreed I'd better wait until I move out. It'll be easier then. Plus I'll find better quality men than any around here. We're way out in the boonies, and the boys in my class aren't really my type."

"God – yes!" A soft voice rips through the night, louder than before, reaching us from the weeds several yards away.

It doesn't help that most of the guys in my small class are taken. Or busy with girls who are more than happy to be their next piece of rotating meat. I'm not interested.

Luke's smirk grows wider, more like a smile crisp with lemon. "How do you know your type if you've never had one?" His blue gaze intensifies, so hard I can't look away.

"A girl knows," I tell him. Vague, but true, one more lie hiding my inexperience. "Not sure why my status is so important to you anyway. It's not like you're coming to college with me, standing over my shoulder, and handpicking suitors to bring me bouquets. You can't stop me from making mistakes, Luke. Everybody deserves a chance to stumble, don't they?"

His arm goes around my waist. My eyes flutter shut. All the frustration pours out of me when his fingers graze my side, firm and wanting, reminding me he'll do whatever he pleases. "Robin?"

I open my eyes, surprised he isn't using my nickname. "What?"

"Shut up." It's not his words, but his kiss that silences me.

Except calling the explosion tearing through my nerves *silence* is wrong.

It's fire, it's ice, it's rain emptied on the soil after a savage drought lasting years. It's everything my body wants, and everything my brain keeps screaming *no* to.

It's quintessentially him, Lucus Shaw, mysterious and ever calm. In control. Focused on taking me over.

His lips come at me softly at first, and his tongue does the rest. It flicks out once, parting my lips, sliding into my virgin mouth when it opens for him. He tastes me good and deep, putting his hunger into me.

Just before he breaks away, I moan, and heat rushes to my cheeks. I only realize after the fact I'd started grinding on his knee, poised between my thighs.

"Jesus," I whimper, as soon as he pulls away. "I thought I was too young for you?"

"Happy fucking birthday, little bird," he whispers, tipping his forehead into mine. He holds it there, listening to me breathe, lust and want and confusion boiling in my veins.

"What's next, Luke? I don't know what to do."

"Go home. Get your friends some water and a shower when they stumble in with their hangovers. I'll see you when I'm home from my first flight. Got at least one reason to come back here instead of staying in a hotel."

He's gone. No hesitation. I can't fathom how he pulls himself away so easily, like it's nothing more than shaking hands.

He's halfway down the path, heading uphill, when he turns back and looks at me in the darkness. I can't see his face, but I know he's smiling.

More than a smirk this time.

He's proud. I'm left happy, breathless, and horny as hell. I kind of want to run after him and punch him in the back of the head, or at least taste his wild lips again.

I don't know what this makes us, if it makes us anything. But it's obvious I won't be leaving the Shaw grounds without experiencing Luke again.

Little bird. That's what he likes to call me, ever since we started having regular encounters in the halls while I'm working, with no time or privacy for anything more than a quick glance and a few words, until tonight.

If only I knew what he really meant with the nickname. Does he want to cage me, or help me fly?

II: Lies, Damned Lies, and Secrets (Luke)

I've heard her voice a hundred times, but never so goddamned beautifully before.

She doesn't know I'm watching her. She's tucked back in a private part of the family gardens, acting out a scene in her sing-song lines. Her soft white dress clings to her in the humid night, tight as a dove's feathers. Half a dozen fireflies dance around her like tiny lanterns.

It's so ridiculous and clichéd I should be smirking. But that was the old Lucus Shaw, pre-Robbi, before I tasted her lips and decided I'd have them wrapped around my cock someday.

I love teasing her. About as much as I adore jumping out when her back is turned, giving her the shock of her life. Except tonight, something holds me back.

Maybe it's the jet lag lingering in my bones. I just got home from my third long cargo haul in just as many weeks. We flew to Barrow, up in the Arctic circle, hauling oil supplies for the men who want to numb themselves at the end of the world with drink and hard labor, whenever the Alaskan cold isn't doing it for them.

Here, just watching her move and smile and speak, I don't think I'll ever know numbness again.

Yes, I'm obsessed.

I haven't seen her nearly enough since the night I took those lips for the first time. Robbi sneaks into my head at the least convenient times, whether I'm a few miles away or a thousand. I can't stop thinking about sweeping my tongue across hers again and again, wondering if our next kiss will be an intermission before I bring my mouth to all the places it hasn't explored yet.

Sex isn't something I ever waited for before. With her, it's different.

She's got me watching every ripple of her body through the weeds like a damned dog with its tongue hanging out. When this agonizing chase ends with my dick inside her – and it will – I want the anticipation shattering in the hottest, sweatiest, most unspeakable fuck of my life.

The girls before Robbi never made me wait long enough to fantasize. Now, I can't do anything else as I stand, every muscle in my body pulling taut, my eyes glued to her as she giggles, climbs onto a rock, and speaks to an imaginary suitor from her script.

"Bedroom? Oh, no. I'm *not* climbing into bed with you, Mr. Petrov. Maybe they do things differently in Russia. Here, you'll treat me like a lady. A very grateful lady who's thankful she's been rescued. Just not so thankful she's going to throw it all away, no matter how handsome you are."

A smile tugs at my lips. It's like she's reading my mind. Screw it, I can't wait anymore, without at least getting my hands on her skin.

She's fake swooning when I sneak up behind her. Whatever she's imagining with her little double agent act, resting in the arms of the sexy spy who wants her, it doesn't prepare her for me.

When I put my hands around her waist and jerk her against my chest, she screams. My palm goes over her mouth, and I gently tilt her face toward me, until I'm drowning in those pale blue eyes. They're so light and soft they almost look grey.

"Wonderfully acted, little bird. You didn't even know you had an audience." I lift my hand off her mouth as she relaxes.

"Luke? Jesus Christ. You're going to give me a heart attack someday!" She's pissed, but it doesn't stop her face from lighting up when she sees me. "When did you get in?"

"About an hour ago. Thought I'd surprise you. Figured you could use the company since you're out here all alone."

"Yeah, I don't know where my parents are." She jerks away from me, rolling her eyes at the constant sore spot with her family.

"Forget it. You've got better because daddy's home."

"Daddy? Ew!" She wrinkles her nose, laughing. I push my hands past her, grab the script, and rip it out of her hands so I can have a better look.

"Cold War thriller, right? *Make Me Say Spy?* The one with the mafiaoso spy who knocks up the American reporter?"

She blinks, surprised. "You've seen it?"

"Used to watch the movies all the time with my brother Hayden. He loved the shit talk and the seduction. I loved the sex and the planes." I cross the distance to her again, putting the script back in her hands before grabbing her wrists. "Finish your scene. Here, I'll be Petrov."

"Come on," she laughs. "What do you know about acting for film?"

"Jack shit. But I know how to make your panties drip. Come on, beautiful. Relax." I put my arm around her waist, resting my hand on her back, slowly gliding down toward her ass until she begins to speak.

"Go ahead and kiss me, Petrov. It won't get you any secrets," she says, doing her damnedest to narrow her eyes. I can't tell if it's part of her character, or if she's hiding her lust.

"I'm not looking for nuclear enrichment blueprints, love. You think this is about war? I'm gazing into your eyes because they're all that's on my mind," I say, trying not to snicker as I make out Petrov's upside-down lines on the page.

"War? You're all about money!" she insists, pushing her hands against my chest. Fuck, do they feel good there. "Don't lie to me, Petrov. You'd sell your own mother for a juicy tidbit to bring back to your handlers in Havana. Whether it's the Kremlin or the Ivanovs paying you more, I don't know and I don't care! I'm not blind. I know what you're after, and you'll say anything to get it."

"Money?" I whisper, bringing my face to hers. We're so

close she can feel my breathing, and I watch her lips bristle. "I want you, love. Keep the secrets wrapped up in your pretty little head. The orgasm is on the house." I pause for about a second before I'm shaking my head, losing my poise. "Come the fuck on! Who wrote this crap? Forgot how sappy this scene comes off. Must've been the actors who made it palatable."

She's laughing. It's infectious. Soon, I'm chuckling along with her, holding Robbi in my arms, my eyes searching her past the giddy tears welling up in her baby blues. "Thanks for reminding me. I have a lot of work to do before there's only one amateur butchering these lines."

"You'll get there someday. Maybe even before I shove my ring on your finger and put a kid or two in you, if you keep working at it." I run my fingers along her side, halfway tickling her belly, halfway outlining her womb because the primal chant to fuck her welling up inside me won't shut up. "About the free orgasm...is this the part where Petrov takes her to bed and knocks her up?"

The amusement on Robbi's face changes. It's less lighthearted, and more serious, desire and restraint mingling in the redness on her cheeks. "As a matter of fact, I think it is. Don't get any ideas, Luke. We're *not* acting out that part tonight."

"You kidding? I've made peace with you hanging onto your cherry until you're forty or fifty." I cup her cheek with one hand, watching her eyelids flutter while I stop just short of a kiss. "I've had virgins before you, babe. You're the first one who's frustrated me like nothing else."

Smiling, she opens her eyes, mirroring the hand on her face with hers on mine. Love how my stubble feels on her fingertips. "Be nice, and maybe you won't be frustrated much longer."

"Like what? A couple hours?"

"No. But I think I'd really enjoy your kiss."

Tease. Delicate, irresistible, cock hardening tease.

Doesn't stop me from giving her exactly what she wants. The little minx doesn't bat my hand off her ass either. I pinch her cheek hard in my fingers while my mouth roams hers, moving my tongue in and out of her mouth in firm, steady strokes. About how I'd like to fuck the rest of her.

She's a lucky woman, making Lucus Shaw wait.

And yeah, I'll wait a little longer for the grand finale, but I'm damned sure staking my claim. It can't be any other way. Whenever she decides to let me have my way, she's going to be mine.

* * * *

I'm on her ass for weeks, and she still won't give it up. I've never met a chick like Robbi. It's infuriating how hard she is to conquer.

We kiss, we touch, I run my hands all over her, and she still stops just short of opening her legs for me. Her resistance also makes my dick throb like it hasn't since I found my first nudes in the library's old *National Geographic* set.

I've never liked hard to get before her. Hell, until I truly began to appreciate my little bird, I never liked a lot of things.

Part of me wonders if I'm quietly losing my mind while I reach under the bed, feeling for the secret key to our future. It's tucked next to the thin black box where I hide secrets far more bittersweet.

I reach for them first. The small lacquered box resembles a coffin. I pop the rickety lock with my thumb, pull out the first letter, and scan over words I've read a thousand times since a servant found them in her old dresser drawer.

Never doubt that you'll do great things, my baby. Whether it's here on earth or up in the air with me someday, you're going to make the world respect you in ways no Shaw has ever done before.

I love you, Lucus. I'm writing this from thirty thousand feet in the co-pilot's seat, on my way across the South Pacific. It's just past sunrise. It's beautiful down below.

Your father's blood means you're guaranteed a hectic, ambitious life. There's a time and place for that. But I hope you have enough of me in you to stop every so often.

Just stop, admire, and breathe, little one.

You'll find your peace when the world slows down. That's where I've often found mine.

Be good to your brothers, your father, and to yourself. Love always. - Mom

I stopped tearing up a long time ago at the note from a woman I never really knew.

Now, I read her words with a sick curiosity in my heart, wondering if she was really as at peace as her words imply. She wrote it during her last successful flight, just weeks before another fateful trip to Alaska, where she met her end.

Mom was always on the go. My brothers say she spent all her time with the family when she was around, but after a few weeks she'd get restless. She'd hand us off to dad and our nannies while she went on her merry way around the globe.

What the fuck was she running from?

A stirring down the hall gives me one idea. It's a woman laughing above a deeper, more masculine sound. My old man growling in her ear.

I don't have to see them to know he's got her in the hallway half undressed, his arms slung around her shoulders, holding her up while he enjoys his latest fling.

I stand up and kick my door shut. I'm tired of this shit, even though it's happened so many times over the years it ought to be normal.

Hayden and Grant tell me he went off the rails after mom died in that crash. I'm skeptical that's true because I've never known him any other way.

Whoever the latest harpy on his arm is, she's giving me a convenient distraction. He doesn't bother me when I'm home, resigned to my long flights in the cargo planes. He hasn't chewed me out for weeks about never going to Milwaukee to take over the Shaw business there.

I'm never doing real estate or finance. I can't settle down in the boring day-to-day business, where there's no room for creativity.

The cargo flights are grueling, and the pay isn't great by my family's high standards, but it's where I belong. It's never been about the money. Regular distributions from my grandparents' trust ensures I'll be stinking rich while I figure out how I'll leave my mark on this world.

Mom's letters are right about one thing – there's too much of her in me. Maybe that's why what's happening with Robbi is insane by any objective measure, but it isn't in my heart.

I push the black box of old letters away, shoving my hand beneath the bed. The other secret I have stowed away there is in a black box, too, but it's smaller, softer, more delicate.

This is the ring I'm going to use when I ask her to be my wife. I'll do it when I see her again, the morning after I take her cherry, which she's hinted is finally mine.

Lightning hits my cock and flows into my blood. I think about all the vile ways we'll be fucking tonight, and then again after she's said yes.

I'll mount her, mark her with my teeth, take her a thousand bawdy, demanding ways over the years to come. She'll learn every single one with my fingers, my tongue, my seething cock buried to the hilt.

Her body isn't enough. It's her heart and soul I'm after, a completion I've never sought before in any of the meaningless girls I've had. Fuck, I want to bring the rapture, the end of my playboy days, every time I think about finding out what makes her squirt. I'll burn her soft, red face into my brain forever while she's coming herself senseless.

Forever, I said. Something I'll never say lightly.

My thumb flips the little box open. I stare down at the ring, an elegant black diamond set in rare gold.

She doesn't like to trot her desire for the dark things out in the open, but I know it's there. If she wanted flowers, candy, and soft kisses like a normal girl, she wouldn't be attracted to me. I wouldn't have her leaning in, dry humping my leg, every time I take her bottom lip with my teeth.

I stand up, closing the box with an audible *snap.* More laughter and footsteps echo in the hallway, dangerously close to my room.

Tucking the ring into my pocket, I bolt across the room, ready to rip the door open and tell them to keep it the fuck down. My drunken ass of a father never blows up when he's tongue-deep in his girl candy, even if I practically spit in his face.

"Oh, Ericka. Bad, bad, *bad* fucking girl. Tease me like that again, woman, and you'll spend the next week without panties in this house. I'll come by personally to make sure every fucking pair is locked up in my drawer."

Ericka? Christ. My hand stops on the doorknob, and I look at the shot glass on my desk. It's still brown from a couple quick nips of good whiskey I've thrown back.

Maybe I'm drunk, taking too much after dad for my

own good. Maybe I heard him wrong.

Not that it's a terrible surprise. I've had a gnawing suspicion in my gut his latest fling was with someone on our property, possibly Robbi's mom. It would explain an awful lot about why her parents work such odd hours.

"Frank – not here! The ladies haven't finished their shifts. My own daughter could walk by and see us like this. We're not supposed to be in this wing of the house, much less doing – oh, my." Her familiar voice melts.

Exhilaration. Moans. Gasps.

Cringe.

"No. Yes! I mean, no!"

"Shut up," my father growls. "This is my house, you're my girl, and I'll do as a I damned well please. I'll drag you out the nearest exit, down the hill, and fuck you in front of your pathetic husband if I'd like. You'll come for me in front of him, with your little girl watching, if you don't pull up that fucking skirt for me *right now.*"

I hang my head, banging my forehead against the door. It's louder than I intend, but of course, it doesn't stop them.

I want to pour hot wax down my ears and seal them up forever. How the fuck am I supposed to live with this not throwing a gigantic wrench into everything?

Ericka curses, gasping her delight as he begins to do God knows what. His words are slurred as usual.

Rage pumps through my heart, savage and relentless. Whatever happens, he's *not* screwing up my plans with Robbi. I've lived my whole life in his drunken, womanizing shadow. I've fought to avoid his worst habits, always looking for the day when I could roll out the gates of the family estate in my car, and never return.

Tonight, it's not so simple. It's not abstract. There's no excuse for the shit he just said.

The asshole just threatened me. No, I don't care if he knows he did or not.

Everything he said, everything he's doing with Robbi's mother, outside my own fucking bedroom, is a death threat to our future.

I don't know what to do. My fists would like to connect with his face, over and over, even at the risk of this clown disowning me.

But a father-son brawl won't really fix the other problem staring me in the face.

The worst suspicions I've had for months about Ericka's situation were just confirmed in the big, sick reveal. I stagger backwards, heading for the other side of the room, where I can't hear their pleasure through the walls.

I'm fighting my worst instincts. They say destroy, but my brain can't see one reason why that'll help. Clocking my father square in his cheating, just-fuck-my-life-up face won't make him any less of a soulless pig tomorrow. It won't make Robbi's mom any less of an underhanded slut.

Disrupting them with a violent flurry of fists is Option A, and it won't do me any favors.

Option B: run to her. Tell her everything. Then take her far, far away from this black pit where she doesn't belong.

Only trouble is, she's a fragile girl. She won't take the rift between her folks lightly, much less finding out the father of the man she's falling for is the reason her parents are heading for divorce.

If I tell her, will her eyes resent me? Will they see my old man ruining her happy life, and not the man who loves her?

"Fuck." I don't know the answer. My fist bangs the wall. No matter how many times I turn the options over in my head, there are no easy answers.

No simple escape. Even if I throw her over my shoulder and carry her away with me after she learns the awful truth, it won't bleach it from her mind. She'll still have family wounds deep in her heart.

Considering the circumstances, she may want to shoot the messenger, too. Who am I to blame her?

Our ring lingers in my palm. It's become like a hot coal the longer I touch it. I clench it and sweat, pacing my private apartment, wondering if the liars in the hall are finally done.

Leave, you idiot, a dark voice says inside me. *You have to get the hell out of here before you do anything else.*

There's some truth to it. My older brothers got away, and it's done them a lot of good.

Right now, it's the only thing that makes sense. For me, for Robbi, for the future I've just decided we're having, we have to get precious space, or we won't have anything else.

I need to go to her, load her in my car, and get us the hell away from this place.

Sure, she'll learn the truth sooner or later, but it won't come from me.

If I get my ring on her hand before she bites the bitter

apple, I know we'll work it out. All the poison seeping in from our parents. It won't ruin us if we figure it out together, with plenty of distance between us and this hellhole.

When I fling my door open and step into the hall, it's deserted. Thank God. They've gone to my father's room to finish what they started. I'm not wasting this precious time while they're distracted.

I have to find Robin, and then check on rooms in Chicago. The city will do, until we have a place to call our own.

If I have my way, I'll be signing the ink on my own plane next week, something it's taken me years to save for. Those wings will shelter us. They're freedom itself in steel, titanium, and the custom gold and platinum trim I've had installed to spruce up the interior. They'll take us far from the sickness unfolding here, and closer to each other.

I love this woman. I wasn't going to say it point blank until I put my ring on her hand, but if that's what it takes to move her tonight, then I'll do it sooner. I'll rip out my heart and push it into her hands, beating and alive, bleeding the hope I have for us into our world.

There's no way this won't be messy.

Forget the perfect choreography of love I've been planning in my head on those long cargo flights. Long as she's mine, we'll find our way, no matter how complicated or painful it turns out to be.

III: One Last Night (Robin)

"We have to leave tonight, little bird. Car's waiting. Come with me." He keeps making the same demand, and I keep staring at him like he's crazy. We're standing in my backyard, close to the path leading to his family's gardens, alone as we always are at this time of night.

"Just up and leave?" I ask, staring at my backpack. "I don't know if I'm ready, honestly."

He catches me in a daze, and takes one wrist in his huge hand, pulling me close to him. "You've finished your classes. You said last week you'd be moving onto acting school next. Robbi, you can do that anywhere. Don't have to be stuck here for another few months while you wait to find out if you're moving to downtown Chicago or Hollywood. Fuck, maybe London."

"London?" I wince. "I don't have the money or the talent, Luke. I think heading downtown is as good as it's going to get."

"Say the word, and I'll pull the right strings," he growls, pushing his hand against my back, sending chills up my spine.

I've heard him serious plenty of times, but this is a whole new level. He won't take no for an answer. He doesn't care about my excuses, my hesitation, or my very sound logic why this is a bad idea. What I can't figure out is why.

Why the hell does he want us to leave so badly? Why tonight?

I stop for a second, staring into his bright blue eyes. They've never been more determined. Tonight, they're unshakeable, even more piercing than usual. He's promising me the universe, and I'm too proud to take a single star.

"This is our second chance. We'll start a whole new life," he says, brushing his stubble against my cheek when he comes close. "Together, we'll make it happen."

"That's kinda the thing. I have to do this acting thing myself," I say softly, hoping he won't take offense. "I can't let you step in. If I'm going to get anywhere, it's got to be with my own talent. If I'm not good enough, if I use your connections, well, I'm only hurting myself. Weakness will shine through in front of the panels, on the stage, or on the screen, if I ever make it that far. I appreciate the offer – really, I do – but all the money and handshakes in the world can't cover for mediocrity."

"You're *not* mediocre, Robbi." His denial comes out so harsh it makes me smile.

If only I believed in myself half as much as he does. We stop moving, eyes lost in each other. Sliding my hands up his big arms, I let my fingers wander, squeezing his biceps. God help me, they're bigger and harder than ever. I think all the heavy lifting on his cargo flights, helping the ground crews get their shipments in and out, are sculpting him into perfection that would make Michelangelo jealous.

"Come away with me," he says again. "Tonight, Robbi. What's it going to take to slaughter your doubts? I'll stand aside and let you shine in the spotlight, if that's what you want. Long as it's with me, I don't give a damn. I'm not up in your face because it's all about jump starting careers. I'm here, Robbi, because I'm sick of these midnight liaisons. Tired of having to keep our love a secret from the rest of this fucked up world because they wouldn't get it."

My heart skips a beat. *Love?*

Sensing the heat in my eyes, he stops and reaches up, running his fingers through my hair. "That's right, beautiful. I said it. I mean it. I love you, babe, and one fine day I'm going to show you it's forever. I'll have my ring on your finger before everybody else starts beating down the door of a world class star."

"Luke…" I don't know what to say.

Love? Marriage? As wonderful as it sounds, it's happening so fast. The heat in my head expands until I'm feeling faint.

Seeking grounding, I push my hands into his, lacing fingertips, and squeeze. His heat, his strength, his sweet stability dashes the questions murmuring in my head.

"You better not just be saying this because I'm about to let you in my pants," I say, narrowing my eyes.

His smirk rises, bringing the heat between my legs up a hundred degrees. "That's exactly why I'm telling you tonight, and you know it. Sex changes everything between a man and a woman, especially when it's more than straight up fucking. With us, it's more than I ever imagined it could be. I want to leave tomorrow. Let the next sunrise start the rest of our lives. Come with me, baby. We can find a hotel downtown, leave all this bullshit here behind."

His happiness wilts when he looks around, gesturing to the bungalow behind me, and then to his huge modern castle in the distance behind him. Grabbing my shoulders, his fingers dig deep, and he comes in, pressing his forehead to mine so hot it burns.

"I don't know. I want to, but..."

"But what? You're still afraid? You think the two ghosts living with you here will ever care about you more than me?" He pulls back, his eyes locked onto mine. "I'm not looking to bring up your family drama. I want to take you away from it, before it drags you down. Not sure what I'd have become if I didn't have so much on my end bogging me down. It's only been that way because I let it, Robbi. That's what I've realized since I started going on those flights – we're not nailed down to these lives. We can fly. Go anywhere, be anybody, and love like the rest doesn't matter because it really fucking doesn't."

"Okay, fine! Whatever. Let's just roll the dice." As soon as the words are out of my mouth, his kiss seals the deal. The soft, sweet fire dashing across my lips convinces me more than words ever will, and they've been pretty convincing too, tonight. "I love you, Luke. We'll leave tomorrow."

"Tomorrow?" Hesitation swells in his eyes. I start

laughing when I imagine everything rushing through his mind, thinking he's just had what I've promised him tonight delayed by a whole twenty-four hours.

"Let's go to my room. As long as we leave by six in the morning, they'll never know. Mom doesn't even come home some nights. Dad just stops in to eat breakfast and cleanup. He sleeps at the bar most nights."

It takes a long stare and a tug of his hand to convince him. Soon, we're moving in through the backdoor, fumbling into the spartan kitchen while his hands move all over me.

Whatever held him back before, it's gone now. Luke corners me, pushes me into the counter, shoving me up on it, folding my arms and legs around him. He buries me in several more panty soaking kisses, then his mouth moves down to my neck, working with more freedom than it's ever had before.

I'm breathless before he lifts me up, slinging me over his shoulder. He's panting too, and my thigh brushes the raging hardness through his jeans. "You'd better be right about your folks staying the hell away tonight. Because once we start, I'm not stopping for anything. I'll violate you seven ways from Sunday with the entire world watching if I have to."

Before I can say anything, he silences me with another kiss. His tongue pushes deep into my mouth, conquering mine, pulsing more heat into me. I'm burning.

I'm in heat, just like an animal. I've resisted him for so long I'm not even bothered by his crude promise. Hell, crude sounds pretty damned good right now.

We're in love, and I'm ignorant about what really goes on between the sheets, but I know I don't want him to hold back anything. I want him to use me *hard,* push me to places I've only imagined, show me the hot white ecstasy I've thought about inside the stars while his pleasure becomes mine.

"There, Luke," I whisper, pointing to the shoebox bedroom straight ahead. He carries me in and throws me down on the bed a moment later, kicking the door shut with a *bang.*

We're alone. His hands are on me. Twisting, stretching, maneuvering off my clothes. I don't stop to help him because he knows exactly what he's doing.

My sweater disappears in his hands as swiftly as my jeans. He swipes my bra open with one jerk, popping the clasp, freeing my aching nipples for his teasing mouth. When his lips come down on the first little bud, I tense, falling backwards on the bed and grabbing the sheets.

Sweet. Holy. Heaven.

I've found it, and the key was always having this man's mouth engulfing my nipple. His teeth form the perfect ring, divine tension, holding it taught while his tongue lashes the tip again and again. My pussy rises to meet his knee, poised between my legs. I moan when he lets me have just a little bit of pressure against my clit.

"Save some of that honey for when I'm in you, baby girl," he whispers, his blue eyes stabbing mine like daggers. "It's going to flow hotter and richer than anything you've ever felt when you're wrapped around this cock. You're still afraid and unsure. I see it in your eyes. Won't be that way much longer."

"No!" My head snaps to one side. I'm a pathetic liar, melting as he cups my chin with one palm, making room for his lips all over my throat. His other hand slides down the curve of my waist, a cool tingle in the wake of his fingertips.

"I'm ready," I tell him, trying to breathe. "For you, I'm ready for anything."

"Correction: you will be soon. Soon, little bird. I'll set you free and teach you how to fly. I'll mend every last fracture in those wings, every fear and doubt you've got left churning in your blood. We don't just fuck with these bodies. We reminds ourselves why we live."

Something is definitely living deep inside me when he starts pulling off my pants. A dozen butterflies take flight in my belly. The simple act of fabric shimmying down my thighs causes my legs to shake.

Sweet anticipation. Sweet and short because he won't keep teasing me forever. Luke's breath flares hot against my skin, summoning goosebumps. His huge chest rises and falls as his face moves between my legs, kissing up my thighs, tasting me and inhaling the hot need surging in my pussy. His hands grip my knees, pulling my legs apart.

Muscles I didn't know I had go taut. He spreads my legs wider, making room for his magnificent shoulders. He reaches straight for my panties, tightens his grip around the lacy fabric, and pulls.

I'm embarrassed when he sees the wet spot. His eyes glow, amused because I'm just one more toy responding predictably to his touch. He rubs his thumb across the stain, drawing a deep breath, before he throws them over his shoulder and plants another kiss on my upper thigh.

"It's been too long, Robbi. You need it bad." he tells me, reading my mind. "Don't stop screaming when my tongue starts fucking your sweet little cunt. It's music to my ears. Remember how much I like it when you're coming too hard to remember your own name."

Lofty promises. If it were any other man, I'd think he was exaggerating.

But Lucus Shaw doesn't BS about sex. Before his tongue sweeps across my swollen virgin lips for the first time, I know I'll be hoarse by the end of the night.

My mouth trembles. I'm holding it in, tugging on the sheets like reins, muscles stretching so tight my ass lifts automatically, tries to escape the maddening pleasure steaming from his mouth.

He doesn't like that. His hands reach behind me, clench my ass, and pull me into his tongue.

Growling, he holds me there, and goes to work fulfilling every last word he promised. Luke buries his face. Licking, sucking, tonguing deep inside me, ringing my clit with his teeth.

I gasp. I moan. I'm trembling when I can't hold back the screams anymore.

His tongue seeks them out, discovering the spots that make sirens come to life in my throat, then working them like mad. He's taking me over the edge in record time, faster than my busy little fingers ever brought sweet release.

Every new movement of his tongue on my tender flesh becomes a word. I hear it in my head when his hungry circles dance around my clit, taking me closer and closer to the edge, before shoving me over.

Fly for me, little bird. Come on my tongue.

Come so fucking hard you soar before falling from the sky.

Like I need the encouragement. My body goes off in a blinding, hot, pussy drenching convulsion. Tipping my head back, pressing it deep into the mattress, I scream for all I'm worth.

My legs quake, threatening to slam shut, but he holds them open. His mouth binds me back to earth when I'm completely gone, lost in the bliss, halfway to the sun where everything is hot and bright and perfect.

Also, *tingly.* Needles dance through my skin, prickling me through the inside out. I wish someone told me an orgasm with a man, the right man, could feel like full body acupuncture.

I'm coming down from the high when I sense his hand on my face. Luke cups my cheek, forcing me to open my eyes. I see him hovering over me while his fingers stroke a few last aftershocks into my quivering pussy.

"I'll never forget your O as long as I live. You're beautiful when you come for me," he whispers, breathing heavy, stopping to run his tongue over his lips. He's still tasting me. "Robbi, fuck."

"I love you, Luke." I wonder why saying it makes me

feel a hundred times more vulnerable than when his face is between my legs. Red, shameful fire beats against my cheeks, turning them raw.

"Good." He smiles, touching his forehead to mine, a subtle gesture I'm loving more every time it happens. "Because I'm going to make you come harder next time, babe. I'll watch your little face blown to smithereens the next thousand times you're coming for me. I'll swallow your screams on our wedding night, on our honeymoon, when we're done with condoms and I'm fucking our first born into you. Love means something because you're fucking mine."

He's insane, but he's right. His words, his promises, they make me shudder with their weight. Emotions fold in my heart, tight like a security blanket, lovingly tucked around me by the only man I'll ever allow in.

"Show me," I say, needling my bottom lip with my tongue. "I want you in me. I've wanted it since the first night you chewed me out, and I hated you. Even when I thought you were an asshole, I wanted it."

I don't know why I'm confessing, spilling my inner secrets all over him. It just makes his smirk bigger, wider and more amused than I've ever seen it. He holds my face, running his hand back across my ear, collecting blonde hair in his hand before he closes it in a fist.

"You shocked the fuck out of me that night. Saw a piece of me I never showed anyone. I knew it wasn't an innocent mistake. Knew we'd either end up taking this thing all the way, loving each other bigger and deeper than the shadows over our own lives, or we'd have to end it all."

"End it?" I ask, when he's done laying another steaming kiss on my lips.

"Yeah. We'd absolutely destroy each other. Scorched earth. Torches, pitchforks, and sledgehammers. Mortal enemies, babe. Who ever charted where love and hate ends? I think they're neighbors, and it doesn't take much to blur the lines."

"I'm glad it's ending on the right side." I mean it. I can't imagine what he'd do to me if he hated me, if he'd pursued me as a monster instead of the man after my heart.

"Wrong. It's just beginning, beautiful. We're not even done with tonight until you've had my dick showing you things my tongue can only dream of." There's a crinkling sound near his legs. I realize he's pulled a condom from his pocket, and he's testing the foil, crinkling it in his fingers. He stops, holding it, and gives me an icy stare.

The time for talk is over, especially with the maddening hard-on bulging between his legs. He climbs off the bed and stands at the edge, pushing his fingers through mine, pulling me up. "Undress me first," he says, relaxing his arms.

I'm feeling bashful again. Amazing how that works, when he's seen me naked for the last half hour. Maybe it's because I've never seen him, and now he's ordering me to undo one more mystery.

I need his hands to guide me. I fumble several times, drawing his shirt off over his huge chest. He's even more gorgeous bare.

The ink is the real surprise. I'd only seen the ends on his arms before, stripes and criss-crosses, never knowing they were just the edges to a beautiful tapestry scrawled all over him. There's a falcon spreading its wings on his chest, screaming at the sky, lightning arcing out to his shoulders. My hands take their time roaming him while we kiss, melting my pussy with new, wet need.

The mysteries aren't all swept away. I don't know what the date stamped on his shoulder in the broken heart means. 2-13-97 probably has something to do with his dead mother. It's beautiful and sad like the rest of him, and I'm so lost in his wild ink I almost forget all about his pants.

"Down, baby, down. I want your lips full of cock. Start sucking, and I'll teach you everything." He puts his hands on my shoulders and gently lowers me to the floor.

Then his fingers are on his zipper, slowly pulling it down, urging me to reach inside while he undoes his belt. My hands warm when I pop the clasp, tugging his jeans to his knees.

My second surprise of the night pops out when I shove his boxers down to meet them.

Lucus Shaw is huger, harder, and more eager than anything I imagined.

Dicks aren't supposed to be like *this,* are they? Hung doesn't begin to describe the thick, angry root throbbing in front of me. It's strong, bigger than life, and maybe a little dangerous. No different than the other six foot something of glorious man it's attached to.

"Stroke," he growls, putting his hand over mine, guiding

my fingers forward. His cock jerks as soon as my fingers hug his tender skin.

I can barely form a complete fist around it. My pussy goes slick from the challenge while I stroke him slowly, up and down, gliding across his length.

It's hard to fathom how he's going to fit inside me, but God willing, I'll take every feral inch.

"Nice and easy, little bird. Fuck, that's good," he groans, letting his head roll back on his shoulders. "Now, put that shy tongue to work like you've always wanted."

My lips part. I start with the tip, tasting him for the very first time. He's salt, earth, masculine to the core. Opening my mouth wide, I lower it onto his length, rolling his swollen head against my tongue.

"More," Luke groans, positioning his hand on the back of my head.

He eases me lower in a slow, gentle bobbing motion. I listen for his commands and his pleasure. My tongue revisits the same places on his skin and his breath shortens. It's hot knowing I can choke a man with pleasure, whenever I push the right buttons.

He's so big, so strong, everything I want. I swear I'll bring him to his knees one day with this mouth, after I've memorized the things that electrify his nerves.

"Yeah, baby. Yeah!" he groans, over and over, just like a mantra, background music to my tongue working his cock. My confidence grows every second.

I'll need lots of practice to perfect my technique. At least I'm off to a good start, even if I can't get more than a few inches past my jaw without tearing up. He's so big it would hurt if I'm not careful.

There's a strange power to sucking him off, a risk that fans the flames building up inside me. A sick, dark part of me *likes* that he can hurt me.

Every time his hand pulls on my hair, I'm reassured he won't. He's in control, introducing my virgin mouth to new delights, teaching me how he wants to be pleased.

It's just like he said – we'll end up lovers, going all the way – or we'll be mortal enemies.

The yin and yang of possibility tastes divine against my tongue. I devour his pleasure, bobbing my lips faster now, each time he dips his head backward, his short dark hair spiking out in the shadows. The blue flames in his eyes are contained, raging inward, because they're pinched shut.

He's focusing on my heat wrapped around him, pulling him deeper into the undertow. I don't know what to expect if he blows in my mouth, but I'm ready to find out.

I can't wait to taste him at his fullest, his peak, his flood.

Can't wait for him to lose it, to make him seize. He'll give in, pouring himself into me, the same way I've surrendered to his tongue.

"Good, good, *good,* baby girl. Sweet fuck!" He's groaning, swearing every other stroke.

I try quickening my speed, but it's all new to me, and it isn't easy. I slow my strokes, focusing my tongue, digging into the spot under his cock's head that causes his entire body to tense.

Please come, Lucus Shaw. I need you.

Just when I'm expecting him to ride my tongue to release, I feel tension in my hair, a hand lifting my head away. "Enough." His eyes are open, looking down, staring in judgment so fierce I blush.

"Was it good?" I whisper, terrified it wasn't.

"No. It was fucking incredible, Robbi. You'll get another crack at making me come down your throat soon enough, but we have more important business." Pausing, he presses his hand against my cheek, holding my face so there's nowhere to look except his eyes. He lowers his lips to mine, painting them in a new brute heat with his kiss. "My cock can't handle keeping you a virgin a minute longer. Stand up, lay down, and spread your legs. I want that cherry, babe."

I'm in a haze as I obey. Cool autumn air brushes against my pussy when my thighs shift open. He finishes shedding his pants and boxers before he joins me on the bed, naked and perfect. The bed is so small holding both of us, sinking under his weight. Perfect for bringing our bodies closer to sin.

He takes my mouth in his. Several kisses in, a slave to his tongue, I hear the condom's foil tearing again, this time all the way open.

My eyes flick down to the space between us. Massive cock in his hand, and he rolls the condom on skin tight. Rearing up, he taps the throbbing head against my leaking pussy, teasing me in long, delicate strokes like a painter testing his canvass.

"Please. Luke, *please.*" I think he wants me to beg.

Whether that's true or not, it's happening, and my pussy is about to kill me with anticipation if he doesn't do something in the next thirty seconds.

"Look at me, Robbi. Need your eyes on mine when I stretch you open. It's a special night for both of us. You're kissing your virgin ass goodbye. I'm having the best fuck of my life."

He's so sure. Confidence is sexy, they say. Must be true because my blood is boiling when he gazes at me again, his eyes narrowed, focused on the prize he's claiming.

His hand comes up, heavy and hot on my cheek. He's holding my face as his hips move forward, one thrust away from breaking the barrier between us. It's a good thing, too, because my whole body wants to thrash. The wait is torture.

"Please." It leaves my mouth like a whimper.

"Love you, Robin. I always will." It's the last words I hear as a virgin.

Luke's hips plow forward. One thrust, and he's in, shoving his thick cock into me. He doesn't stop until he's reached the hilt, his heavy balls resting on my ass, shifting my pussy to accommodate him along the way.

Holy shit. It's incredible. There's a soft, sharp ripping sensation when he's in, rooting his thickness deep inside me. Yes, it hurts, but the pleasure shadowing the pain is worth it, a promise of bliss in the stinging depths.

"Fuck me," I say, wrapping my legs around him, urging him on.

His nostrils flare. The hand on my cheek moves down, gently to my throat, cradling me with a tender, awesome power. One more reminder we've chosen to be lovers, when we could be each other's total undoing.

I let him savor the moment for twenty seconds before I start moving my hips into his. The motion makes his eyes widen, drilling into mine.

We're fucking like real lovers now, finding our rhythm. Flesh tangled, breath pouring, sweat steaming from our pores.

A dozen more strokes, harder than the first, and the pain recedes with every thrust. New pleasure fills my veins, simmering my nerves. I'm digging my teeth into my bottom lip, ecstasy pooling around my womb, an inferno refusing to be contained for long.

Wrapping my arms around his broad neck, I use the extra leverage to fuck him back. Maybe it's too much, too soon, but I don't care. My pussy takes him better each time our hips collide.

Every thrust leads me deeper into a wild, primal mode I didn't know I had. When he rears up, lifts my legs, and throws them over his shoulder, giving his cock more depth and more sweet friction, I'm panting through clenched teeth.

"Oh, Luke!" I cry out, hands on his arms, fingernails cutting into his skin.

Oh, God. It's sex as it's meant to be: uninhibited, wild, exciting to the very end.

And my first end, my crescendo, comes with the bed quaking. He fucks me harder and faster, slamming his big cock into me, his balls clapping my ass in steady, rough beats.

I'm going over the edge, breathless and mouth open, lips frozen in a silent scream. Hot blood floods my extremities. My pussy tightens around his pistoning cock, clenches, and electrifies.

Luke never relents while I'm coming myself into the next universe. His thrusts power through it, coming harder all the time, especially when my pussy clings to him like a glove. It's sweet, rampant madness massaging my walls, bringing every inch of me off into the white hot yonder.

His thrusts only slow when I'm coming down, letting me catch my breath. Then he positions himself lower, pinning my thighs around him, before he slides one hand underneath my head to fist my hair.

"Wake the fuck up, beautiful. We're not finished yet," he growls, pulling my blonde locks.

No, we're not. My body knows when he starts to rut in harder, slower strokes, dragging his pubic bone against my clit. New delicious fire kindles in my depths, bringing my muscles back to attention, turning me into his willing virgin slave anew.

I want him to come.

I need him to come inside me.

Both my hands go to his face, raking my nails through his stubble, begging him with just my eyes while my third orgasm of the night is building stroke-by-stroke.

"Please, Luke. Please. I need to feel it."

"You'll get it, and you'll fucking love it, babe." He stops moving, adding one more round of torture to our loving. "Move like you want it. Show me how bad you've got it before I give it up."

Whatever shyness and shame is left in me fades. I don't recognize myself anymore when I'm pinching him with every limb, folding myself around him to move my pussy against his cock, drawing his length in and out and over the moon.

Come for me, beautiful bastard, I think to myself. My teeth pinch together so tight I'm afraid they'll break. I'm struggling to hold back my latest release before he erupts inside me. *Please. Fucking. Come.*

He doesn't understand. It's no longer a want, but something I need.

I need it to know we're real.

I need it to know we'll always have this love.

I need it to know I'm making the right choice, running away with him tomorrow, leaving everything I've ever known for wherever he leads.

There's a flash of smirk on his face before he moves with me again. This time, there's nothing held back. His cock fucks into me with a crazy, bone jarring force I swear shakes the entire house.

My eyes roll back in my head, and there's no way I can hold back the inevitable for a second longer. The fireball in my belly bursts, spilling bright, orgasmic heat into me again, and his growl becomes a roar through the maelstrom.

"Robbi, fuck!"

Just in time. I'm smiling as his cock balloons, adding his heat to mine. He ruptures in thick, fiery jets I swear I can feel hurling out of him even through the condom.

My pussy convulses, sending shocks into every muscle, every extension of who I am.

Toes to fingertips to the edges of my soul.

Yes, it's ridiculous. Cheesy. Clichéd.

I'm the virgin girl responding like a violin's strings to a virtuoso's touch her very first time. Coming so sweetly, our bodies in tune, giving as much as they take. Making beautiful music I'll never forget for the rest of my life.

I don't care what anyone says. It's real, damn it, and I relish it all night as he bends me over, folds me around him, puts his mouth between my legs again and again.

It's just before dawn when we're finally spent. We've barely said a word all night, speaking with our flesh instead, lost to the world's depressing complexities in each other.

"Sleep for a few hours," he tells me, shoving my hand off his cock when I move to make him hard again for round…round what? I've honestly lost track. "If we don't get out of here by six, like you said, there'll be hell to pay."

He's right, as much as it makes me pout. I snuggle into his chest, using his scary falcon as a pillow, hand laid over the mysterious date stamped on his shoulder. "Goodnight, Luke. I know I'll have sweet dreams thanks to you."

"Get used to it, little bird. If there's nightmares rolling around in your head after this, I haven't done my job." His face moves into mine.

We kiss one more time. It's love, salt, and sugary sweetness. The kind of kiss that hurts every time you remember it as your last because it's so real, so honest, so fucking perfect.

If I'd known what was coming next, I would have kissed him again. Maybe the next one would've been a little less immaculate, and wouldn't weigh on my heart like a back breaking boulder tethered to the past.

* * * *

There's a crash. Pounding. Screams.

I wake up in a cold sweat to an empty bed. Luke is already up, pulling on his boxers, stumbling to the door and stopping there with his fists flexed.

"Robin! What're you doing? Wake up, wake up! We have to leave *now!*" Mom's voice. She's pounding on my door again, slamming her fist into it like no tomorrow.

"I said back the fuck away, cheating whore! You're not taking her. You're not taking my little girl!"

My heart jumps into my throat. The other voice is dad, boiling with rage. I'm blindsided. I think it's the first time I've heard my parents together in months. Never like this.

"Luke..." I look at him, shirtless and beautiful as ever, not knowing what to say. "Let her in. They're going to find out."

"You sure?" He lifts his eyebrows, a surprised look that would be sexy if he weren't standing there half-naked, just as confused as me at the commotion outside.

"Robbi, please! Hurry!" Mom again, giving the door another round of violent slaps.

"Just a second!" I yell back. I'm up, throwing off the covers, stepping into the closet for fresh clothes. He waits another minute while my parents turn on each other.

I can't make out the steady stream of curses, insults, and accusations. At first, I think my father's completely lost his mind.

He's drunk. There's no doubt with the way he's slurring

his words. Nothing else explains why he'd be rampaging through the house, screaming at my mother, accusing her of high crimes and atrocities.

There's just enough time to get dressed. Luke throws on his outfit, and peeks out the window, looking toward his car. It's still there, untouched. If my parents have noticed I'm not alone in here, they haven't said anything. Hell, they haven't said anything about it through the screaming.

"Robin Marie Plomb! I said, open up! *Now!*" Mom again. More desperate than before. This time, when her fist hits the wood, it doesn't stop.

"Back off, bitch! You're scaring her! She doesn't need your damned help." Dad again, roaring, closer as it sounds like he tries to grab her, and throws her against the wall.

The chaos doesn't stop until Luke stomps over, grabs the knob, and practically rips it off its hinges. Dad has her against the wall, digging his fingers angrily into her shoulders, just like I thought.

The early warning in my imagination does nothing to blunt the pain tearing through my heart. *What the* hell *is happening here?*

They've never had a screaming match, much less laid their hands on each other in anger.

My mother's red, tear streaked face eyeballs us in shock when she sees Luke standing there. It takes her huge eyes a couple seconds to look behind him, following the trail to me. Dad doesn't move, loosening his grip ever so slightly on her, just enough to let her drop, and pull herself away from his drunken hands.

"You." It's all she says when she's free, before she fixes her eyes on me, and doesn't let them waver.

"Get your things together, Robbi. Pack some clothes. We're leaving right now. I'm taking you far, far away from this fucked up place."

"Leaving? Why?" I'm stunned, confused, and frightened all at once.

She ignores Luke, pushing past him, sneering at me. "No more questions! There'll be time to explain everything later. We have to pack!"

She's serious. If flying into my closet and ripping shirts off their hooks is what she calls packing, anyway.

I'm too stunned to move, much less question yet again what the fuck is happening.

"Ericka!" Dad breaks his trance and comes staggering in, knocking a few things off my nightstand as he runs into it. "Cheating fuckin' bitch. I told you to leave her alone. You're not going anywhere." His words are slurred. An empty whiskey bottle hangs limply from his hand. "Wha...what're you doing here?" he slurs, noticing Luke for the first time.

Mom never lets my man answer. "Danny, I'm not talking about this here, in front of her! For the last fucking time – get *out*! Leave us be, or I'm calling the cops."

Ever the guardian, Luke moves between my parents and me. We watch the hot mess unfolding in front of us.

My parents in the closet, trading barbs, tangled in the clothing. One of my dresses covers dad's eyes as he stumbles through the chaos. He grabs onto the fabric, trying to prevent himself from toppling over. It doesn't help. He goes down on the floor slowly, and I wince, listening to fabric shearing apart.

"Look what you've done, you drunken idiot!" Mom shrieks.

I throw my fists up, just as Luke grabs me, wrapping his big arms around my waist. I start hitting him because he's the only one in sight. I don't care that he might be the only one here who makes sense.

"I'm not going anywhere until somebody explains what the fuck is going on!" It's my turn to scream. I pump my fists in the air, starting to shake. It would be worse if it weren't for the manly security blanket wrapped around me.

Mom kicks her way out of the closet, a fistful of my clothes slung over her shoulder, gripped in both hands. She stops in front of us. Dad is still stuck in the closet, wrestling with dresses, quietly cursing every variation of 'fuck Ericka' he can.

"Let go of that boy, Robbi, right this instant! I won't let you make my mistakes."

What mistakes are those? My face cranes to see Luke as I twist in his arms. He's looking past me, into her eyes. They're sharing a look like they both know something terrible I don't.

"With all due respect, Mrs. Plomb, your daughter's an adult, and free to make up her own mind," Luke tells her. "I think you ought to walk the fuck out of this house, and take the drunk with you. He needs help. It's going to take a lot of counseling to sort out your shit."

Mom doesn't say a word. Her feet begin moving a second later. She walks up, stops in front of us, and reaches past me. Luke grunts when her hand lands on his cheek, so forcefully it echoes through the entire house like a gunshot.

"Release my daughter *now,* you spoiled, fucked up brat. This isn't your fight, and she's much too good for you. I never should've brought my family to this place. Never should've let my guard down for an instant. Never should've gotten involved with your disgusting rich father and his stupid, *stupid* promises!"

"There it is!" Dad bellows from the closet. "There it fucking is! Least you're not afraid to kick me in the nuts one last time confessing, Ericka."

"Like you have any balls to kick," she sneers, before turning her attention back to Luke and me. "Robin, please. I know this doesn't make any sense. Mistakes were made. I've been selfish, put myself above your own well being, and I'm done with that today. We need space. We can't stay here for a second longer. I have to get you away from this place, away from *him,* before the Shaws and their filthy hands ruin everything."

It sounds like they already have. I wonder why Luke is so quiet. His whole jaw line glows red, hot like burning metal from the scorch mark she's left on his face. He doesn't even reach up to rub it. He just stands there like a sentinel, holding me in his fading grip, staring her down.

"You heard your husband. Leave her the fuck alone," he growls, resting his chin in my hair.

"No. I won't allow another Shaw to use my daughter

and throw her away. That's all your family knows how to do. Call the police now, if you'd like. I'm taking her away for her own good. You'll need a restraining order to stop me from protecting her!"

"Mom!" I can't take it anymore. I cut in, before he can say anything, stirring her up more. "I'm not going with you until you explain what's happened. I'm sorry you had to walk in on this. I don't know what's going on between you and dad, but I –"

"She cheated! She's a liar, a whore, a goddamned backstabber!" Dad roars from the closet, finally up on all fours, still too tangled in my dresses to crawl toward us. "Don't listen to a word she says, honey. Tried to get the truth out of her for months. Took Frank Shaw handing us both a pink slip to find out she was fucking him all along!" His fist slams the floor.

His rage is overwhelming. I don't know whether my lungs are going to explode first, or my eyes from the fiery tears I'm holding in.

Their marriage was never good. They'd been growing distant for years, especially after I hit my teens. But if there's any truth to this, if my mom was cheating – and with the head of the Shaw household, Luke's father – then I've just been hit with a bigger blow to the gut than I know what to do with.

"Stay back," Luke warns again, pulling me several steps backwards. "Both of you." He nods toward my dad on the floor, twisted in my garments.

"Sure, Mr. High and Mighty. I'll just fold my arms and

wait while you take off with my girl. I'll pretend you didn't know about us the entire fucking time. Like you didn't know what your father was doing to me, strong-arming me into his bed. Like you haven't already gotten her wrapped around your pathetic little finger, something you've inherited from *him.* Tell me, boy, would you have dumped her for your next mistress as soon as you had her brainwashed? Maybe a married woman, like the kind your father likes? Or does that gene skip a generation?"

Luke says nothing. He continues to hold me, daring her to say or do something that'll give him an excuse to make good on his warnings.

"Come on. You're not blind, boy. I heard you slinking around the house at least a dozen times when I was with your father. You knew, and you did nothing, because it's business-as-usual in your twisted world."

Knew what? I'm struggling to keep up with her nasty words. There's an evil conviction in her voice. It scares me.

He couldn't have known about my mother cheating. He would have said something…wouldn't he?

I spin around, freeing myself from his greedy arms, searching his eyes. "Luke? Don't tell me you knew about this? It isn't true!" Denial is poison, and it stings my tongue with every word.

There's a long silence. He lowers his head, staring at the floor, shifting uncomfortably. "I wanted to get you out of here before something like this came down, Robbi. I knew you'd be hurt. Yeah, I had my suspicions for awhile. But I didn't know anything for sure until yesterday. I just knew it'd break your heart when you found out the hard way, and I tried to save you from that."

My hands go up, covering my mouth. I'm breathing into my hands, hard and heavy. "You knew. You *lied* to me."

"Lied? No, baby, no. I did you a favor."

He's lying right now. "*Favor?* What the fuck is wrong with you? You thought I wasn't strong enough? That I couldn't handle the truth? Jesus. That's all I've ever wanted. Honesty. It's part of love. When you said you loved me, I thought you understood." I look at him, tears welling in my eyes, wondering how we can already be worlds apart. "You lied. How do I ever trust you again?"

"Because I tried to do the right thing, and I fucked up, Robin." He stands up straight, pain tightening his jaw, grinding out every word leaving his mouth. "I'm sorry. You have to believe I am. Look, this doesn't have to change anything. We don't need to let this bullshit come between us. You're not thinking straight because it's hitting you in the face right now. It hurts too much. Let's get out of here, babe. Clear your head. Get you the fuck away from this drama, this insanity."

I'm backing up on instinct. I don't realize I'm on top of my mother until she grabs me, locks her arms around my waist, and holds on for dear life. "He knew the entire time, Robbi, and he didn't say a thing. Don't believe him when he says he only found out a day ago. How many times did I see him lurking out the corner of my eye when I was with Frank? Oh, he knew, and he kept it to himself. He wanted you for something else. I hope you didn't give it to him, but it's not your fault if you did. That's what the Shaws do. They lie."

Luke bares his teeth, his lips peeling back in a snarl. My mother looks him dead in the eye, unrelenting, her words coming hot and painful.

"They blackmail. They bribe. They make you do things you never would in your right mind. They treat women like their personal toys. Ultimately, they break them, just like they take a hammer to everyone's lives, and they never care who picks up the pieces. I'm so sorry. I'll apologize up and down for my part, but I think you'll understand I didn't have much choice after I tell you the rest. But I'll own my part in this, unlike him. I'm still your mother, and I love you. Leave with me, Robbi. We'll figure out the rest. Please. Trust me."

She's hurt me almost as much as Luke. So has dad, for that matter, drooling on the floor in his drunken, confused rage. His leg continues to kick helplessly at my clothing wrapped around him, but he's stopped yelling.

Decision time.

I break eye contact first. Luke won't take his eyes off me. He's staring, hoping he can make me reconsider, hold me to him by sheer willpower in his gaze.

That's what I expect to see when I take one last glance at his face. But it's not fiery determination. It's pain, defeat, and maybe a little panic.

He's just watched the world he tried to save me from go up in smoke. He doesn't know how to fix this. He doesn't know how bad he's hurt me, and there's no combination of words he can find to make me forgive, forget, or trust again.

We're both fucking lost. That's the last thing we have in common, standing in this rubble. Unsure who's going to make the next move, but certain it's going to be a terrible one.

I'm standing in the middle of a three way wreck, a pileup. It's brutal proof I'm the most blind, gullible person on the planet, or at least anywhere in the Shaw's vast empire.

Yes, that's ego talking. Raw, scorched, wounded pride.

I don't know who to trust.

With everything happening around me, I'm not even sure if I ought to be trusting myself.

My hands go to my chest, covering the bitter throb behind my ribs. I'm going pale from the emotional bleeding, the wounds everyone in this room inflicted on me.

It hurts to think. I have to get out of here before I go insane.

I can't go with Luke. I also can't stay with my well meaning, but alcoholic father, who seriously needs to find his way into rehab. If he's right about being off the Shaw payroll, we'll all be evicted in a matter of days. Maybe hours.

"Robbi..." Luke says my name. There's an edge in his voice. His eyes are big, bright, and pleading. Strong, perhaps, but his power isn't enough.

I can't feel the adoration in his gaze anymore. Only lies. It belongs to a man who said he loved me, but doesn't love mean openness, honesty, as well as strength?

How can I trust him when he's been manipulating me?

How can I trust him after his family ripped a gaping hole through mine, and he knew it was happening?

Was *love* one more lie?

My head is spinning. I need to leave the room before I suffocate, choking on pain and dishonesty. Throwing my arm around mom's shoulder, she hurries me out to her car. Tears blur my eyes.

I don't dare look back. If I do, I know I'll see him standing there, working himself into a quiet rage as the loss sets in.

If he ever loved me, he'll be hurt. I don't know why, but the thought of seeing it makes me feel worse than knowing he straight up lied.

I don't totally break down until we're on the interstate, leaving the grim Shaw estate in the rear view mirror forever.

Liar or not, I'll never forget the look on his face. He betrayed me, and he knew it.

Whether he was sorry for himself for getting caught, or just sorry, I don't know. I don't care.

Trusting Lucus Shaw was my biggest mistake. Loving him was my second. I'm not letting him back in my life long enough to make a third.

IV: Remember Goodbye (Luke)

Present Day

Weather clear. Altitude just shy of thirty thousand feet. Plane on auto-pilot. I won't have to man the controls again until we're in California, on the home stretch to the studios around L.A.

It's good leaving Oregon behind. I just dropped my older brother, Hayden, outside Portland. He's there to kiss and make up with the redheaded honey he married on a whim. She left him in a huff over a big misunderstanding with another woman, just when things were getting real. I thought he'd lost his mind, until I saw how serious he was about the chase, bringing her back and making it right.

That's his problem now. Mine is making sure the biggest break of my life knocks down the doors I've been staring at ever since I got into the industry.

What would Miles Black be doing right about now? It's time to start thinking like him.

Heart throb. Player. Billionaire. Dark and broody as a vampire without the fangs and coffins. Book boyfriend to about a billion women – damn, does he get around – and now he'll be their fantasy on the silver screen.

Correction: *I'll* be their Casanova.

I've got the troubled billionaire act down, at least. I've wondered if it's talent landing me the role, or destiny, considering how many things I've got in common with this fictional man-whore.

I reach for the folder on the passenger seat. Everything my agent laid in front of me is there. It's as good a time as any to review the supporting cast before I touch down to sign off on the final details, and show up for the first shoot.

Opening the folder, I flick through the papers inside, looking up names on social media. There's Aaron Harkness cast as our villain, a two-timing Senator, a Hollywood legend if there ever was one. I'm two names down the list when my finger comes to a dead stop.

Robin Plomb, Allison Evers.

What the fuck? No.

It can't be. I hesitate, reaching for my phone, before I decide to stop screwing around with a snort.

It's a freak coincidence. Another actress with the same name. It takes the internet awhile to load up here in the sky. Her face materializes on my screen like one of those old porn pics from the nineties, loading several rows of pixels at a time.

Her mouth hasn't even shown up when I realize how utterly screwed I am.

"Fuck." I mouth it silently, staring out the cockpit, into the pale blue wild over northern California.

It's her, all right. I'd know those pale blue eyes anywhere. They're almost grey now that she's older, more beautiful than before, glossed with a sheen of worldly sadness.

I'd never mistake Robbi for anyone else in a thousand years. How the fuck could I?

She's burned in my head, stamped into my grey matter, like the last time I saw her was just yesterday. Her features are there, and they're all the same, even if they've become a little more refined.

Blonde hair, cream skin, high cheekbones, and full lips. I'll never forget how they opened on our first and last night together, gushing pure pleasure, a melancholy warm up to tragedy.

These memories are cruel. I take a long, brutal pull of the plane's oxygen while the rest comes rushing back.

Me, standing in her parent's bungalow, that clueless fucking kid who watched his best laid plans crumbling to ash.

The hurt in Robbi's face when she found out I hid the worst. I couldn't give it to her then, couldn't break the awful news. She stormed out, her eyes wide open to my fatal mistake.

Watching her cheating bitch of a mother usher her away from me, sending the venom reserved for my old man into me. Running out the door when it was too fucking late, their car disappearing down the road leading out our gate in a huff of autumn leaves.

Crawling back to that house, defeated, still chasing a ghost romance in my mind. Helping her drunken, bawling father up from his mess in the closet. Keeping him from throwing fists in my face while I called an ambulance.

Hurling the ring in its box at the wall so hard it left a hole.

Limping home with my grief. Seeing my old man, drunk and already into Ericka's bubbly young replacement, fawning all over him.

Shaking my head because I could've stopped this fucking tragedy, I could've told Robbi the truth about her mother, and I didn't.

The last savage call I had with Robbi on the phone. Accepting scorched earth. Slamming my fist into my hideous old man's face for what he did.

Leaving the house for the final time, hearing his pathetic excuses through the blood running down his throat, the last words he ever said to me before I saw him on his deathbed just a few months ago.

I still don't want any part of the inheritance Hayden keeps working like a dog to save. It's tied up in our scheming step-mom's hands, Kayla, a woman dad met who was finally his match, more soulless and conniving than him.

I fly on, my heart sticking in my throat. Briefly, I think about what would happen if I walk away from this shit.

Just turn the plane around, land in Klamath Falls, and forget I ever accepted the male lead in what's bound to be a billion dollar hit.

Too bad Hollywood isn't forgiving. There are no second chances where agents and studios are concerned. I didn't pour my soul into supporting characters and low budget comedies over the last several years for nothing.

I can't walk away now. I won't submit to fear.

If I have to get up close and personal again with the woman who ruined love for me, so be it. I'll be sure to sink my teeth into her lip when it's time to stage the kiss.

* * * *

Two days later, I'm on the set. Ready to face her. I don't give a damn how beautiful she is, or how much history is bound to ignite the atmosphere as soon as we're in the same room.

This opportunity isn't slipping away.

I half-expect Robbi herself will bow out. She never had the stomach for the hard things, like forgiveness.

I make the rounds, meeting the production crew, the makeup people, and the director, Pierce Rogan. I say a few words to Aaron Harkness, tell him how much of an honor it is to work with him.

Director Rogan's infamous work ethic is already showing. It's the first film I've worked on where there's hours to get our bearings, instead of days.

The man doesn't waste time. Fine by me. The sooner we're rolling, the better.

"You'll have to wait until this evening for introductions with Ms. Plomb," an aide to the producer says. "I'm sorry for the delay. Some personal business kept her from arriving before the shoot."

"Fine," I tell the woman, taking my spot on the stage,

practicing my kinky billionaire power pose.

Is it really? Fuck no.

Seeing Robbi for the first time in five years when the cameras are rolling is anything *but* fine and dandy.

I don't buy the line about personal business. It's more likely she's deciding if she can go through with this, face me again when there's so much on the line. Both our careers are in the hands of the same sick twist of fate.

I'm dressed in a ten thousand dollar tux, standing stiffer than a board, gazing down on my imaginary empire in the green screen. They'll fill in the Chicago cityscape later, after we've been there to shoot for real.

Let's do this, I tell myself, flexing my fist so hard the Rolex tightens against my wrist.

"*Bare,* scene two, take one. Action!"

I turn around slowly, placing my hands on the sleek marble desk in my office, meant to resemble a Fortune 100 CEO's. There's a screen built into it, my own private tablet connected to the cameras in the building. They'll fill in the details there on a green screen, too, but I do my best to imagine what the script says I'm supposed to see.

Allison Evers. Robbi. Coming up the elevator for her interview as my new secretary.

The stage crew simulates the elevator's *ding* a few seconds later. My cue to do a slow, sexy turn, allowing a smirk to crease my lips.

She's there. Adrenaline surges in my blood, and I can only imagine what's happening under her skin. I watch her walk toward me without the slightest hesitation in her step.

I step casually from behind my desk, pulling out a chair for her, and holding it. "Ms. Evers, I presume?"

"Guilty," she says, taking her seat.

Robbi never takes her eyes off me. I hold her gaze, searching for the things I'm expecting.

The fear, the disbelief, the attraction it's taking every fiber of her being to suppress…there's fucking nothing.

I braced myself to see the pain I caused, the loss, maybe half a decade of disappointment since our puppy love days were abruptly cut short by our family shortcomings. The reality is a lot more simple, and it shocks me to hell and back.

There's an actress doing her job. Nothing more.

Okay, so she wants to keep this professional? I roll the next scene over in my mind, everything I've memorized.

The cameras pan over me, taking their time to catch a nice, long view of my suit hugging my body from the ass up. If it weren't for my old flame adding her gaze, I'd enjoy being eye candy for millions of lovely ladies.

"My resume, sir," she says. Her eyes drift down to her purse as she digs through it, returning to meet mine when she's holding a slim cache of papers.

I snatch it out of her hand, give it a good shake, and snort. It makes it over my desk when I fling it over my shoulder. I listen for the crunch as it hits the floor.

"You don't think I read your bio before you came to talk turkey? I already know you look good on paper. Stand up." I motion, putting my hands evenly at my sides, fondling the edges of the desk.

My make believe secretary rises. She does the slow, sensual turn written in the script. My eyes are glued to hers, searching for what's real, roaming her curves with a furious need to find out.

It's been too long. My fingers tingle, remembering what it was like to have her lush ass in my hands. The prickling sensation flows into my lips, tasting our bygone kisses, and then it slips into my ears. For a second, I re-live how she lit up every time my mouth found its way between her legs, or smothered her nipples. Those moans are like a ghost whisper now.

Hell, this whole encounter makes me feel haunted.

"Mr. Black. Sir?" She sounds scared, but I know it's just acting.

I stop in front of her, grabbing her chin. There's a spark. It's not just my imagination – it's fucking static.

Robbi flinches. I hold my hand on her face, looking into her eyes while they're trying to escape mine, giving my best broody billionaire smirk for the cameras. "Do you follow orders?"

"Orders? Why, of course, sir. I've served several chief executives since I started interning in tech. Read their recommendations. You'll see they use the word reliable a lot. That's me. If I'm fortunate to work for you, I'll never let you down."

"I'm more interested in your appetite for risk, Ms. Evers." I narrow my eyes.

"Please, sir. It's Allison. My friends call me 'Ali.'" She turns her lips up in a mousy smile.

Sweet fuck. I don't know what makes my cock jerk harder – hearing her call me *sir* over and over, or listening to the nervous, husky giggle that slips out her mouth.

If only it were real.

"Walk with me." I grab her wrist, leading her out through the yawning glass doors at the back of the set. It's supposed to open onto a spacious city balcony, but as usual, we're left to imagine it until the boys in graphics work their magic on the green screens.

We'll be filming in Chicago soon. Why they can't find a place to stage Black Corp's headquarters there, I don't understand. Fortunately, it isn't my job.

We head for the very edge of the balcony. I stand behind her, arms around her waist, feeling how she tenses. I can't tell if it's because my hands are all over her for the first time in years, or because she's a damned good actress, pretending she's looking at the pavement a hundred stories down.

"If I told you to jump, would you?"

She turns around, her best shocked look on her face. My eyes go down to those rosy, full lips. It takes a lot to suppress something rough and primal rising up in my throat.

"Jump? Are you crazy? You're insane, sir, with all due respect."

Her legs open, ever so slightly. Better for me to lean into her. I put my fist in her hair, tipping her gently against the glass banister, passion dripping from my eyes into hers. "Congratulations. You've passed the first test. I want an obedient secretary, not a stupid one."

Remembering the script, I get closer.

Our lips are only inches apart when I pull away. I let go in a quick jerk, allowing her to stand. Taking several strides back toward the door, I wait for her voice before I stop near the entrance.

"Test? Um, I don't understand, sir. Forgive me, but…" She pauses, doing a slow blink before opening her eyes. "Are you really some kind of fucking maniac?"

"Yeah, that's how it is in this business," I say, straightening my tie as I turn around. "And if you play your cards right, I'll be the best boss you've ever had."

One more second. Our eyes stay connected across the ten foot gap between us like magnets. Their energy pulls and pulls, but never collides.

"Cut!" Pierce's booming voice rings out over the speakers. "Marvelous job, you two. Let's take a break before we get a few more angles."

The cameras are off. I'm stuck waiting. I imagine she'll do a dozen things when she walks up and talks to me as Robbi, instead of Ali, for the first time in our five years apart.

Will she be cruel, or magnanimous? Excitement surges through my veins. I'm left wondering if I'll get her hot little hand crashing across my cheek, or just some muddled words about putting it all behind us breathed into my ear.

I listen to her tall black heels hit the floor. She isn't even looking at me as she stomps past, quick and deliberate.

What the fuck? Before I know what I'm doing, I've got my arm out, raised in a gesture meant to stop her.

But she's already gone, passing through the makeshift office, back through the cameras and the lights that will be our constant companions for the next few months.

Robin Plomb just snubbed me.

Forget Miles' line about playing her cards right. There are no rules here, and I don't even know what game she's playing.

If we're going to survive the next six to eight months together, I'd better learn fast.

* * * *

"Seriously, Lucus, what the hell was that?" My motor mouthed agent, Jim Golder, looks like he's about to throw the cup of water he's holding in my face.

We're back stage, taking a breather, just like the director said. "What?" I say coolly, pretending I don't know.

"Uh, our Ali, Miles. I haven't seen passion like that since…ever. If I didn't know better, I'd swear you've been inside her last week." He pauses, wiping sweat from his brow, knocking down his water in one gulp. "Come on, man. I've seen you in those low budget romantic comedies before. You never connected with any of the girls like her. What gives?"

"History," I tell him, looking up as I dust off my sleeve. "Don't worry, it won't affect the role. Everybody thought we looked good today, didn't they?"

He hesitates. "Well, yeah. But damn, my man, if you keep looking at her like that, I think you two had better hash it out over a glass of wine or something. These things have a way of exploding and ruining everything. Only a matter of time before the tension makes things awkward on the set. They're going to want sex scenes soon!"

Shit. Like he has to remind me. My cock comes alive through my frustration, remembering its one night taste of the woman I wanted to marry in another lifetime.

"I'll handle it. You handle your business, Jim."

He stops, pivots away from me in his polished shoes, and throws his hands up. "Touch-y! Okay, Casanova, I'll trust your better judgment. But I'm telling you, if I start seeing a wet blanket on the flame you're supposed to have on screen, we've got *problems.*"

He's out, leaving me alone. I have another half hour before the filming resumes. Just enough time to reach into the nearest drawer, pull out the bottle of scotch I've stashed inside for the tough moments, and take a big swig. I drink from the neck like it's a canteen.

No, I'm not like dad. I don't need it to medicate.

It's there to sand the edge off. I'm hoping it'll keep old emotions in check when the memories hit.

Today, they're merciless. The worst one comes just as the booze hits my stomach and melts into the fireball.

Our last phone call, five years ago, just days after she blew Chicagoland forever. I'd been dialing her furiously for days. It always went to voicemail, until one day I heard her frigid, hateful voice on the line.

"Stop calling or I'm going to figure out how to block your number."

"Hello to you, too, beautiful." Dead silence on the other end. No laughter, no derision, no reaction whatsoever. "Can we talk about this? I realize I fucked up, Robbi. I should've told

you about our parents sooner. I took matters into my own hands, trying to protect you, and I'm sorry."

"Drop the martyr act, Lucus. Mom told me what he did to her. Every fucking detail. She was weak, yeah, and maybe she should've went to the police. But he's a monster."

"It's what he does," I growl, frustration pulling my teeth into my cheek so hard I taste blood. "I can't help it. I can't control him. Dad's a reckless, womanizing, drunken piece of shit. He's always been the same, and it hasn't gotten any better with age. I can't apologize for his mistakes."

"No? So, it's business-as-usual then? Wow. You're right about one thing: there's no apology for doing nothing *while a vulnerable woman got blackmailed into sleeping with him."*

Vulnerable? Blackmailed? What the fuck is she getting at?

"I'm not following," I say, leaning against the wall with one hand. "She wanted to be with him, Robbi. When I found out, I heard them laughing. Heard them all over each other. Whispering the nasty, lovey shit I don't even want to remember. My old man's an idiot who left his morals behind twenty years ago, but it takes two to tango."

"Tango?" Her voice hisses over the line. "Mom told me he threatened her! Threatened her job and then swore he'd tell dad, too, if she didn't keep what they were doing under wraps. She said you'd side with him, as soon as I told you the truth."

Rage tears through my head. I don't know what to believe.

What she's telling me is, it wasn't an ordinary affair. If it's true, there are only two possibilities. Either my old man's even more twisted than my brothers and I think, or her mother's a bigger liar than her drunken father insisted in his last screams, before the paramedics hauled him away.

"I'm on our side, babe. Nobody else's."

"We don't have a side, Luke. Not anymore. I can't be with a man who dismisses what that freak did to my mother as 'tango.' You think she's lying to me. Covering up affairs she never had, at least not with her own free will."

Whoa. Fuck.

"Robbi...slow down. I'm not ruling out anything when it comes to him. He's broken hearts before and stayed the fuck out of my life except when he wants to talk business. Still, you've got to admit, this doesn't add up."

"What doesn't? Enlighten me!" She's breathing hard, on the verge of a full panic breakdown.

"Where's your dad in all this? He came crashing in that day everything went to hell. Screaming, drunk, crazy, but certain she'd screwed him over. If my old man did what you just said, don't you think she'd have told him?"

She's quiet while several heavy seconds tick by. "You can't trust a word he says. He's in rehab, for Christ's sake. Long road to recovery, if he ever gets there at all. He did it to himself, Luke. If he hadn't been so miserable and selfish, and ran from our family's problems to the bar, he would've realized what was happening sooner. He would've protected her."

She's in denial. There's a hideous realization setting in, so deep and sad I feel it in my bones like creeping ice.

I'll never reach her, even if I can find out the truth, and prove it. Nothing will overturn her mother's lies.

Whatever my father did, it's blown a hole in her life so wide it might be mortal. It certainly will be if I stay with her, keep her boiling in this fucked up drama, taint her with neurotic bullshit that's synonymous with the name Shaw.

"I can't help you with this," I say, my voice like a whisper. "Have a nice life."

"Wait!" I'm about to hang up when I hear her voice, desperate and shrill. "Wait, wait, wait, wait, wait! Luke...that's it? You're telling me I'm wrong, and you're fucking giving up?"

Bingo.

This is how it has to be, I tell myself. Anything else is so damned complicated I don't know where to begin. I just know any more mistakes in the web of complexity will strangle her alive.

She deserves better than this. Better than my fucked up family. Better than me.

"You said it yourself – how can you trust me after this?"

"You're right. I can't." I hear her sniffle. Half a choked off sob leaks out before she kills the call.

If the hangar wall I'm leaning on wasn't made with solid steel, I'd break my hand punching through it.

"Mr. Shaw? Fifteen minutes!" A production aide knocks on my door.

I'm back in the present, fresh salt rubbing old wounds raw.

"Be right out." I sigh, standing up, fixing my suit.

It's the same kind of tacky penguin outfit Hayden and Grant love wearing all the time. It's never fit me. I feel naked without my jeans and bombardier jacket, but at least wearing this thing reminds me I'm supposed to be someone else.

On this set, I'm Miles Black. He's a very lucky billionaire bastard because he never loved and lost.

* * * *

She's ice, but we sizzle. We do virtually the same scene from a few more angles, taking the entire afternoon. On our fourth take, Pierce calls it quits, walking onto the stage once the cameras are done.

"Hold up, love birds," he says in his booming voice, before Robbi scatters from my embrace. "We have a very special guest with us this evening. I'd like to introduce –"

"My dears! You've brought my lovelies to life, and I'm so, so grateful." A strange, short woman with frizzy red hair going everywhere walks up, throws her arms around me, and beams through thick spectacles.

Next thing I know, her lips are on my neck, pecking at my throat again and again. She drops me just as quick, walks over to Robbi, and does the same thing.

There's no mistaking her.

"Ms. Frieze, it's a pleasure," I say, tucking my hands back into my pockets. A handshake won't really do after that introduction.

The author beams. "I'm delighted to meet you, too, Miles. You know I'll be calling you Miles from now on, okay?" She smiles like it's the most natural thing in the world.

I learned a long time ago to smile right back at creative insanity. "Whatever you'd like."

Pierce clears his throat, steps between us, and puts his

hand around the woman's shoulder. The genius behind *Bare* stares at us like a dieter spending their cheat day in a candy shop. "I hate to put you two out since it's only our first day, but I'd like you to head down the hallway for a quick promo shoot with marketing. The studio wants to get going on posters, teasers, and all that good stuff right away. We'd also like to give Ms. Frieze something to go home with since she's graced us with her presence today."

"There's nothing more graceful than watching art come alive," she says, never taking her eyes off me and Robbi.

Not at all creepy or crazy, I lie. Eccentric. That's what they always say about the artistic types, right?

"Of course," Robbi says, dipping her head in a small bow. "How do you need us?"

"Standing next to the hot tub we've got set up down there," Pierce says. "A lot more naked, if you don't mind. This one's hitting social media first, and it needs to be *hot.*"

My eyes flick to her. Finally, I see something I recognize. A slow, burning shade of red lights her cheeks, and it lingers, even as she smiles at the director and the world famous author.

"Let me go with you, Robbi," I say, lifting my arm to take hers.

She pulls back, careful to catch herself before she creates an obvious scene. Her eyes leave no doubt about what she's trying to say. *What the fuck are you doing? Back off.*

"Thanks, but I have to powder my nose first. I'll meet you there." She turns, walks past me, and never looks back.

Angry as I am, I can't help watch her ass bobbing as she

moves down the hall, slipping into the restroom that's closest to the secondary set where we'll be doing our promo shoot.

I had that ass, once. How many times have I thought about owning it again over the years? Must number in the tens of thousands.

Part of me is going to enjoy this, having her plump cheeks in my palms again. Maybe a very *big* part of me. The other part wonders if I'll die of frustration first.

Only one way to find out.

V: Accidentally Again (Robin)

There's no avoiding it. I'm going to be getting naked for him again, after I swore I'd never give Lucus Shaw another morsel of my heart, much less my body.

Too fucking bad. The rest of the world doesn't care.

It also couldn't care less that I'm holed up in the restroom, watching my own bewildered eyes in the mirror, trying not to stamp my heels and scream.

No, keep it together. I can't afford to do less. I have to take this thing scene-by-scene, day-by-day, one hateful glance at a time.

As soon as I'm finished washing up, I dry my face, and tell myself I'll forget his lies the instant I've left this bathroom.

It doesn't work.

I head into my changing room, slip out of my clothes, and into the thick burgundy robe they've provided. *It's just business,* I remind myself, as if it's possible to forget the intense, sexual tension that's about to cut my patience to the bone.

The tragedy five years ago is all I can think about when

we're face-to-face again. Or skin-on-skin, I should say.

Luke just has to be shirtless. He's gotten a head start disrobing according to the photographer's instructions.

He's standing next to the hot tub with the carefully placed glasses and the overflowing champagne bottle, watching my eyes pop when I see his perfectly sculpted labyrinth of muscle and ink. I haven't lost myself in it since the night I lost my virginity and the morning I lost everything else.

His smirk freezes me when I stop at the edge of the set, one hand poised on my silk belt. I close my eyes as I pull, letting it drop, knowing his eyes are on me every agonizing second.

"Looking good," the photographer says. "Now, if you'd like to embrace your lady, Mr. Black, we'll keep this short and sweet."

When I open my eyes again, he's staring through me. Somehow, I find the courage to move my feet, heading toward him, into his sultry embrace.

My skin sizzles where his fingers touch. It's a struggle holding my eyes open, keeping them on him. I'm so conflicted and ashamed I wonder if any amount of money is worth *this.*

Whatever happened in our five years apart, my body hasn't forgotten his touch. Familiar electricity runs through his fingertips into me. Every nerve crackles, blisters, sings as his fingers dig into my skin, firmly but gently. My breath becomes shallower. I focus on the black pools in the middle of his gem blue eyes, the ones that betrayed me so many years ago.

"Beautiful, just beautiful, you two," the photographer says again, more clicks and flashes going off like bombs around us. "Robin, I'd like you topless for the next shot, if you don't mind."

I do mind, prick. I mind a whole hell of a lot, but there's no way around it without raising a career sinking fuss. I hesitate, my hands going behind me, stopping on my bra's clasp.

Once it goes, there's nothing between us except my black panties, now becoming painfully wet between my thighs.

Luke's hand glides gently down my back, stopping just short of my ass. He lifts an eyebrow. "Think of me as Mr. Black, *Ali.* No hard feelings," he whispers.

Easy for him to say. Even easier to hide the hard-on pulling at his trunks. I catch the faintest glimpse of the bulge threatening to peak out of his waistband when I look down, popping my bra off.

More cameras explode all around us. Luke wraps his arms around me and pulls me close, just enough to hide my bare breasts against his chest, exactly like the photographer wants.

I tip my head back, trying to look like we're in the throes of passion. It's actually a small relief to put distance between our faces. My nipples graze his hard muscle. They're hard as diamonds.

The asshole has to be enjoying this. I take quick, tentative glances at his eyes, searching for the boy who used to torture me and love it. Amazingly, I only see a man doing his job, no different than a model posing for a junior art class.

I'm not sure why that's so infuriating. How can he go through the motions, without even being hot and bothered?

"Marvelous!" A woman's voice rings out behind us. It's Frieze again, here to enjoy the show. She's carrying on a quiet conversation with Pierce next to her. "Oh, Photographer Man, can you get them to do the pose we talked about? The one where their lips are oh-so-yummy-close? My fans simply adore those."

We stop. Luke and I both look at the photographer, who twists his lips sourly, before he relents with a smile. "You heard the good lady. Let's see the pose, even if it ain't great for marketing."

Luke's hands clench my back tighter this time. Goosebumps rise on my skin, circling his fingertips, peppering their way down my spine. I whip my head forward, staring into his eyes, watching his face move closer to mine.

Jesus. I can't breathe.

He bends me in his arms, tips me over the edge of the hot tub. His lips are coming, so close their heat burns on mine, without even touching.

"Hold," he whispers, closing his eyelids.

Mine flutter open again. There's no more than the faintest gap between our lips. Every sense I have dies in a cloud of smoke.

Hot, forbidden memories flood my veins like slow moving lava. I still want him, damn it. Rather, my body has no solidarity with my heart. It's happy to go tense, steamy, and wet when I'm locked in his embrace, a prisoner to the past and my own very present desires.

I think it's the hate boiling in my heart that keeps me from pushing my lips just a little further, straight into the irresistible storm of his mouth.

No matter how sexy he is, how well he calls to my senses with his mad inks and muscle, I'll never forget our unique pain. I'll never forgive him for hiding what he knew, for letting his father prey on us, or for abandoning me in the end.

How can you trust me after this? I hear his last question in my mind, dark as the day he said it.

"What?" I snap, giving him a vicious look, before I catch myself. I'm hallucinating. The bad memory too vivid.

"I said, *trust me,* Robbi. We're done." He pulls his hands off me, motioning to the crowd breaking up around us.

The photographer has his back turned, checking over his precious marketing photos. The numerous aides, plus the director and author, are gone.

We're alone in the bustle around us, two almost naked enemies pretending to be lovers. I turn the hell around without another look at him, pick up my robe, turning my body to the nearest exit. Before I can get very far, his hand goes around my wrist, and jerks me backward.

"You look like you could use a drink," he says, picking up the champagne flute and tapping its side with his thumb. Bubbles course through the fluid, more chaotic than the rage unsettling my blood. "No use wasting the props."

"No thanks," I say, ripping my hand away from his.

"Suit yourself." He shrugs, lifts the champagne to his mouth, and takes a long carefree pull. When he's finished, he frowns, staring into the glass. "This crap isn't quite like I remember. Too coarse. Enough to give a man heartburn and make him regret drinking it, if he isn't careful."

His eyes find mine. *Real subtle.* I'm seething.

"I'm not your damned champagne. Don't care what you remember about me," I say, leaning in, whispering raw hate through my teeth into his ear. "Stay away from me, Luke. I'm not playing your games."

He blinks, as if I've just told him the evening forecast instead of a serious warning. "It's not all bad, Robbi. You're not the girl I remember. You're more beautiful than her, and a hell of a lot stronger, too. Makes me think there's a chance we just might pull this off, without letting past experiences derail it."

Past experiences? Really?

I can't read him anymore, no matter how long I gaze into his bottomless blue eyes.

Is he warning me back? Being sincere? Or just trying to get under my skin without shredding it?

I don't know, but I'm not waiting to find out. As soon as he lifts the champagne glass to his mouth again, waiting for my response, I throw my robe around me and move.

His eyes never leave me the entire time I'm leaving the set, heading to my changing room.

I hold it until I'm safely inside.

Then, and only then, do I let the tears wreck the makeup caked to my cheeks.

I knew I hated him. But I never knew how deeply until this afternoon, when I had to bare myself for this cold, unflinching savage man.

If he wants the games, I'm stuck with his rules. Luke cares about his career, but losing a few million if the movie goes bust means nothing to him. I have a lot more at stake. I'm forced to tread lightly if I want to get anywhere at all without a fatal trip that sends me crashing down, obliterated on the ruins of our past.

He'll be there to break my fall, one way or another.

He'll cut me. Make me bleed. Yes, *bleed*, just like the very first words I ever heard on his lips, when I intruded on a life I wish I'd never walked into.

Lucus Shaw would be intolerable enough as a complete stranger. He'd threaten my body and my mind.

As my ex, the only man I've ever loved, he's a quietly screaming sword pointed straight at my heart.

* * * *

There's a three day break from the studio. Plenty of time to practice lines, explore the town, and get ready for the flight to Chicago, where we'll be filming the next few parts on the ground.

It should be easy. Something I've done a thousand times in my brief, but devoted acting career.

Instead, I'm too restless to spend more than an hour or two glancing over the next few scenes, always with wine or strong espresso. My go-to drinks aren't helping me internalize a damned thing. Uppers, downers, and plain old water can't wipe away the fresh burn marks Luke left behind.

I'm pacing the living room in my rental when my phone rings. MOM lights up the screen, leaving me to sigh, and lean on the counter while I take the call.

"How's my little actress doing?" she beams, as soon as I press the button to connect. "I feel privileged you're still taking time out of your busy schedule to take my calls. Why aren't you out in the California sun if you're not on the set?"

"I burn easily, mom. You know that."

She laughs. We make the usual small talk about how I'm settling in, finding my way around L.A., noting all the restaurants on my very long list I have to try.

"Oh, you'll never believe this," she says, later in the conversation. "Remember Hayden Shaw, the older brother, who came to see us once or twice? He landed himself in hot water. Some kind of fling with an heiress. He ran out on her and the baby she's carrying, chasing the wife he cheated on. It's been the talk of the town here in Chicago the last couple weeks."

I stop, pinching the edge of the counter so hard my fingers hurt. "Yeah, well, that's a shame," I say, trying my best to sound calm. Like I'm not in ground zero of another Shaw storm hellbent on upending my life.

"They're all sick. Every last one of them," she says coldly. "Anyway, I'm so, so happy for you, darling. All the things we went through when we lived and worked on their estate...it's almost worth it, just to see you where you are. Happy, safe, successful, and free from idiots so rich they think they're entitled to use the world and its women as their personal carnival."

"Let it go, mom. Dwelling on the past or the present drama from anyone named Shaw won't do us any good." I wish I could follow my own advice, instead of using it as a convenient escape from straight up hypocrisy.

There's a long pause on the end of the line. "Maybe you're right. Sorry, I'm being insensitive. I know the anniversary of Danny's death is coming up. Squawking about the Shaws is the last thing we need to think about."

Two years next week since dad met his end in the hospice. He went down empty, drunk, and heartbroken to the very end. Rambling about his cheating whore of a wife, blaming mom for everything, telling me he never should've agreed to work for any of those freaks.

Ugh. I hadn't even thought about it until she reminded me.

"Honey?"

"Yeah, I'm here. I'll do something to mark the occasion, don't worry. Maybe go out to his grave since I'll be home for the next couple weeks filming."

"If you need anything, just holler. I'm always here for you, even with this. Whatever happened between me and Danny, you have my support. You know it's not his fault he turned into a rambling, broken lunatic by the end, right? Frank Shaw drove him there. That horrible, selfish man ran us straight off the cliff. He's dead now, too, and I'm glad. I framed his obituary earlier this year, did you know that? If it wasn't for the security at the Shaw's posh tomb, I'd go there personally just to spit on his fucking grave!"

"Mom…come on. We don't need this drama."

I have plenty to deal with by myself. Every wicked day I'm playing Allison Evers.

"Sorry, sorry, you're right. I can't help but get a little giddy every time I hear about their misery." She takes a long breath. "Keep up the amazing work. Tell me everything. We'll try to do lunch one day when you're in town, and the firm isn't breathing down my neck."

She's serious about her work. It's her taken years to claw her way into law after going back to school and landing a new career. Whatever her other weaknesses, I admire her a lot for adapting.

"Got it. Talk to you later," I say, but she's already gone.

I try not to dwell on the strange relationship between my mother and me. *Try.*

Always her favorite word when there's a chance to spend time together, outside the mandatory holidays and birthdays.

It hasn't been the same since I left Chicago, found my way west, and watched dad deteriorate from afar in one useless rehab facility after another. On the surface, everything looks fine. She dotes over my career success, helped pay my way through acting school, and gushes over me on the rare visits to extended family.

It's not okay. She's never come clean about everything that went down in the Shaw house, and I'm too afraid to ask.

I love my mother. I respect her. But we're not open or

honest, and maybe we don't need to be.

Hearing about more Shaw drama is the absolute last thing I need in my life. I'm too busy worrying about what I'll say when mom finds out who's playing my lover on the screen.

It'll be hell explaining – or pretending I can.

She'll never understand what would cause me to work with Lucus Shaw. And how could I blame her when I don't understand it myself?

* * * *

"Do you want to see my dark place, Ali? You can't keep your little nose out of places it doesn't belong, so I think you do. Hell, I'll do you one better. I'll make you *feel* it." I pause, mouthing Luke's lines from the page in my hands, cringing internally when I imagine him saying them to me. "God. I can't do this."

I'm a mess. My head is swimming. I've polished off half a bottle of good moscato looking over the script. It's getting harder to sink back into my shy, submissive, painfully curious Allison role.

Harder, I realize, because everything is an act of surrender to him.

Even if it's pretend, I'm handing Luke total power over me on a silver platter.

"This isn't going to work," I whisper to myself, throwing the thick binder onto the coffee table, watching as it slams shut. "Seriously. What the fuck am I doing?"

I'm a day away from the next shoot in Chicago. I'll

probably have some time off once I get there before filming resumes. The studio is having emergency negotiations with the production crew over salaries, something that's bound to tie things up for weeks. There's rumors they might strike.

I don't know whether to welcome the down time, or despise it because it's preventing us from getting this over with.

For now, it might be what I need to save my own skin. I haven't managed to memorize half of what I should this week, much less capture the tone, the emotion, all the non-verbal extras that go into a successful part.

I'm too busy thinking about him, and his stupid family. I stay up late, buzzed, my eyeballs glued to the shitstorm about his older brother all over social media. Just days ago, the entire world thought Hayden Shaw was a spoiled, cheating bastard. The #DeadbeatBillionaireDaddy not-so-eloquently captured in the hashtag lighting up self-righteous Twitters and Facebooks everywhere.

Now, his baby mama is recanting everything. He's had a press conference, and he's bringing his woman, Penny, home to the windy city.

The sensational blunder and lightning romance has turned into the biggest celeb love story the tabloids have seen since Prince Silas overseas settled down.

The media was wrong about Hayden Shaw. He's not the cheating, irresponsible, fabulously wealthy shit they claimed. I guess the devil has a sense of humor, or else one of the Shaw brothers actually has a heart.

Whatever the truth, it's not helping my predicament

here. It's just feeding an obsession I shouldn't have.

I stare at the clock. Eight p.m. Still early enough to deal with this boulder rattling around inside me as I struggle with the script, or at least humiliate myself trying.

Reaching for the manila envelope next to me, I pull out the studio packet, and start digging through contacts. It takes me a minute after I've found his number to send him a text. My fingers hover over my screen, burning because there's no better option.

This hurts like hell, but I type my message and hit send.

Robbi: We need to talk. Are you free tonight?

I throw my phone down, freeing my hands to rub my temples. *This was stupid.*

He probably won't write back, or he'll do it when he's at the airport tomorrow. He'll tell me we can meet up in Chicago, some quiet place downtown, just like the few times we spent time in the city together in 'the old days.'

I muddle through the script for another twenty minutes. Ms. Evers got caught rifling through her billionaire boss' contacts, and she's found out more than she should about the kinky, elite parties he used to attend.

Curiosity killed the cat, according to the old cliché. Fitting for a plot that's full of them. Only this time, it won't kill me. Death would be too merciful.

Rather, it's going to get my bare ass spanked by a man I loathe in front of half a billion people.

I really shouldn't have poured myself a fourth glass of wine. I'm worrying about the risk of winding up like my alcoholic father when my phone pings loudly, bringing me out of the stupor.

My eyes go to the screen, heavy with more than a little dread. He replied.

Luke: Dreadnaught Wine Bar. Nine thirty. How does that sound?

Miserable. I want to come clean, tell him I'm drunk, and I never meant the request for a meeting. Not for real.

But if I don't get on with this and try to make peace, or at least come to some kind of understanding, my career is torched along with my nerves.

I write back, telling him it sounds fine, and head into the kitchen to drink some water. It goes down cool, refreshing, easy. Just the freshness I need to make it to my bedroom, where I tear open my closet, digging through the few outfits I haven't packed yet for the trip tomorrow.

I close my eyes, try to control my breathing, and make a solemn vow with just my clothes as silent witnesses. Three simple rules I make up on the spot stand between making this meet the groundwork for a truce, or a complete shit show.

Don't let him get to you.

Don't get wet.

Don't think about the past.

If I can follow through on three simple rules, I might walk away without Luke holding an atom bomb over my head. I won't let the questions and doubts I'm turning over in my head rule me.

Searching the closet gives me one more before it's over, though. *What the hell do you wear to a meeting with a man who destroyed you?*

* * * *

"You're five minutes late," he says, as soon as I take a seat across from him. "Not like I can blame you. I'd drag my feet, too, if I'd decided to show up for more punishment."

Taking extra care to tuck the plain grey dress I've picked out under me, I flick my hair behind my shoulder, and stop myself from asking if this was a bad idea. "The punishment doesn't technically start until our next scene."

"Oh, yeah. I've read the entire script. The sick, repressed part of me should get an extra spring in my step when I'm tanning your sweet ass with my bare hand, Robbi." The monster in front of me doesn't even hesitate.

He stares, waiting for my cheeks to give up the hot, red shame that used to come whenever he made these promises in the past. I can't control it, however I try. At least the dress I'm wearing is very carefully selected not to rile him up more.

"Look, we have to get through this, or we'll be replaced. That's why I'm here, Luke. Have you heard about Pierce's track record with actors who under-perform? Let him down, and you're out the door. No do-overs."

"That's what we're doing?" Raising an eyebrow, he sips his wine while I put in an order with the waitress. As soon as she's gone, his glass comes down, and his wicked tongue moves again. "I thought you'd come by to make friends and catch up. It's been a long time, babe."

Babe is a barb. I close my eyes a second longer than I should, recoiling from the insult. It's a miracle I recover without slamming my hand across his cheek.

Folding my hands neatly, I lean in, and smile. "I'm not your babe, jackass. We're co-workers, and the fact that we're both in this film is the only reason I'm sitting here across from you. Don't think I came here tonight for anything else. I want to work this out like professionals should."

"This?" His smirk hits me between the eyes and makes me see red. "What exactly is *this* anyway? We've hobbled our way through two easy scenes. We still have a whole fucking movie that's going to take a year to finish. What do you propose? Giving ourselves a lobotomy so we don't think about what happened?"

No, you idiot, I want to say. *I want you to shut up, play along, and...shit. I guess I don't have a magic solution for easing the tension between us.*

I'm seething when the waitress sets my wine in front of me. I pluck it from the table, pouring half the glass down my throat in one swallow.

"That's new," he says, his smirk becoming a thin smile. "When did you learn to hold your liquor like a pilot? Usually the only guys I see that thirsty are the ones soaking themselves in airline lounges after their shifts."

"I'm not sure." I pick up my glass by the stem, slowly turning it in my fingers. I look at the insufferable mischief in his handsome eyes. "Wasn't too long after you decided to walk out, leave me behind, and thought you'd come knocking five years later with both our futures on the line."

"Please." His smirk fades. He flattens his hands against the cool table. "I can't change what happened, and neither can you. Don't know how to make what happened between my old man and your mom right, much less everything that went sour with you and I."

"I'm not asking to undo the past, Luke. I'm just hoping we can talk this out, come to an understanding, get on with this movie, without every scene feeling like we're drowning in our own fucking awkwardness!" I'm raising my voice. I stop, take a deep breath. He's *not* baiting me into making a scene.

"And how do you propose we do that?" His knuckles go white as he presses his fingers into the table, leaning forward. "We were almost engaged, once upon a time. We threw it all away for our own good. Grim survival. It's served us well, hasn't it, Robbi?"

Engaged? I grab my wine, quickly swallowing another sip, before I choke on the sudden lump forming in my throat. *He's toying with me to the point where I can't hide it, and I hate it.*

There's no question now. Coming here and doing this was a bad idea. I secretly promise myself I'll never let too much wine make decisions for me.

"It has, but silence doesn't fix everything," I say. "It isn't fixing this, when we have to work together, doing the kinds of scenes coming up."

"It's just sex." He shrugs, motioning to our waitress for a refill. He waits until she's gone before he looks at me again, new mischief sparking in his eyes. "You've grown up. Matured. Surely, you've moved past the childish place where you think there's something magical and sweet about fucking? Hell, we're not even doing it for real. It's make believe for the cameras."

"There's *nothing* magical about dealing with you!" My drunken hand slaps the table. I blink, embarrassed, pulling it back to my lap. "You're not taking this seriously. I don't know why I came here."

I reach into my purse, digging for my credit card, ready to pay up and find the closest taxi. His hand comes down on mine as soon as it's on the table, knocking my card gently out of my hand. It goes spinning towards me.

"I'm paying, and we're not done," he growls. "Sure, I'm being a little standoffish, but I'm not here to antagonize. It doesn't give me the rise it used to. Let's figure this out, Robbi. Seriously." I know that tone.

It's softer, almost caring. The same one he used to take when he'd pushed my buttons to overload. Frozen, I look up, locking eyes with a man who seems destined to torment me in new ways I haven't imagined, regardless what happens here.

"How do we make this work?" he asks.

Finally, the million dollar question. It's actually worth at least eight figures in this case for both of us, knowing what the film will gross. It doesn't have any easy answers.

I try to give it one. "Come clean. Apologize. Tell me you're able to see a professional who deserves your respect, instead of the clueless little girl you abandoned when everything went haywire."

"Abandoned? That's really what you think?" Luke leans back, picking up his glass, studying the liquid inside as it swirls a dozen shades of red in the light. "I cut contact to save you from the quicksand, Robbi. I'm not defending it, and I damned sure won't sit here and apologize. I did the hard thing, the right thing, the *only* thing that kept us from making a nasty situation ten times worse. I couldn't fix our fucked up families. You wouldn't hear me out, much less forgive me. What else was there to do except walk away, and get on with our lives?"

He's full of himself, but it's the most honesty I've had in years. It reminds me what I've forgotten about these kinds of frank, brutal words. They hurt, yet the pain fixes nothing.

"I waited for you to make it right. I thought we'd find our way through, however bad it hurt. Believed in all that 'love conquers all' crap because I lost my faith in everything else, especially my parents. You let me down." I look at him slowly.

Luke doesn't look at me for several seconds. He's staring at the black tabletop, a mirror for a graveyard of regrets that can't be taken back.

"If you don't understand why it went down the way it did, you never will," he says, shifting in his chair. When his hands come up, he's holding his wallet. "I'll work with you, Robbi. We'll be professionals. We'll be good together. And then we'll walk the fuck away like we never had to do this. I'll ease off the teasing, if you'll stop putting me on trial every damned time we're on the set. I left scars I can't erase. If you think I'm here to smooth them out with therapy, you're asking for the impossible, and we're both wasting our time."

I can't meet his eyes. It hurts too much. Plus he's left me no room to maneuver when he's led me headfirst into a wall.

"I'll see you in Chicago," he says, standing up. He throws down a crisp hundred dollar bill, more than enough to cover our drinks and a generous tip. "Have a nice flight."

Yeah, I'll get right on that. I'm sure I totally won't need to use the plane's barf bag when I'm holding in this venom, not to mention the ache pulsing from our failure tonight, new pain seeping into my blood from old wounds picked open.

"I won't, you bastard, and I haven't had a nice life either!" I'm on my feet, echoing the eerily similar words he said when he left me last time after him.

Have a nice life, he said, before I hung up the phone forever. I never imagined he'd turn his variation tonight into a weapon, proving he's gotten crueler with age.

Swearing after him is useless. I can't even see him anymore. I haven't noticed how much the place has filled up, and he's conveniently disappeared through the crowd loitering in the front, waiting for their spots.

So much for the three simple guidelines I told myself I'd stick to for protection. Luke tore them all to shreds with just his glance and a few harsh, honest sentences.

Let him get to me? He's ruined my poise. Left me crying and ashamed, pushing through a crowd of strangers to the door.

Wet? Yes, I fucking am. All the hate in the world can't

extinguish the shameful flame in my belly. It crept between my legs while his eyes were on me, spotlights beaming dangerous sex. The cool night breeze reminds me it's there when it sweeps through my dress, and there's nothing I can do.

And as for *thinking about the past*...it's all I think about on the cab ride back to my apartment. I can't stop obsessing over how he told me we would've been engaged if things hadn't gone to shit.

What ifs hit me again and again, hard as they are relentless. If he hadn't left me behind, we might've had a completely different life – an existence where we're still lovers, instead of exes who can barely hold it together long enough to keep our dreams alive.

That's what hurts most when I'm alone, staring at the script and nursing my impending hangover on mineral water.

There's a world out there where our love never died, and we're living our happily ever after. I see it every time I close my eyes. Luke's strong arms wrapped around me in our big house, two and a half kids, the third coming along nicely in my second trimester.

I push my fingers into his while my wedding ring glows underneath the perfect light in our dining room. And when I turn around to plant a kiss on his lips before we sit down to eat, I see my best friend.

Not my enemy.

Not the man I'll never come to terms with.

Not the cruel, teasing motherfucker who's pretending to

make peace after letting me know what we could've had, if only I'd been able to forgive him.

There wasn't much chance before. Now? I never will.

I'm going to get through this movie hating him. Even when the script says we're supposed to be naked, or tearfully confessing our love at the climactic end.

Movies like *Bare* have easy, storybook endings made to look like they're hard fought victories for the masses.

Real life? That's fucking complicated.

More than anything, I hate how I'll never find the happiness I could've had with him, and I'm never going to get over what we've lost.

Our talk tonight showed me the truth. Unfortunately, it's worthless, and love is just one more *what if* crushed under its wheel.

VI: Unleashed (Luke)

Robbi Plomb is murdering me.

I'm coasting along in my plane several days after our talk over wine. What should be a long, relaxing flight in the helm from L.A. to Chicago makes my guts churn instead.

I can't stop thinking about the way I walked out on her at the bar.

Walked out for the second time.

Shit, I haven't ever stopped thinking about the day I decided to walk out of her life.

There's a storm building over Nebraska. Dense, thick clouds with thunderheads lighting up the underbelly of my plane every time the wind whistles below. My hand tightens on the controls, and I clench my jaw, trying to make myself focus at a time when a pilot needs his wits most.

Too bad they're a million miles away in another time and place. Every time I blink, I hear our last argument over the phone again, where I told her to *have a nice life* without me.

I remember marching up to my old man's office after the crap she said about him blackmailing her mom. If he really did something to Ericka against her will, then I vowed I'd make him pay. My fists were hungry for pain already because he made me lose her.

I remember like it was yesterday, as vivid and monstrous as seeing her explode in rage the other night.

I kick down the door. He's lying on the floor alone with his blazer open, an almost empty bottle of scotch at his side. Surprise, surprise. I expected to find him with the new girl, the tart half his age he's already replaced Ericka with.

The door swinging off its hinges doesn't get a reaction. Neither does walking up to him. Dad doesn't even open his eyes until I press the toe of my shoe into his ribs, hard enough to make him squirm.

"Lucus?" he groans, lifts his hand, trying to block the dim light like it's a desert sun.

"Up." I don't wait. I knock his hand away with mine, grab him by the wrist, and pull him to his feet. He wobbles. Growling, I shove him into an overstuffed leather chair in the corner, standing over him so he doesn't think he's going anywhere before we're done.

He's sickeningly light. The strong, smug man I remember as a kid has probably lost at least five pounds every year since the bottle became his ritual. Booze and melancholy atrophy his muscles and his heart one day at a time. The shit eats down to his soul, too, I'm sure.

I should feel sympathy, but today I can't. There's no room for anything except the raw, angry need for answers. And then violent revenge if I don't like what I hear.

"Really, boy? You're resorting to common hooliganism to

push me around now?" He sneers, turning up his face, angling it so I get a perfect view of the bruise I left on his jaw the other day. "What is it this time? The girl, she's left you, hasn't she? You'll realize in the years to come how big a bullet you just dodged when you're done mourning."

I reach down, grab him by his lapels, and shake the miserable old fart until his lips stop moving in protest. "Shut the fuck up. I'm here to talk about Ericka, asshole, and you will answer my questions."

"Or what?" he whispers, his eyes going wide and lucid. "You'll finish the job you started on me last week? I'd like you to explain it to your brothers, boy. How you beat your poor father, crippled him, or worse. I'll cut you out of the inheritance, and your grandparents' trust! You can spend your days in jail. Probably an improvement over your flights to the ends of the earth."

"Do it. I don't give a shit." I slam him back against the chair, digging my hands into his shoulders, letting him know I mean business. "Robbi told me some things. She said you forced yourself on her mother."

"Forced?" He snorts, a vile frown twisting his lips. "One drink was all it took before the bitch was all over me. Typical star struck gold digger. As soon as I brought her up to my private balcony overlooking the gardens for an evening nightcap to talk bonuses, she had her tongue down my throat. My, that woman could work it, but I guess you know a thing or two about that with the younger, hotter daughter."

My hands move like lightning. I slam him deep into the chair again, baring my teeth. "Shut. The. Fuck. Up."

"You're after the truth, aren't you? This is it."

"Stop lying, old man. You blackmailed her. You made her suck your drunken cock. Told her you'd throw her out on the streets, just like she fucking said. You –"

"Of course, Lucus. It was me. I'm the lone monster in this. Not the woman who laughed when I warned her about her husband on my payroll, before she opened my belt. Not the woman who showed me utter lust in her eyes when I took her in the library, rough like she wanted, and told her I'd fuck her in front of that sad, weak prick she married."

Fuck.

I close my eyes, remembering the day I learned the awful truth about them, before everything went to hell. I don't trust anything he says, normally, but now he's reminding me what I heard with my own ears.

No. No, damn it, I'm not letting him off this easy.

One hand grabs his shoulder, and the other goes around his throat. I start squeezing into his Adam's apple while he looks at me with the same sad, eerie calm. "You better not be lying. I'm only going to let up once when I let you speak again. Tell me the truth, the whole truth, all the fucking truth. Tell me you forced her into it and come clean, if that's what happened. Dad, I need *to know."*

When I let go, I see the scariest thing in my life since cutting Robbi loose. Hot tears stream down the lines in his cheeks, and his face dips to the ground while he chokes for air.

"You've got me, boy. Guilty as charged. Yes, I seduced her. I made a play, knowing she was a married woman. She took the bait, sure, but she cast the first glance the day I hired her.

She gladly took the money I offered after every trip to my bed. Took it with a smile on her lips and a kiss to my cheek, told me it was for her little girl's college. Just a classless, willing whore – the kind I always jump at." He lifts his head, all his inner turmoil boiling in his eyes. I take a step backward. "Let's be straight – you're not here for the truth, boy. You've come to watch me suffer, to witness a break in the wall, and now you've fucking got it. Are you happy?"

I'm disgusted. I just don't want to throttle this asshole until he stops breathing anymore because I know he's telling me the truth about Ericka.

I turn my back and start walking away when I hear the thud on the wooden floor. Stopping near the door, I turn around, see him shuffling toward me, crawling on his knees. He grabs my trousers, pulls on them with his hands.

"Forgive me, son. I'm a terrible man, and I live every damn day of my life knowing it. I miss her, you know."

"Who?" I whisper the question, shaking my head, even though I know the answer.

"Helene. She reigned me in. She made me happy. Made me better than the pussy chasing maggot I've become, who can't go three months without new skin sharing his bed." He lowers his head again, mumbling the part that causes my heart to drop like a deadweight. "And there's so much of her in you it makes me want to puke. That's the real reason I can't stand the fact you won't follow in my footsteps, and can't form a normal goddamned business like your brothers. Hayden and Grant are too much like me, minus the flaws. You…you're her blood, her spirit. I'm ashamed I've let her down every time I look at you."

It's hell giving him the stern look, showing none of the emotion ripping through me while he quivers and sniffles. I pull his hand off my leg and reach for the doorknob, clenching the cold metal in my palm.

"Forget this ever happened," I say, looking past him to the old picture of mom and her plane. He keeps it on his desk, a piece of his humanity lingering like an idle ghost. "Get some fucking help, dad. Rehab. Counseling. Whatever it takes. If you don't learn to control it, whatever your malfunction is, you're going to destroy yourself one day with too much booze or the wrong woman."

* * * *

I know I've let her get under my skin when I'm thinking about the last real talk I ever had with my father in the middle of a storm. Turbulence doesn't care about my woes.

A gale reaches up beneath the plane and slams itself into the underbelly. Sensors I've put off maintaining start to hiccup, screaming warning lights. I grab the controls, my eyes flicking over the mess on the panel, trying to guess which one is real while rain beats down on my windows.

I'm thinking about Robbi again when another warning illuminates and begins screaming.

STALL.

This is no mistake.

The plane drops like a ten ton anchor, nose-down, into the black, stormy atmosphere howling around it. Sweat drips into my eyes as I grab at the controls, trying to recover pitch, pull the fuck up before I'm vaporized on impact.

It's like an out-of-body experience. My fingers jerk the lever as hard as I can. Sweat pours off me. The metallic smell of pure adrenaline fills the cabin. Every instinct I have focuses on saving my aircraft and my life, but my mind is a thousand miles away.

I'm there, and not there, if that makes any sense in what-the-zen-is-happening sort of way.

Death has a way of making a man see everything with crystal clarity. My entire life doesn't flash before my eyes. Just the most important parts, the ones with her.

I see the first time I screamed at her when she walked in on my edgy music. See the other night when I slammed the door in her face a second time, walked away from the minuscule opening she left for me.

I see my mistakes, my dreams, my disappointments. They're written in time, but they seem so fluid with my life on the line, like it isn't too late to erase anything.

I did it for a good reason…right?

Fuck, if I could do it all again, would I?

Yes, I tell myself, clenching my teeth. I've known all along her bitch of a mother lied to her. Ripped her away from me and blamed it on my dead father. She was a willing co-conspirator all along.

I knew, and I owned that knowledge. Didn't have a choice.

I kept her away from me. I kept her safe. Kept her sanity intact and saved her from being dragged into the self-loathing shadows that were a constant drag on my young life. Pushed her out of the family drama poisoning her life, all so she could have a good one without me.

Tore my own heart out protecting her from pain, shielding her from me, and it still wasn't enough. Because the improbable threw her into my life, forcing us to share a spotlight when we should've had our own.

Separate sunrises, and sunsets. Separate lives. Separate road leading her to a man who'd make her happy, without my problems, and would take me to the place I've always sought for some shred of peace.

So far, I haven't found it. I never will if I don't *pull out.*

"Pull the fuck out, damn it!" My whole body hurts down to the bone, trying to right the plane, just a few thousand feet before recovery becomes impossible.

Lightning flashes near my right wing, blinding me. When I open my eyes, ready to see the ground threatening to kill me, I'm drifting upward again.

My heart doesn't beat normal until I'm flying steady, heading into the calm blue morning ahead. It's twenty more minutes before there's sun reflecting on the wings. That's when I start laughing like I've lost it.

You almost died, you magnificent bastard.

I'm wide awake. Wondering. Thinking about how insane it seems that I can't just walk right up to Robbi, tell her the damned truth, wait for her apology, and get on with our lives.

I'll come to my senses when I'm on the ground. But up here, after I've just survived a brush with the end, it seems like anything is possible.

I'm still shaking off my stupor, under two hours to

Chicago, when the satellite phone in my ear goes off. "Hello?"

"Hey, brother." It's Grant, his voice as crisp as the big smile he always wears, peaking through his lumberjack beard. "Hayden and his girl are square again with the public. Thought you should know. He's already talking about having a proper wedding reception soon, and he wants us both there."

"Fine. Good riddance to the baby mama drama," I growl into the mic. "Not that I really give a shit what's tarnishing the Shaw name this week."

Grant chuckles. "Lucky for you, Hayden and I care enough for the three of us. You'll get your inheritance out of the trust soon, too. Kayla's fled since Hayden found out she put the bitch trying to derail his marriage up to it. He would've sued her into the ground with the statement he got for the court."

I close my eyes, wincing when I think how it went down. Kayla was dad's last woman. A gold digger of the highest order, and one he was stupid enough to marry before he croaked. She would've gotten everything, if Hayds hadn't forced her to flee the country, relinquishing her claim to our trust.

Sometimes, I'm afraid the fateful confrontation I had with my father led him down to disaster. The poor SOB fell for her plastic looks and very eager doting. Fell for it so hard he married her, wrote her into his trust, and almost screwed Hayden's real estate empire to ruins.

"I don't care about the money. Glad it's wrapped up, for your sake."

"Yeah, well, there's something else." His normal jovial tone disappears.

"Don't tell me. You're flying to Alaska next week to fight grizzlies with your bare hands because tromping around in the Maine forests aren't enough." Why my brother spends his free time out of New York City in the wild, I'll never understand.

"Fuck you," he says with a laugh. "It's Hayden's Penny. She's got herself a bun in the oven. Hayden told me himself last time we talked."

"Smart enough to run circles around the big guys on Wall Street, and you still haven't figured out how babies are made." I stop yanking his chain for a second to allow myself a smile. It's perfect timing with the sun splashing into the cockpit, warming my face. I pull my sun glasses over my eyes. "Seriously, that's great. Always thought I'd make an awesome uncle."

"You and me both. Just thought I'd let you know, Fly Right." He calls me by the old nickname he's used ever since we were boys, and I discovered my budding fascination with flight. It's a savage irony since I'm anything but perfect, the black sheep of the Shaws. "See you soon at the reception. Heard you're going back to Chicago for your porno."

"It's an erotic romance, jackass," I snarl. "Won't even be an NC-17 rating by the time the studio gets through with it. We're making art here, whenever we're allowed to get back to it, after they resolve their union issues."

"Uh-huh. Remind me again when I have to see your balls hanging out at the world premier."He pauses, letting his words sink in.

I'm about to lay into him, tell him he's a fool for thinking there'll be any full frontal nudity in our production. But it's Grant's job as my eldest brother to bust my balls. I take the brotherly sucker punch with silence.

"Honestly, brother, hope you kill it. Keep up the great work doing what makes you happy. I'll see you soon. Try not to crash that thing." He cuts the call.

Another Shaw. A new generation, and a clean slate. I think about the baby, wondering what it'll be like to have a nephew or a niece. It doesn't matter, as long as the kid coming from Hayden and Penny winds up happier than my brothers and me.

Children aren't even on the radar. Haven't given baby making much thought since I went looking for Robbi's ring, thinking about our future. There's no settling down when I'm playing lead with an ex who hates my fucking guts.

Despite my wink from death an hour ago, it might be for the best. There's no fixing what went haywire between Robbi and me years ago overnight.

Hell, there's practically no chance at fixing it in a thousand years.

What's done is done. I have to work with her, get on with my life, and stop second guessing.

Maybe I'll always have questions, what ifs, and second guesses. Maybe they'll fly out and hit me in the face whenever I let them, like when my plane spirals out of the sky.

Having them boxed up neat in a dark, secret place I

control is no sin. I'm only in danger if I release them. If I let them consume me.

Then there's no excuse for fresh mistakes. And any attempt to re-kindle an old flame that's better off extinguished would be the biggest fuck up of my life.

* * * *

One week of negotiations turns into two, then three, then five. I hate being back in Chicago, especially with nothing to do. Riding the city's L-line like a normal person and casual flights over Lake Michigan get old after awhile. I don't do the fancy balls and limo rides to cross the streets like a normal billionaire.

I take a couple trips out to the old place in the country with Hayden and Penny. They're selling our family's old estate now that Kayla is out of the picture. Their reception in a couple weeks is the last time we'll gather there as a family, before it passes into the new owner's hands.

Good fucking riddance. That's what I think when I wander through the overgrown gardens, walking down the path to the rundown bungalow.

It's like a historic marker where everything went wrong in my life. I've never told my brothers about the trouble with Ericka that cost me Robbi. Hayden and Grant have a rosier view of dad than I do. They were older, lucky to leave our ancestral mansion behind before his drinking and skirt chasing led him off the rails.

I'll let them keep their memories untarnished. There's a large tree with its branches stretched over the old servants' quarters. A single robin sits on it, singing into the lonesome evening.

I should look up and think some symbolic shit about the beautiful little bird who got away from me. There's nothing. Sentimental, mopey thoughts left my head years ago.

Turning my back, I walk, heading to the car.

There's no rebuilding what was ruined here. I have to stay strong when it's time to work again.

Looks like the time has come when I see a voice mail from my agent, Jim. "Studio says we're back in business, my man! They want you downtown tomorrow, and they're pretty picky about making up for lost time. Pierce is in a bad mood with these delays. Be on your best behavior."

My best? I don't know how to give anything else to the biggest break of my life, even if there's a mad, sexy obstacle I never imagined.

I can't bow. Can't break. Can't ever stop to think how I'd lure Robin into my embrace, put her where she belongs, and slam the door shut. Not even if a tiny whisper deep inside me won't let go of the idea.

I set my little bird free for a reason. There's nothing more important than remembering why.

VII: Bruises (Robin)

One Week Later

"Bad girl, Ali," Luke, or Miles, rumbles the words into my ear. I'm pinned against his breakfast bar counter. He's standing over me, my hair in his fist, staring out the window at the Chicago skyline stretching on forever. "We have a certain corporate culture around here, and there's *zero* tolerance for espionage. Did you think I wouldn't find out about the snooping you did? That I wouldn't discipline your sweet little ass?"

His hand comes down hard on my bare, rippling ass cheeks. Insta-scream. The impact burns, totally unhinged.

It's a louder and more intense spanking than the script calls for. My moan slips out, just as over-the-top. So much for keeping it together. It was supposed to be a whimper, a virgin girl set to get a very kinky introduction to ecstasy by her billionaire boss.

This is more.

More, because I *was* that girl with him, once upon a time. Now, I'm stuck pretending love and hate aren't rending me in two with the man I abhor plowing his harsh palm into my ass.

"Mr. Black, please!" I yell, shaking as my fingers grip his desk. "I'll never do it again. I've learned my lesson! I was curious. Worried. I thought the whole company was going down in the D.C. investigation when I saw the Senator's name in your contacts. It's not my place, I know. Forgive me for caring."

Luke pauses, pacing a neat circle around me. He walks to the corner of the luxurious penthouse, grabs two black cords from a drawer, and walks back to me. Ali Evers stuck her nose too deep where it didn't belong, into Black Corp political contacts, and now she's being confronted. It's my job to pull off the scared, lovestruck virgin girl act seamlessly.

"Caring? You think I need your sympathy more than common sense? When I hired you, I thought you'd know better. Thought you knew to respect my damned privacy!"

My pussy tenses, helplessly excited when I see him from the ground up.

Polished black shoes. Charcoal trousers. A dark jacket with a burgundy tie tucked down the middle, one that's going to be wrapped around my wrists in the near future.

"Seriously, you want to go there? Talk about privacy?!" I spit the last word. "Like I haven't caught you trying to look up my skirt when I'm standing on your glossy marble floor at just the right angle. Like you didn't push me to the wall last week before your meeting, brushed your lips on mine, and told me there's no room for flirting at the office?

Like you haven't hit on me every day since I started working with this…this weird dynamic. I don't even know, Mr. Black. You keep going to this dark place, and I swear, you want to bring me with you."

Funny. If I avoid his face, I swear the emotions are easier to tolerate.

But then his blue eyes appear next to mine again, deep as oceans, and just as unforgiving. "Do you want to see my dark place, Ali? You can't keep your little nose out of places it doesn't belong, so I think you do. Hell, I'll do you one better. I'll make you *feel* it."

He starts binding my wrists and ankles to the small leather sofa, stretching my arms and legs to conform to its shape. It's conveniently disguised as household furniture, but it's able to accommodate much more than sitting.

I close my eyes, searching for my happy place. It's safety, where I'm able to pretend Lucus Shaw is just Miles Black, a meaningless name whose emotional appeal is strictly pretend.

I grit my teeth, hoping it doesn't make the muscles on my face twitch for the cameras. *It shouldn't be this fucking hard.*

Oh, but it is.

I thought the weeks off filming would do me some good. I relaxed, I did yoga, even tried meditation. Every defense fails me now thanks to Pierce insisting on the spanking scene. Weeks of dread and anxiety, replaced by real, up close and personal glances from Luke. Plus the unbearable reality – being stripped bare in front of him yet again.

"Close your eyes, my curious little dove," he whispers, bringing his lips so close to my ear his breath blows warm against my skin. I tremble. "Secrets are a two way street, and the dark places sometimes swallow you whole. I want you to count for me, love. Once for every sin I'll make your ass pay for."

It's over the top. It's dangerous. But I do it.

The next time he brings his hand down on my ass, I jerk tight in my restraints. My neck cranes, and I let out a half-moan, something that's not in the script.

"One!" I cry, wondering if this is even acting anymore. I don't have to imagine what Ali feels. I'm as scared, turned on, and vulnerable as she would be, the tense knot deep in my body coming undone as his palm crashes into me again.

"Two!"

Two, you bastard, I count to myself. He's still using a lot more vigor than his part calls for when he's spanking me.

My eyes pinch shut, and I bury my face in the leather beneath me. *Three, four, five!*

Those numbers are muffled. So is the climax building in me, a slow moving boil seated in my womb, hot and wet and rampant when it comes.

Luke used to hint he'd introduce me to kinky things when we were young and stupid. Neither of us ever thought it would happen like this, lovers-made-enemies following studio instructions, his willing prisoners for the next few minutes, or however many retakes this scene needs.

Oh, God. What if Pierce needs retakes?

I have to get this right.

Luckily, my body doesn't need much extra motivation. It snaps back against his hand during the next few whacks. I'm face down, growling the words into the leather muzzle under me, legs out and spine arched when I call out the numbers.

"Six! Seven! Eight – oh!"

Oh, mercy.

Spittle flies from my lips when he hits me again, leveling his force on the red target he's painted on my right cheek. "Nine!"

It's either great acting on my part, or completely terrible. Worse, I'm dangerously close to coming. Something I never signed up for when I walked in for this scene.

Sure, I'm supposed to pretend Miles Black just gave me the most mind blowing orgasm of my life when it happens in the next thirty seconds.

But I'll never forgive myself if it goes off for real. He's standing over me, taking a small break, studying my aching, red buttocks beneath him. He walks to the front of the bench, pushes his rough fingers through my hair, and pulls my head up just enough to press his lips into my ear.

"Three more, and you're done." He lets me drop.

My wrists move in the restraints, finding the tension I need to resist.

Resist, damn it. You've spent your adult life trying to resist Lucus Shaw and his terrible memories.

I tell myself I'm *not* losing control. It'll be over soon. I'm not going to be in a sweaty, tender, post-orgasmic haze when he's done smacking my ass and lifts my head for the famous kiss.

I don't know who I hate more: Isabella Frieze for writing this crap, or my own body, hot and bothered, lurching into total mutiny.

"Ten!" I scream it, bristling when I feel the sting his hand leaves on my left cheek.

"Eleven." I'm exasperated. The threat of having to re-do this scene can't stop the earthquake rolling through my legs. His crisp palm bites my right cheek, and I'm dying holding it in.

He takes his sweet time. Somewhere behind his character's steely expression, he's smiling. Deep down, he's loving this. It would make me sick to my stomach if it wasn't numb with butterfly wings beating like mad.

My pussy throbs, swells, digs into the thin layer of fabric covering it. The slightest friction will send me over the edge. There's no denying it.

"Twelve," he says, his voice soft and firm. "Make sure I hear you, Ms. Evers."

I hear the clap when his hand crashes across my entire ass. But I don't feel it for half a second.

Then there's fire. Dense pleasure reaches up underneath my skin and throttles me, surging up my spine, catching me by the throat.

"Twelve!" I barely choke out before my face hits the bench, colder than ever with this inferno chewing through me.

My eyes are wide, frantic, trying to hold in the chaos threatening to tear me in two. My body lurches in the ropes, tight as can be, before their tension slams me back to earth.

I let out a primal scream of release. I'm writhing for several seconds before I collapse, and then Luke's hand is on my cheek, angling me up to touch his forehead.

We share a look. I hear his voice in my head, his taunting blue eyes given speech. *Fuck, that felt good. You still want me, don't you, little bird? Admit it.*

Yes. No.

I'm not even sure.

My eyes are confused. They want to go everywhere except his gaze, offering the true release I've barely managed to hold in.

"Keep digging, Ms. Evers," he says, a satisfied smirk hanging on his lips. "You've got no choice. You're in too deep. I thought you might end up here when I picked you for the job, and I was right. Are you ready to assist me? I'll need your help with more than conference calls and scheduling appointments."

"What help? How?"

"Senator Bluhd. He's at the top of my private shit list because he's a target. I'm going to bring him down, and it has nothing to do with his investigation into my company."

"Trafficking," he says, brushing his bottom lip against mine. His eyes turn dark and serious. "I'll show you the details soon. You've shown me you're not afraid of the dark. The Senator has done some *very* dark things. So have I, if I'm being honest, but I've never hurt an innocent. This is your chance to back out. Tell me, Ms. Evers, are you up for what I'm asking?"

I pause, let the slow, tense breath I've practiced come, and then drown myself in his eyes. "Only if you start calling me Allison."

"Deal. One last condition in the fine print, Ali. I *will* be inside you soon." His hand crawls down my neck, curling his fingers into it. The perfect hold for guiding me into his kiss.

Christ, what a kiss.

Five years of lost love, pulsing hate, and ruthless confusion break the instant his mouth moves on mine. It's more intense than it ought to be, but hell if I care.

This isn't Ali and Miles savoring each other for the first time.

It's me, Robbi, locking teeth and tongue with the man who's left a greater imprint on my life than he deserves.

It's magnetic. Forced. Inescapable.

Luke growls when his tongue finds mine, sweeps over it, and reminds me how good he is at making me weak in the knees when I least want it. It's a miracle the orgasmic bomb I suppressed just a minute before doesn't reignite.

My breath hitches into his. He pulls my hair. Something soft and sticky sweet leaves my mouth, a moan slipping into his. He devours it, pushes his fingers through my hair one more time, before his fingertips burn a trail down my quivering cheek.

"Cut, cut, cut!" Pierce bellows from the sidelines, entering the set.

I hear him slapping Luke on the back. He's congratulating him.

I'm the one who deserves the accolades for stopping myself from surrendering more lewdly than any screen will tolerate. For not coming *for real.*

"You okay, Robbi? Hell of a job you did." The director's hand taps my back. He whistles through his teeth to the production crew. "Hey! Get over here and get this shit off her, if you please."

I'm still shaking. He crouches down, smiling when we're face-to-face, a boss' pride in his dark brown eyes. "You need anything?"

"Water," I whisper. My throat is cotton. Dehydrated because it seems like I've lost half the fluid in my body between my legs.

There's a wet spot I quickly cover up when I'm back in my robe, arms and legs freed from the cords, sitting upright on the bench.

"Here's your water." A big hand that doesn't belong to Pierce or any of the production crew pushes a bottle into my hand.

"Thanks," I mutter, refusing to meet Luke's eyes. It's too much. I'll blush the second I look at him after what just went down.

He conquered me again, and I despise it. Not Miles Black, but Lucus Shaw, destroyer of hearts and dry panties everywhere.

"Darlings!" A voice squeals behind him, a prelude to Luke being jostled aside by Ms. Frieze's plump hip-check a second later. "I must say, that scene was absolutely glorious. Just how I imagined. You're doing the devil's work, making my wicked dreams come true. Can I get a selfie for my fans?"

I'm really not in the mood, but who am I to deny the

author behind our movie's creative spark anything?

We link arms while she fishes out her phone. I force my biggest fake grin while Frieze holds her phone in front of us, her in the middle, grinning like a Cheshire cat who's just doubled its weight in tuna. I see Luke in my peripheral vision, giving her doting fans a more authentic smile than anything I can manage.

"Cheese!" Her flash goes off. Photo over, she turns back to us, reaching up for an affectionate tug on Luke's ear before she looks at me. "My, you're lucky to have him as Miles. I think we're going to have to share, Ali."

I'm really smiling this time because it's so ludicrous. "He's all yours when the cameras aren't rolling, Ms. Frieze. Thanks for the extra promo."

Luke shoots me a darker look while she trots away, humming to herself. I think it's the movie trailer's test score, still in the works before it goes out to theaters in a couple more weeks.

"I'm glad we're together again," he says when we're alone. "I feel at home on this set."

Pursing my lips, I look away. Frankly, I'm not sure what the hell I feel when I'm in his presence.

"Talk to me, Robbi," he says, stepping up, palming my cheek. "I think we lit the screen on fire today, and we're going to do it a lot more as long as we keep going like this."

Twisting away, I stumble backwards. Just *who* does he think he is, putting his hands on me when there's no reason? We aren't shooting a scene. There's no reason I should tolerate it.

"What?" he snaps, eyes narrowed, crossing his arms.

"I don't have anything to say to you that isn't in the script." I need to get out of here.

He isn't letting me go that easy. As soon as I turn and start moving, he's next to me, escorting me to the hallway backstage.

He's *not* coming into my dressing room. I'll slap him across the face and scream bloody murder before he pushes us that far.

"It's the stress, isn't it? That's the trouble with all this time off while they were mucking with the production crew's contract. Causes you to turn things over in your head, and overthink."

"I'm not overthinking anything, Luke," I say, quickening my steps. He matches my pace exactly.

"Then what is it? Surely, you're not upset about what went down at the bar last time we saw each other?"

"Of course not. I've gotten over it. You were straight with me, and I appreciate it, even if I didn't like the delivery." Lies, lies, lies.

"Lighten up, Ali." He breathes my fictional name, slipping seamlessly into Miles Black mode, stopping next to my dressing room door. "You've got this. I've got this. The whole fucking world is going to see us under control when the teasers start next week."

As much as he's rattled my nerves, he's right. I've managed to survive another day on the set without a complete meltdown.

Then he says what makes my nerves do more than rattle. "Why can't we be friends?"

Friends? Is he out of his mind?

"Sorry, I don't need more of those. I'll be...amiable," I say, choosing the word carefully. "Look, I've got to go. They want me back in a few hours to film the scenes with the Senator."

"Okay, Robbi. We'll do it your way." He steps closer, puts his arm against the door, over my shoulder. "Big finale's coming up in a few weeks, the one where I make good on my promise. Remember: I *will* be inside you soon."

Fuck. There's the familiar lust, the release I suppressed on the set. It's rising up in a hot, wet blush between my legs, resonating through my body.

I hate his words. I hate his smirk. Hate how he still makes my body turn against me, and he *knows* it.

I'm too stunned to even curse him out, call him a pig, or slap him across the face.

I'm helpless as he turns away, starts walking, and looks over his shoulder to say a few parting words. "Take care of yourself this evening. Senate scenes should be a breeze after what I did to your ass." His dominant hand twitches at his side, like I need a damned reminder.

I dart inside my dressing room and slam the door shut. There's a small bathroom attached. I head right for it, dropping my robe on the way.

After putting up with his crap all day and getting dirty, a shower sounds divine.

But first, I really, really need to rub one out.

* * * *

I will be inside you soon. I can't stop hearing it while the water pours down my neck, steamy and warming. Rivulets crisscross my skin and twine around my nipples, two puckered stones where the throbbing is worst, except for the greedy nub between my legs.

The memories come hardest when I'm fingering myself. I haven't done much with men since the night Luke broke me in.

The flings I've had on campus and in bars were never as good as him, if I'm being brutally honest.

I miss his mouth. I miss his fingers. I miss his enormous cock fucking me senseless.

Inside me soon? The bastard already is.

He's lodged in my brain, my heart, and my soul. I don't know where the line between love and hate blurs, but it's happening while I shove two fingers deep inside my pussy, and frig myself to his furious smirk.

I. Fucking. Hate. You.

Yes, I swore off those lips. I wasn't supposed to taste them again after all these years apart. Craving them definitely wasn't on the agenda.

I can't help it. Just like I can't help the repressed climax welling up inside me with every stroke, one that won't be held in much longer.

Say my name, little bird, I imagine him saying, slamming his hips into mine, shoving me harder against the wall with his strong, focused thrusts. My cunt sucks my fingers. My eyelids flutter shut while more water kisses my lashes. *Say my fucking name if you want to fly.*

"No!" I shout it, flicking my thumb against my clit. My thighs pinch shut, clenching my hand, and the white hot fire crests higher, sweeping my fight away. Resistance isn't an option anymore. I'm jilling off to the man who's everything wrong for me. "Fuck you, Luke!"

Cursing his name pushes me over the edge. I taste it when it rolls on my tongue.

Taste every nuance in his vile, addicting kiss.

"Luke, Luke, Luke – oh, fuck!" Machine gunning his name isn't easy when pleasure turns my lips into a breathless ring.

I keep chanting it anyway, a twisted mantra. It mirrors the rough desire lashing me from the spot between my legs. No, more than desire, and not just there.

It's the tingle he's left on my ass, the hot wanton power in his impact when he tenderized my flesh with the fury in his palm.

He fucking owned me today.

I'm afraid he might own me still tomorrow – especially if I can't stop coming like a rocket every time I let his stupid, smug face feed the fire between my legs.

I'm later than I should be getting out of the shower. I dry my hair and change clothes, eager to stop by the production place for makeup so they can re-do my face.

I need to look normal for the scenes where I'm spying on the Senator. Not like a woman who's just let her hate fantasy fuck her brains out.

When I open the door, I gasp. There's Luke, standing against the wall, looking like he's just left the world's best rock concert. "What the hell do you want?" I snap, pulling my baby blue skirt tight and low.

God, please. If there's any justice in this world, tell me he didn't just hear me screaming his name in the shower.

"Left your purse and your water on the stage," he says, stepping toward me with my stuff in his hands. "Thought I'd be a gentleman and hand them off."

The look he's giving me means one thing: he heard. He knows. And I'm screwed without a goodbye kiss.

"Thanks," I mutter, snatching them out of his hands and hurrying away. "Sorry, I'm going to be late."

I don't bother looking back. If I do, I know I'll see him lined up against the wall again, watching my hips bobbing until I'm out of sight.

* * * *

"You know the drill around here, doll. This ain't Chicago. Everything comes to light in D.C. sooner or later. Let's save ourselves some time. Tell me the damned truth. Who sent you?" Aaron Harkness is old enough to be my father, a silver fox if there ever was one, and an incredible actor. He's an amazing Senator Bluhd, distinguished and unsettling. My heart swells with pride working with him.

"The agency, Senator," I say, backing up against the wall as he corners me. "I'm just an intern. They told me I'd get a better shot at an interview if I came to you directly, made the extra effort to get my resume in your face. With all due respect, your record isn't any secret around here. Everyone knows how much you love action."

"Action? Is that what you call a break-in?" He does a good job flashing me a scary look, and I do my best damsel in distress. "Try harder next time. Nobody who's anyone in politics keeps the important stuff in their filing cabinet since Watergate. You'd better dig if you want to nail me to the wall, or I guaran-fucking-tee I'll do it to whoever you're working for first."

He does a smart turn, and walks away, back into the hallway flanked with green screens, where they're going to fill in the cavernous government decor later.

"Cut, cut! We'll do a few more takes tomorrow, but I think we've got ourselves a start," Pierce announces, using his director's megaphone.

It's been a long day. I'm ready to head over to my rental and see about meeting mom for dinner when I hear a familiar voice behind me.

"Robin? Talk about a small ass world." It's a familiar Shaw voice, but not the one who's made my life a muddled hell.

"Hayden! I'm surprised you remember me." I smile, extending my hand, noticing the curvy redhead at his side.

"How could I forget your hospitality? You made the summer visits home bearable. I'm sure Grant agrees." He looks at the woman, his arm around her waist. "Penny, I'd like you to meet one of the servants my father employed, Robin Plomb. And Robin, this is my lovely wife. Soon to be the mother of our little girl in the next six months."

I nod politely, shaking the woman's hand. She's wearing the biggest diamond ring I think I've ever seen. "Pleasure."

"All mine," she says. "I'm *hooked* on this series. Can't wait to see how it looks on the big screen!"

He's married, kind, and as handsome as I remember. It's a shame Luke can't share his manners – not that he has anything to make up in the looks department. All three of the brothers are hella gorgeous in their own right, and Luke has that extra *something* causing endless frustration and shameful liaisons with my fingers.

"Say, you're not the female lead, are you?" he asks, eyes narrowing. His are a little brighter than Luke's, but they're nearly a match.

"I am," I tell him proudly.

"Stars all over the place! Wow. Can I have your autograph, too?" Penny pulls out a pen and a photo from the binder underneath her arm. She smiles sheepishly. "My wonderful husband said I'd be meeting all kinds of famous people today. I really came here to get Mr. Harkness' autograph – he's been my mom's favorite since *forever* – but I'd love to get your signature just the same. Never know how much it'll be worth some day when you're a household name."

She winks. I laugh and sign over my spot on the photo of the cast she's holding, one of the promo shots we did the first week.

When I look up, Hayden hasn't stopped staring, stroking his chin with one hand. "Why the hell didn't my brother say you were working together? 'Good looking blonde,' he told me. Figures."

I freeze. I don't think either of the older brothers who

lived outside the home know about the bad blood his father caused with our families, or the summer love I had with Luke.

"Great question, maybe you should ask him!" I offer, hoping my exaggerated grin doesn't look suspicious. "Need me to point you to his dressing room? He's probably back there, if he isn't in the lounge backstage."

"No big deal. We'll find our way around," he says. I hold my breath, hoping the billionaire developer will just let it go. "Shame you and your folks disappeared before my dad re-married that year. I never got a chance to thank you for helping out."

"Oh, that's sweet, Hayden. Don't worry about it. It's been awhile. I've come a long way from being a part-time maid on your family's property." I flick my hair over my shoulder, doing my best pompous starlet impression.

"Yeah, we all have," he says, barely any humor in his voice.

Penny laughs. "Good luck with the movie. Come on, let's find Mr. Harkness before we see Luke!"

"Whatever you want, love." He oozes all over her.

Deep down, I'm jealous. These two have the fairy tale ending I wanted in my younger days.

But that was before his pig of a father ruined everything, and the love of my life covered up the bitter truth. Before sheer coincidence thrust him back into my life, and forced me to gratify myself to his evil allure in what's supposed to be my sanctuary, my place away from filming stress.

This can't go on, Lucus Shaw, I tell myself, heading for

the lounge, praying I won't see him there. With my luck, he'll be flirting with one of the servers. *If I have to scream your name in the shower one more time with my hand between my legs, you'll ruin me a second time.*

VIII: Drawing Lines (Luke)

I heard everything.

When I say everything, I mean it. The panting, the screaming, the steam roiling her skin while she let out the muffled cry through the door. Same breathless little chirp she let out when we fucked five years ago, rutting like animals in heat past dawn.

I knew I'd gotten her hot and bothered slamming my hand against her ass, but I didn't know it went beyond that until I knocked, nobody answered, and I pressed my ear to the door.

Fuck, she came so hard.

Coming like she's wanted for God only knows how long. Coming like she needs it. Coming just for me.

Couldn't even stop herself from screaming my name through the hissing shower. It doesn't take much effort to hear everything in these tiny dressing rooms with their shoebox bathrooms. It's a lot harder stopping my cock when it tries punching a hole through my trousers, more alive than it's been since this morning, when I watched her whimper and writhe while I spanked her sweet ass.

My palm tingles. I feel her there still, waiting for the stinging kiss from my fingers.

Sure, I knew part of me wanted her. Didn't realize how big that part was before I had her under me, under my control, making music I'd long forgotten with her pleasure.

A knock at my door brings me out of my lust crazed stupor. I throw on my bombardier jacket, a second skin I've had to shed too often lately for the film, and walk over.

"Hayds, you're right on time," I say, moving aside for my brother and his wife. I haven't seen them since the big wedding reception about a week ago. "Enjoy seeing a side of fame that doesn't involve building skyscrapers?"

He motions to Penny. "Give the lady an autograph already without getting too full of yourself."

Smiling, I take the large rectangular photo of the crew she shoves toward me, complete with one of his five hundred dollar gold trimmed pens. "Please, Luke, for my collection today," she says.

"Anything for my niece's mama." I hold the pen's cap between my teeth while I sign.

"Oh, why didn't you tell us how huge this is for you?" Her bright green eyes are awestruck, beaming. "Can't believe we ran into *the* Pierce Rogan! He's a genius. Everything he does blows up big. Hayden said you were working on a movie, but he never said blockbuster!"

"Don't jinx it, now," I say, re-capping the pen and pushing it back into her hands with my autograph.

"You kidding, love? If Luke's head gets any bigger, he won't be able to fly all over hell anymore. There's only so much room in the cockpit, and his ego already takes up a lot of space."

She laughs, tugging on his fingers. They share a glance that makes me just a little bit envious – I'm not going to lie – and then she whispers in his ear before turning back to me. "Mind if we catch up later? I'm trying to chase down Mr. Harkness to get a signature for me and mom."

"Anytime, Penny. Try the little balcony out back, behind storage. The man loves his cigars. I've seen him there plenty catching a smoke before his scenes."

I smile. He gets in a few good brotherly jabs now and then, but the middle child has nothing on Grant. "At least I can take to the skies whenever I want, Hayds. How's it going with the sale on dad's old place?"

He frowns. "I like real estate a whole lot more when I'm signing off on something commercial. It's a lot of work dealing with the crews cleaning the place up, especially when they're sprucing up a fifty million dollar estate. We've got ourselves a buyer, though. If he doesn't jump ship at the last minute, it'll be out of our hands by the end of the month."

"Good. Didn't mind showing up to your reception there, but fuck if that place doesn't still make my skin crawl," I say, straightening my jacket. I sit next to the tiny cabinet where I've stashed a couple bottles of whiskey, motioning. "Drink to celebrate?"

"You know I normally don't. But since this is technically a day off..."

My brother shares my smile as I pull out two glasses, a

little ice, and splash gold scotch over the rocks. We clink glasses, then see who can knock back their shot faster.

I win. No contest when I've done a whole lot more of it than he has lately.

"I'll miss the old place," he says, settling into a chair next to me while I refill his glass. "I know you had a tougher time there than me, but it'll always be part of us, Luke. You can't deny it."

"I can, and I will. I'll bury those fucked up memories as deep as I need to if it means getting on with my life. I don't remember what it was like before mom died, or before dad's demons took him to hell. What I remember, history or not, doesn't do shit for me, bro."

"Fine," he says grudgingly, tipping his glass to his mouth. "Speaking of the past, we ran into someone familiar on the set. You remember Robin Plomb, right?"

"Of course. I kind of have to see her every day, considering her role as my kinky secretary while I'm playing Miles Black."

"Kinky secretary…Christ." He chuckles, shaking his head. "I'm not sure how you're pulling this thing off with a straight face."

"That's why you got the brains for development, I got all the talent, and Grant got…well, whatever the hell he's got. It's called acting. I take it seriously. Believe me, I'm not oblivious to the jokes on the late night comedy shows and the bullshit in the tabloids – same ones who tore you a new asshole not so long ago over Penny and the fake baby mama drama. This isn't porn, Hayds. It's a service to millions of women around the world I'm grateful to get wet. If it makes my star fly a little higher in the end, everybody walks away happy."

He smirks for a second, but then it disappears. "Fair enough. You respect what I do, and I'll return the favor. Seriously, though, why the hell didn't you say anything about Robin?"

Because if I told you our history, Hayds, you'd lose your shit, I think. *You'd either throttle me with your bare hands for covering up the truth about our old man, or you'd punch me square in the nose for my stupidity, leaving her behind.*

Hayden and Grant have both done well for themselves with serious careers raking in tons of money. Hayds, however, is looking like the most serious one of my older brothers period because he's settling down. The family man he's becoming doesn't need more baggage.

"I forgot," I say simply, downing more whiskey. "There's a lot on my plate lately. Hell, you were barely home much in the years she was with us. Didn't think you'd care what some employee of dad's has been up to since she rolled out the family gate."

"Care? It's a small fucking world! Don't you think it's an insane coincidence you're getting naked on the screen with a girl who used to work for us? I mean, what are the odds?"

"It's crazy," I concede, trying to figure out the bewildered look on his face. "But I'm not sure what you're getting at."

I mean it, and I want it to stop. He can't start digging into corners better left forgotten.

The past can't be changed. Won't do him any good

knowing dad was a boozing, lying piece of shit who might've done something unforgivable to Robin's mom. I'm not completely convinced by his confession years ago.

"You put her up to this, didn't you?" he says, laying a brotherly hand on my shoulder. "Shit, Luke. I used to hear her singing, or practicing her lines in those plays years ago whenever I'd come home and sit by the gardens."

"Yeah? And so?"

He smiles, exhaling slowly. "So, I think you've done something amazing for this girl, pulling on your connections to get her in, and you don't want the credit. Whatever, I'll let you play modest. Just know that you're less of an asshole than I thought, and I'm happy about it. There were times when I thought you'd never figure yourself out. Thought you'd either take off with a biker gang, or wind up in the same place as mom, flying where you shouldn't on the wrong night because you've got nowhere to call home."

I stare him dead in the eyes. "You're the one who used to cage fight with the fucking Grizzlies," I growl, not sure I like the direction this is going.

He still sees me as a kid, one who'd take off with an outlaw motorcycle club or some shit, instead of just playing with them like Mr. Older and Wiser did.

"Guilty," he says, straightening in his seat. "I'm not here to patronize, and I know you don't need my approval. Still, I just wanted to say, besides the movie role…it's things like what you did for Robin that makes me proud we're family."

"You can't be proud unless I kiss ass and do public charity?"

"No. Fuck, this is coming out wrong," he says, eyeballing his whiskey and slamming it on the table. "I'll be honest. Grant and I watched dad self-destruct after the plane crash. We worried he'd left us something genetic, something that'd rub off in the worst ways. We got over it when we found our careers, but for you, our little brother…we were scared, Luke. But today, when I'm sitting here, I'm goddamned glad you're proof we were wrong. We had no reason to be. You've got more sense and a bigger heart than dad at his best ever had."

"Thanks. That's big of you, Hayden." Using his real name for once instead of the pejorative makes him smile. Inside, I'm annoyed, but only one response makes sense: shut up. I'll let my older brother think I'm becoming a little more like his perfect ass if it means keeping the truth about Robbi and what happened with dad under wraps.

His phone pings. He reaches into his pocket, pulls it out, and sighs. "Looks like Penny found Harkness. I'd better go make sure she's all right. Just between you and me, I hate letting her out of my sight while she's living for two."

"Congrats, again. Can't wait to meet my niece in the next few months."

He thanks me one more time, and heads for the door. I open it for him, but he stops, reaches into his jacket pocket, and pulls out something else. "Almost forgot. While we were cleaning out the house, we found a bunch of old security tapes."

"Tapes? I thought the systems were wired to show the feed to security, without recording?"

"Nah. Dad was a lot more paranoid than anybody thought. There's footage, Luke, boxes upon boxes going back about ten years."

"Christ. No wonder he knew to chew me out every time I snuck out of my room in high school."

"There's at least a couple boxes from your wing of the house. Don't know what to do with the damned things. The cleaning crew found this gem sitting on top of the crates. I thought you'd want to destroy it yourself."

Dread fills my gut. His eyes say it all. There's either something very private or very fucking embarrassing on the small black tape in my hand.

"Thanks, I guess," I tell him, preparing to close the door.

"You're welcome. That's what we do in this family. Look out for each other."

He's gone. I tuck the ghost on tape in my pocket, wondering if I have an old camcorder and a cable laying around so I can find out what the hell had his eyes shining like he's seen too much.

* * * *

Later, on the way home, I swing by a media conversion place that tells me how to connect the old camera I've rented to the TV. I know I'll probably smash the tape after I see what's on it. Still, there's a part of me that's curious, and I can't resist the urge to look back through time.

It takes a second for the screen to lose its green intro color. Then it's there, my younger self sitting at a desk in the library with mom's letters. I must've pulled them out of their box and brought them on a rare journey outside my room. I watch myself turning over her letters from the old box, the one that's now stashed in my storage vault in LA.

Fuck, there's sound. My ears prickle. My younger self hums the last of my edgy ballads before I left that phase of my life behind. I close my eyes, remembering the bitter, hopeful words.

If you ever loved me, bleed.

Just don't bleed like her.

Leave me a smoking crater before you leave for good.

As long as you open your heart.

As long as you love.

Then bleed.

Amazing how shitty lyrics stay with you for years. It's the last summer I lived with dad, shortly before the heaven I had with Robbi became hell.

When I hear the knock at the door on the screen, I open my eyes. "Come in!" My younger self says.

It's her. Dressed in black and grey, the modest clothing she wears on her evening shift.

My younger self stands, moving out from behind the desk to greet her. Robbi walks straight into my arms, a smile on her face, wiped away a second later when I take her lips. We kiss like I hadn't had her lips every damn day I wasn't on a cargo plane. I kissed her harder every time in the long, teasing build up to the lone night we had together.

The kiss hasn't broken when I grab the remote. I punch the off button, having seen enough, even though it's basically over with my young self taking her arm, leading her outside. Probably into the gardens, where we used to walk together, talking about our dreams.

Enough. I don't wait for the screen to turn black before I walk to the balcony door, tear it open, and step outside for fresh air.

She's getting to me, and I know it. No, not just her, but the past itself.

Everything I tried to ignore, torch, and smolder. That's the thing about love. It's a vicious, indestructible parasite. It sinks its hooks in, crawls into your skin, and only lies dormant until the slightest breeze of memory wakes its thirst for blood.

Did I say breeze? Fuck, more like a hurricane.

Every day I'm plodding through new scenes with her hits me in the face, storms into my blood, reminds me I can make all the lofty, secret promises I want, but it's useless.

She was right the night we sat down weeks ago over wine. *We can't go on like this.*

After seeing the tape, watching the happy ghosts moving on the screen, I have to take action. As soon as I've refreshed my lungs with cool Chicago air, I go inside, tear a page from my notebook, and find a pen.

I haven't put this much thought into writing anything since those crap ass pity songs in my youth. These words *will* move her.

If they can't win her back, then they're damned sure going to make her cry.

IX: Here It Comes (Robin)

It's an easy week. *Too easy.*

I work with Harkness on scenes with the Senator most days. Ali Evers earns his trust, discovers secret leads on the trafficking cartel he's working with, and, of course, falls even deeper in love with her broody, spank-happy billionaire foil.

But I haven't filmed the next parts with Luke yet. He's nowhere to be found around the studio, which should be a relief.

It isn't. Actually, his absence leaves me unsettled, and I can't for the life of me understand why.

The next scenes are going to be horrible, and I think we both know it. I've looked over the final script. He's due to strip me naked, haul me into bed, and take my virginity in the hottest scene the family friendly groups doing the film's ratings will allow.

It's worse than reliving what we had, and lost. In character, Miles Black is supposed to knock me up.

I should be relieved he's gone. But a restless part of me just wants to get on with it, get it the hell over, and move onto the final action scenes so we can do our wrap up, and never have to see each other again.

I'm coming home from coffee with my agent, Bebe, when I see the small manila folder slid under my door. Seeing his crabbed, familiar writing in a black pen hits me in the gut. There's no name on it, but I'd know his handwriting anywhere.

READ IT, the words scratched on the front say. My fingers tremble when I slit the edge with a knife. I catch myself, annoyed with my nerves, and slam the utensil on the counter.

Christ. It shouldn't be this bad. I'm shaking like a junkie who's just picked up her latest fix after swearing off a bad trip.

It's not such a terrible analogy. For me, Lucus Shaw *is* that bad trip. And whatever he's trying to say in this letter promises nothing but another walk through the seventh circle of emotional hell.

I *could* ignore it. Rip the thing up, throw it in the trash, and forget about it until we see each other again for our baby making torture on camera.

Yeah, and maybe I'll become stronger than a heavyweight boxer with special forces training tomorrow. Sighing, I pull out the contents. It's a single sheet, surprisingly.

Robbi,

You're killing me, and we have to talk. I know I walked out on you at the wine bar. I know I did wrong. I know you think I'm enjoying it every time we get naked, kiss, or pretend we're in love for the screen.

Guess what? Everything you know is fucking wrong.

We have to come to terms about the past. If we don't, somebody's going to walk from this film before it's done, and it'll probably be me.

I told you the first time we saw each other after our break you were strong. You've only proven it the last few weeks we've worked together. I'm man enough to say it. Admit you're maybe a little stronger than I am when we're out there on the set, living the lie the script says.

I know you've got your limits, though. Know you let your pain out privately, drain the wound when you're alone in the shower, fucking your fingers and screaming my name like you've missed me more than life itself.

I can't continue playing games, and neither can you. We have to get our shit together.

We met when you heard me asking my dead mother if she still bled for me, wherever she is.

Next time we meet, I want us bleeding together. Let it the fuck out. However angry, dark, and therapeutic it needs to be.

I'm taking my plane on a joy ride over Lake Michigan tomorrow evening. I hope you'll show up. There's no better way to re-connect and find your basic humanity than when you're freed from gravity. Let's talk.

Yours, L.

I'm done.

Done, done, done, done, and *done* with his crap. The paper crumples, tears, and screams in my hands with a noise like the world I've known coming apart.

I toss it across the room before I hold my hands over my face. Dramatic? Yes, and I don't fucking care.

I'm giving him another chance to make this right when the outcome couldn't be clearer. Letting him drag me into another heart-to-heart thousands of feet in the air will end in ruin for the plane or my emotions.

I'll do my job. I'll smile for the cameras and put my lips on his when I need to. Yes, I'll even rub my clit behind closed doors and howl his name through clenched teeth if that's what it takes to keep my sanity.

Luke won't break me. I'm not giving him the chance.

* * * *

Okay, I lied. It's less than twenty-four hours later, and the chase is on.

I'm in my car, gripping the steering wheel so hard my knuckles turn white while I'm flooring it to the airport. The one thing that will make me feel like an even bigger fool than racing to see him against my better judgment is if he's already airborne.

The dream last night changed my mind. I re-lived the past. Woke up in a cold sweat, wide awake after seeing Luke next to me our first and only night together.

How gorgeous he was laying there, a rare smile on his lips, his strong arm around me. I laid there late in the morning, an hour after he'd fallen asleep, just listening to his heartbeat with my ear against his massive chest.

We'd made each other happy, once.

Why did it stop? Why, five years later, do we bring ourselves nothing except endless pain and frustration?

If the dream wasn't enough to make me re-think my visceral reaction to his letter, the questions are. They suffocate my heart because I can't answer them.

Maybe I'm about to make the second biggest mistake of my life, getting in his plane. But I'd rather land on solid ground again in a mess of tears than wonder without answers.

It takes half an hour to get through the airport, out to the private section of the tarmac he's given me. I'm over ten minutes off the takeoff time he listed. I don't know whether he's taken off yet or not.

At first, I don't recognize him standing next to the big silver jet. When the sunlight hits his eyes, turning ocean blue to sky, I'm not sure how I ever missed him.

He's breathtaking in pilot mode. His leather bombardier jacket hugs his wide shoulders, billowing softly in the breeze, just like the dark crop of hair framing his strong face.

My heart skips a beat, and I hate it. The dream last night has nothing on seeing Lucus Shaw in the flesh again when he's at his finest.

He's standing next to the plane, waiting past his takeoff time. If I didn't know better, I'd say he almost looks disappointed. He thinks he's delayed his flight in vain, waiting for a no show.

I hesitate, waiting for him to turn and start heading up the short staircase to the plane's cockpit before I shove the glass door open.

Last chance to back out with your ego intact. No, it's not even an option.

"Wait!" I call, running several yards, waving.

He turns around just in time. "Robbi?"

My smile vanishes about as quickly as the surprise on his face. The fact that I'm climbing up the stairs means it's really happening, and I'm not sure either of us expected it.

"Glad you could make it," he says, stopping when we're both on the top step. "Even if you're so late I was two minutes from leaving without you."

"I'm here to talk, Luke. Talk, just like you said in the letter. Don't pull anything that makes me regret it."

It's only talk. A negotiation seeking an understanding.

It doesn't mean we're hunting second chances.

"Come on. I'll help you get strapped in," he says, taking my hand and leading me inside. When he pushes the metal door shut and turns the heavy lock, it's just him and I, free from the rest of the world.

* * * *

I've never been in a cockpit before. It's bigger than I expected, a small passenger plane with a cabin behind us, leather seats, a bar, and a very noticeable bed. Passion makes him fly the damned thing himself when he's rich enough to afford a pilot.

The décor is about as tacky as his personal style. Black designed to look textured like marble, gold flourishes cutting through the darkness, adding its color.

I'm in the co-pilot's seat, but there's nothing fancy about it. It's much closer quarters than I imagined. His hand brushes mine while he works the controls. The plane rolls smoothly down the runway, picks up speed, and brings us high into the sky.

I'm enjoying the ride so much while we rise I almost forget why I'm here. I remember as soon as he gives me his famous look, kissing the skies above Lake Michigan.

It's time, his eyes say, before he speaks. "You hate me for what happened, and you should."

Ouch. So much for easing into it. I clear my throat, taking an extra second to think before I ruin the wild blue yonder up here with a shit storm.

"Luke, it's not like that. I don't know if I hate you. There were times when I was sure I did. But if I really hated you, deep down, we wouldn't be taking this flight. I wouldn't be doing this movie."

"Five years to sort it out, and you still don't know?" He sounds incredulous.

"It's not like we had sex scenes the whole time to figure it out! We kept our distance. We forgot. Before this movie, forgetting was just fine. Wounds healed and formed scars. Ideally, I'd have kept it that way."

"I ripped them open, didn't I?" He puts his hands on the yoke in front of him, slowly executing a turn. I look down, avoiding his eyes, watching the sunlight glisten on the lake below. "Believe me, babe, I know how it feels. There are a few things you tore to hell, too."

"Me?" It comes out harsher than it should. God, if he's brought me up here to dump the blame on my head, I swear I'm going to use his skin as a parachute. "Like what?"

"Discipline. Control. Sanity. I'm losing them one-by-one every day we're on the set, Robbi. You've got me so hot and bothered I should be a steamed fucking clam. I told you in the letter, someone's going to walk if we can't get the tension in check. We need to keep it professional if we're finishing this film."

"Well, excuse me, Mr. Sensitive. I'm sorry I got you so twisted up you went peeping tom on my dressing room the other day."

His smirk is showing. I think I'm about to prove to the F.A.A. spontaneous human combustion can bring down a plane. "Technically, it's not peeping if I only used my ears. I never set foot in your room once, Robbi."

"Technically, I think you're a huge asshole. You're not helping anything. Why are we even here?"

He doesn't say anything. Then he reaches for one of the levers on the plane, pulls it hard, and sends us careening toward the spotty clouds covering the sparkling water.

I'm screaming. "Are you out of your mind?!"

The plane turns. I'm not sure why the sky looks so different until I realize we're upside-fucking-down.

"Why are we here, Robbi?" he asks, repeating my question with an eerie calm. "Because I'm done playing games. I'm done pretending there isn't this insane love-hate spark between us that's more exasperating than this stupid trick I learned at an air show will ever be. I'm sick – sick to my gut – acting all the damned time, even when I'm not reading off a script. I can't stand not knowing what's real, where our character's lines end and the truth between us begins."

I'm hyperventilating. His heavy hand comes down on my arm and squeezes. Then he moves it down along my forearm, pushing his fingers through mine. "Open your eyes," he says.

I do, and everything is right with the world. The sky is where it should be, and so is the water. Now that my life isn't flashing before my eyes anymore, I'm *pissed.*

"Asshole, why?" I say, tightening the grip I have on his hand, digging my fingernails into his palm so hard I hope they cut.

"Because I want you mad. Anger means honesty. Every time we sit down and try to sort this out, we end up papering over it until it all boils over next time. We both walk away in a rage, and that can't continue. It's not doing us any favors. Up here, there's no walking away."

That's it. I'm trapped in the sky with a manipulative

lunatic. I hate how he's right, even when his sanity is questionable. I shove his hand away, balling my hands together on my lap. Fine, I'll play along because there's nothing else that'll make him land this stupid plane.

"Okay, okay. You want mad?" My fists clench, digging into my thighs. "I'm tired of being jerked around after what you and your fucked up family did to mine, Lucus. What your father did to my mom, it wasn't your fault, but *you* let it ruin us. You walked away. You decided I wasn't good enough, or I was too much trouble after you'd had your fun. You tossed me away. How the fuck am I supposed to ever get over it? I mean, really? Especially when I have to re-live the best of us acting in this stupid movie?"

When my voice dies and the echo stops, I realize I'm shouting. *Good God.*

It's outrageous what he does to me. No man should call to my baser senses, slip beneath my skin, and stir rage and want in equal measure. No man should throw them together, amuse himself with the chemical reactions I can't hide storming in my blood.

I tell myself I'm not his toy. I'm not here for his amusement. I wish I knew *why* I decided to take him up on this stupid offer.

"I tried to protect you, Robbi. Pushed you away because you deserved better than being tied down to the fucked up drama." He speaks slowly, his eerie calm holding. "Hurt like hell, if you want to know the truth. So did confronting my old man. I went to him as soon as we got off the phone. I was ready to kill him if he really did what your mom said."

I don't even know what to say to that. My eyes study him, trying to figure out what he's after, but I think I'm actually getting the truth. Can I handle it?

"My father was no saint. I'm not defending his bullshit. The man drank himself stupid, he went through women like expensive scotch, and he almost wrote off our whole family fortune to a huge gold digger before he left this planet. But he told me he never blackmailed her, never forced Ericka into doing those things. He said she came willingly. There was no arrangement he trapped her in."

There it is. The biggest question of my life, reaching up and slapping me across the face. I want to rush to my mom's defense, but remembering how dad reacted, refusing to speak to her after the divorce, leaves just enough doubt.

"That's crap!" I'm shaking when I spit it out. "You can't tell me it's that easy, believing what he said after all these years? You said it yourself – the man was nuts. Both our fathers were. Both unreliable."

Luke doesn't say anything for about a minute. "I don't know what to believe. I just regret the damage it's done. Whatever happened between our folks, we're the ones who suffered."

I'm about to sink my teeth into him again, but the bastard has a point. "So? It's not like it could've gone down any other way. There's no coming back from everything that happened. We suffered for them, sure, and they hurt us both. But you're the one who ruined us. You let me go for good."

"Did I?" he says, pausing just long enough to roil my

thoughts. "I let you go, true, which was a huge fucking mistake. Nobody ever told me it was for good."

"No!" I say it so quickly I almost bite my tongue. "No, Luke. This isn't happening again. It's impossible. We're done. No mending fences."

"If you're so sure it's impossible, then you're right to ask why we're wasting our time sailing the skies. I might as well turn this thing around and take us down. I'm better off hashing out how I'll tell Pierce to find a replacement for Mr. Black."

My heart catches in my throat. He can't be serious about quitting…can he? "Come on. This shouldn't mess with your career, or mine. You're right about one thing – we don't need to be enemies."

I don't know why, but thinking about getting naked for a new actor playing Miles fills me with dread. Much more than the fear welling up when I think about doing those scenes with the man next to me.

"I'm a Shaw, Robbi. You're forgetting I've got the greatest consolation prize in the world if I walk. I blow my chance at fame, at art, at anything, I'm still living out the rest of my days as a no name billionaire. That's nothing to whine about. It also gives me a whole hell of a lot of freedom."

"No. It isn't fair. Money or not, you've worked just as hard as me to get here. These chances only come up once in a lifetime if you blow them. You know how unforgiving this industry can be. Besides, our faces are already showing up all over the place. If you quit, we'll have half a million of Frieze's fanatics beating down the studio doors tomorrow.

You're their Miles. They love you."

"I'd rather face a mob of angry women than more shit between you and me. I know how to deal with pissing people off. Rarely did anything else growing up. Fixing deep hurt, putting a muzzle on this desire we're pretending doesn't exist...that's a hell of a lot more complicated. Where the fuck do I begin?"

Damn you, I think. I'm softening the longer I stare at his tragic face. He's trying so hard to keep it in, to betray nothing, but the mask of calm he's wearing tells too much. "By knowing this helped."

He looks at me intently. "What do you mean?"

"This talk. It felt...good, I guess, to let it all out. We don't have to hate each other or die inside every time Pierce tells us to perform some new torture. I can't deny there's a part of me that's still attracted to you, Luke." I pause, knowing full well I'm risking inflating his ego bigger than it already is. "But I can deal with that. It's the other tension surrounding the past that's so fucking difficult, but believe it or not, I think we've made some progress today. I understand where you're coming from, and maybe you get me a little better, too."

He smiles, pulling the shades down over his eyes. "You're right. If we keep this up, we'll get by without more awkward moments where I hear what you do in the shower.

My cheeks burn. "Can we please stop talking about that?"

"Sure. I'd much rather find out what's real, anyway, if I'm going to be honest." He takes us lower, around the

Chicago skyline's edge. I see the Shaw Glass Tower below, the one Hayden owns, another landmark in the city's imperial majesty.

"What do you mean, what's real?" I ask. "You're so vague."

"Don't worry about it, little bird. We figured ourselves out a long time ago, when we had something. By the time this movie's done, I think we'll do it again. We'll both walk away wiser when we find out where we really stand." Hearing him use the old nickname makes tears nip at the corners of my eyes, and they're not all sad ones.

"Luke, what are you talking about? Where we stand on *what?*" I turn away, suppressing the outburst, looking out over the place that's promising me a second chance.

"Everything," he says. "Everything that matters."

Second chances. If that's what he's offering in his own cryptic way, then I've got a lot of thinking to do.

* * * *

Later, at my apartment, I'm decompressing from the fucked up flight.

I left the ground convinced I hated his guts. Now...I'm not sure what I believe.

It doesn't get any easier when my phone lights up while I'm drifting off on the couch, thoroughly exhausted after today's insanity. It's mom. I almost let it go to voicemail before I take the call at the last second.

We had a quick late night dinner at a place downtown the other evening. She said she was going to get around to checking out the promos for the movie this week. I guess she's calling to give me her opinion. Part of me is actually curious what she thinks.

"Robin, what the hell do you think you're doing?" Her voice is hurt. Angry, and trying not to show it.

So much for sleep. "What's wrong?" I say, a weight in my stomach telling me I already know.

"I saw the posters. The trailer today. God. Lucus Shaw, baby? Have you lost your mind?"

Shit. Panic takes the floor out under me. I scoot to the edge of the couch and double over slightly, trying to clear my head, come up with answers I don't have myself.

"It's purely professional," I say weakly. "Look, when I took the part, I didn't know he'd been cast to play Miles Black. He's been...okay to me. So far."

At least if I can call 'okay' being lifted above Lake Michigan for a brutal self reflection.

"It's too late to turn back anyway, mom. We're almost halfway through." I sniff, trying not to let my nerves weaken me. She's staying eerily silent on the other end. "I can't back out without ruining my career."

"I want to talk to your agent," she says, shifting into the no nonsense tone I heard as a little girl.

"Excuse me?"

"Bebe, isn't it? Put her on the phone. I'm getting you out of this. I don't care how much time or money it takes."

"No, you're not," I say, standing as anger's heats my blood. "I'm not a kid anymore, mom. You don't have to tell me for the millionth time about all the evil things that went down between you and Frank Shaw."

"You think this is about that evil bastard and *me?* Like I don't remember how I pulled you away from him the day we left that horrible house? I know you two had sex."

Even after all these years, lying about the obvious, the shameful truth heats my face. Burns it hotter than ever because sex with him has been on my mind more than it should be.

"That's all in the past, mom. You don't have to come running to protect me. I'm a grown woman. I know what I'm doing in my industry. There's no way I'm ever letting Luke do anything you'd have to worry –"

"The past *is* the present if you're telling me you're not stepping down. Every day you're with him, you're in danger, honey. Has he touched you? How many head games has he already played?" She's frantic.

A sickening knot pulls tight in my stomach. I regret what happened in the plane today, when I almost decided to shake the past. Whenever I hear mom's voice, I'm reminded what kind of evil stamp the Shaws left on our lives, a monstrous shadow she'll never get to leave.

"It's kind of a romance film," I say, downplaying the erotic part. "Obviously, there's physical contact. We work off the script. We're professionals. I never let him do anything that isn't written down. Our director, Pierce, has the highest standards. He'd never allow any funny business either, mom." The last part is a lie – probably. But I don't know what else to say to win her trust.

"I don't care about his damned standards, Robbi. What

about mine? I want you out of this, before it's too late. There just *has* to be another way you can make your mark in Hollywood."

I pause, trying and failing to find words to make her understand, that won't piss her off. There are none. "Well, there isn't, mom. I'm finishing what I've started. I'm not backing down because we're supposed to consider every minute with a Shaw a dance with the devil. I'll wrap up my scenes with Luke, see him at the award ceremonies if we're that lucky, and never deal with him again. Easy."

"Easy?" She pauses, sniffing back what have to be angry tears. Way to make me feel guiltier. "Easy was how your father and I had it before we ever took jobs with the Shaws. I'm telling you, that place was cursed. Not with black magic, but with human evil I've tried my entire life to keep away from you."

She pauses. I should take advantage of the gap in the conversation to reassure her, tell her the past isn't repeating itself, but I have no proof.

I have no fucking proof…do I? For all I know, Luke could be setting me up for my next great fall, especially if he's even half as bad as his father.

"Keep working with him, then. Don't listen to me. I'll let you get burned, Robin Marie, and if you continue on with a man like him, you absolutely will."

The phone clicks dead. I throw it on the couch, crashing down on the opposite side with my face in my hands.

There's no winning this. No understanding it. No truce, and no peace.

Every time I've found my escape from being hopelessly fucked, I'm hurled back into the same battlefield. Caught between the love, the hate, and the man who leaves me a broken mess over ninety percent of the times we interact.

I don't know when the stalemate will ever end, but it has to be soon.

* * * *

"I never should've sent you alone, Ali. I'm going to kill him." Miles Black scoops me up in his strong, heavily inked arms. His fingers gingerly touch the fake bruises and scratches on my skin, injuries my character sustained running from Senator Bluhd's guards with the files from his office.

"I never should've sent you alone," he says again.

"I had to," I say tearfully. "Please, sir, don't blame yourself."

He stops just before we're in the bathroom with the massive windows overlooking the summer beauty outside. His eyes bore into mine, but it's not a fictional billionaire looking at me. It's the real one, the man I loved. "Miles. No more of that sir and sado crap tonight. I'm cleaning you up, baby, and then we're making love. What you've deserved from the start."

No, not Miles Black, but Luke. There's a heart wrenching note to his tone far greater than the script calls for. For a second, I'm worried Pierce is going to butt in, and make us re-do it.

It's like I can feel his inner anguish as he carries me into the bathroom, unclasps my robe, and guides me gently into the shower. My face heats against the wall. I'm grateful Ali doesn't have to watch him undress because I think right now I'd blow it.

I don't look at him until he steps into the shower, naked with me, reaching to turn the nozzle while his other arm goes around me. "This ends here. No more pulling you into my world, my danger, my pain. You're not my secretary anymore, Ali. You were never meant to be my spy. You're going to be my wife and the mother of our children."

The shower hisses to life. I'm not sure whether my heart or my pussy melt faster as I lean into him, hazy warmth flowing around him, brushing his rock hard cock with my ass.

Of course, we're both wearing skin-tinted body shorts from the waist down. But it leaves nothing to the imagination when he comes in close, moving his hardness against me, grabbing the silk cloth off the little hook next to us.

He washes me while the shower beats down on our skin like frothy tears. Thank God, too, because I can't hold in all the emotion. It slips out through the cracks in my heart, beckoned by this stupid scene that means more than Pierce will ever know.

The shower's steady beat hides my real tears. The soft growl spilling from his throat hides the moan that leaves my lips when they open, excitement and sadness oozing out of me in equal measure.

His hand lays the washcloth against my thigh. He glides it around slowly, moving his fingers between my legs, pushing against the fabric the CGI will touch to naked glory later.

There's no need for him to use as much pressure as he does. No professional reason, I should say. The desire, the touch, the possessive flick of his strength…that's all Lucus Shaw, and I'm ashamed to say I love it.

I want to turn around and kiss him right now. But the script says Ali is too tired for that, too broken after escaping her near beating from the guards. I'm also scared for what's coming next, when he's done cleaning me.

Luke's hand keeps moving. His touch is electric, fierce, so damned real I don't have to fake anything when the shower's beat grows to a shrill crescendo in my ears.

I'm coming on his hands through my panties. He's loving it, devouring me a little more at a time as my breath comes out in desperate huffs, jaw clenched tight, trying not to cry out his name and ruin the entire scene.

When the hot, swift fire sweeping through me recedes, I flatten myself against the wall, trembling a little more than I should for the scene. Luke turns off the water. Grabbing me by the shoulders, he leads me gently through the opening in the thick glass door, wrapping me in a towel as he wipes the last water droplets from my face.

"God, you're beautiful." He says his line, but it's so much more than words crafted by a dialogue editor.

It's honest, heartfelt, and no, his eyes don't lie. Neither do his fingers when they sweep over me again, more softly than before, tucking my wet hair back against my head. Then his face moves in.

My eyes go wide because he's not supposed to do this. There's no kiss written into this scene, and I don't know why the hell he's risking going off script. *Oh, crap. He wants us to do it again, doesn't he?*

I'm frozen. There's no room to do anything except play along. If the improv with his needy lips doesn't completely offend Pierce's perfectionism, then throwing a fit over it certainly will.

I kiss him as Robbi. Not Ali. Slinging my arm around his neck, pulling him in closer, sharing a beautiful moment that's either going to get us praised or yelled at.

When he breaks away, his eyes glow the same way they do when he smirks. Amazingly, Pierce hasn't screamed at us yet. The cameras keep rolling. I'm smiling, and not because I have to, when he lifts me into his arms, carrying my naked body to the huge bed just outside his master bathroom.

He never breaks eye contact as he lays me down. I don't realize how hard I'm breathing until my breasts go plush against his chest. Both my aching nipples sizzle when they touch his skin, willing slaves to the screaming falcon inked on his breast.

"Is this what you want, baby girl?"

Ali, I try to tell him subliminally, knowing he's going off script again. *You were supposed to say Ali.*

I don't know what's real anymore. A hundred death defying drops in his plane won't tell me, won't tell either of us, more than his kiss.

"Yes," I whisper, my voice shaking as I mouth Ali's lines. "I want it all, Miles. Give me a baby."

Give me the children you promised years ago, Luke.

I'm begging. Shamefully, relentlessly, openly begging

him in my touch, my kiss, my every caress.

I keep waiting for Pierce to scream 'cut' through his megaphone any second now. Especially when Luke's hand drifts between my legs while he's taking my bottom lip with his teeth, pulling my mouth open for his tongue.

None of this is in the script. We're playing with the most exquisite fire possible.

His fingers go down, dipping into my panties, and pull. He shifts his legs, making sure his body blocks what's really happening. My bare, wet pussy rubs his cock through a single thin layer of fabric when his hips roll forward. He makes me feel his ridge, his hardness, his furious desire racing through every insatiable inch of him.

"Fuck me," I moan, a silent whisper I'm praying the cameras can't see.

My hips betray me for the final time, lifting up, grinding into him. My eyes shut before the hot red flush taking over my body swarms through my blood.

I fake another orgasm on his thrusting hips, just like the script calls for, but barely. If it wasn't for the last razor-thin layer of his underwear between us, he'd be inside me, and then I'd be coming on him for real.

The cameras wouldn't stop us.

Neither would the pain. Or the past. Or my mother's horror. Not even my own fucking shame.

He watches me intently as I fake my O. His forehead presses mine, and he's growling. Probably because he knows I haven't given it up for real.

His cock rubs violently against my pussy, dry humping

me into submission. Sex is taking over. I can't remember what's supposed to be in the script anymore as he takes my hands, throws them above my head, and pins them down.

"Come for me, babe," he whispers, lowering his voice just enough for the part that comes next. "I said come, little bird. Do it. *Right. Fucking. Now.*"

My heart might be drowning in a moral dilemma I'll never resolve. But my body hears his command perfectly, and it obeys without question.

My pussy convulses. He grinds his cock into my clit so hard it lifts me off the bed, my arms slung over his neck, legs locked onto his. I'm rocking, losing, surrendering to his latest gift of white hot ecstasy.

The last thing I see before the pleasure becomes blinding is Luke's intense eyes burying me alive. He stares down, all love and blue fire, his pupils pinpricks because he's struggling to hold back his own release.

My fingernails dig into his skin. My whimper becomes a scream. There's no fade to black, just white hot lust hurling colorful stars across my field of vision. I'm swallowed up in the thunder booming in his throat, the soft, crisp creak of the bed beneath us, my own sweat becoming lava as it runs down my skin.

He'll kill me, this man. That is, if there's anything left to kill and destroy after coming like this on the set, in front of the voyeuristic cameras, and then for a billion people if this scene makes it to the final cut.

Could I be the first mainstream actress to win an award for best orgasm?

His breath brings me home to earth, and so does another sound. It's Pierce, coming toward the bed, saying something I can't fully make out yet. Luke runs his fingers through my slick blonde hair one more time as he rears up, rolling off the bed and sitting to hide his erection. He throws a sheet over my legs just in time to hide the swollen mess between my legs. My thigh brushes the wet spot I've left on the sheets.

"My God, boys and girls. Haven't seen passion like that on this set since I did *Make Me, Woman.*" He extends a hand.

Luke takes it, smiles, and sucks in a deep breath before he answers. He still hasn't replenished his oxygen. "We've been practicing in our off hours. Seriously an honor, Mr. Rogan. I'm aware I took some liberties that weren't in the script –"

"Lucus, you shined. Take all the creative license you want when we get to the final sex scene at the end of the film, if you'd like, as long as you leave the story to me."

"I wouldn't have it any other way. Robbi?" He turns, reaching for my hand to give it a squeeze, urging me to say something.

I hate having to remember how to form words after the most savage, orgasmic loving of my life. "I gave it my best. I'm glad it paid off."

Pierce grins. "Lovely lady, there's going to be a whole new category at the awards for best sex scene by the time we're through."

My stomach crawls into itself a little. I'd honestly much

rather be remembered for something else.

Good motivation, at least. The big finale is coming up, where Miles takes down the Senator, exposes his human trafficking to the world, and rescues me once more. Mustering the same passion in the action scenes as the sort I've just had between the sheets shouldn't be hard – especially with Luke by my side, looking at me the way he is now, one eyebrow askew as he waits for me to crawl naked from the sheets.

I wait for Pierce to disappear before I make sure my panties are pulled up. Then I slink away, stopping near the hallway as a whole new ache begins between my legs. Luke stands, moving to the side, waiting with his eyes on me while the production crew swoops in to clean up the set.

My teeth pluck my lower lip. I wonder if it's time to breach the last boundary between us. His look makes the decision, every part of me tingling as his gaze traces my curves, starting at my legs and moving over my bare breasts, across my neck, along my cheek.

I can't stop my fingers shaking when I lift my hand, fist forward, beckoning him with a single finger. *Come to me already, you irresistible bastard. Make me come undone. No more cat and mouse.*

He almost pushes several men out of the way as he makes a straight line for me. There's no cat in his stern footsteps, but a falcon swooping in on its prey, hungry and determined.

When he reaches me, he grabs my hand with a jerk so tense it drops my jaw. "Your room, or mine?" he growls.

"There's less crap on your dresser," I say, knowing how

much makeup, lotion, and empty water bottles are all over mine.

"Who said I'd need a horizontal surface? If you're lucky, I won't fuck you through the nearest wall when I spank your clit with my balls for teasing me on set."

Holy shit. "Um, me, teasing? Like you're not the one who started this?"

"Like your nipples haven't been calling to my mouth from the second I ripped open your robe?" He reaches up, grabs my breast. I'm almost jumping out of my skin, swatting at his hand. "Luke! Not here. People."

"Fine. Let's do it your way. One crappy studio wall between us and the world, and it *will* be rocking."

I'm smiling, doing my damnedest not to blush as he leads me out, unsure whose skin feels hotter to the touch. This is about how much he compromises, and as much as my body will tolerate.

I'm in heat. I'd never admit it and inflate his ego more, but if he wasn't leading me away, I'd be leaping in his arms, without even caring who sees us.

* * * *

He isn't kidding about the wall.

As soon as we're in his room and the door slams shut, Luke hoists me up, backs me into the nearest corner, and kisses me into submission.

Those lips...holy shit. Even after all these years and so little experience cut short, he knows me.

He knows my body, reads it, and reminds me who it's always belonged to.

His kiss comes sultry when it should, rough when it needs to, and always, always *hard.* His teeth, his tongue, his entire mouth owns mine, while his thick hands slide down my body. Who knew foreplay could be equal parts torture and delight?

I want him in me. Hell, I *need* it.

My hand reaches between his legs, tugs on his boxers, and I swear there's fire beaming out my eyes when they lock on his. "Fuck me, Luke. Now."

He smiles, moves his hand between my legs, and slips his fingers into my panties. Lightning zips through me when he brushes my clit, cups my sopping wet pussy, bringing the touch I've craved for years.

"You think I've waited all this time to hear those words, and let you give the orders?" He kisses my neck, teasing and furious, working his way down.

I'm about to tell him he can walk the hell out if he isn't going to get inside me in the next sixty seconds. But then his mouth pulls my nipple into it, clenches down with his teeth, and I can't think about my pride at all.

If these are second chances, count me in.

If it means more steaming kisses, more of his body pressed against mine, more of those aggressive hands owning every inch of me, then I'm done fighting.

I arch my back, pushing my hips into him as he sinks down. When he spreads my legs, he looks up with a *you are in fucking trouble* intensity causing muscles I didn't know I had to tense in anticipation.

"Ride my tongue, babe. Show me how bad you missed

it the last five years if you want me inside you tonight."

He's as crazy as this ultimatum. But there's nothing insane about how I melt into him when he flicks his tongue through my folds, pushing my legs apart with his huge arms. He buries his face, tasting me like a starving man, smothering my clit in desperate licks calling to my thighs.

They quiver. They clench. They take the rest of me down with them when release comes embarrassingly fast.

I'm coming on this gorgeous asshole's face for the first time in half a decade.

Did I say *asshole?* No, angel. I'm not sure how they're different anymore.

I tip my face to the ceiling, push my desperate hands into the walls for support, and scream.

It's all coming out. The hate, the pain, the loss, and the sorrow. The urge to get it right this time, to love him the way we should've loved before.

Mostly, the animal need to have him rise up, slam his hips into mine, and hate fuck me into next year. Going off script lit a fire that isn't dying anytime soon. Not before I take every seething inch of him, skin-to-skin, and bring him off deep inside me.

Ali's the one with baby fever, according to the movie's plot. He doesn't know I've got it for real, a hundred times worse, and the pulse between my legs throbs with wicked intent every time I think about leaking his come.

"Fuck me, Luke," I whimper. "Please!"

He comes up wearing a full smile. I taste my cream on his next kiss, and he delights in it. "Just like old times. How the hell did we survive without this?"

His full, naked hardness rubs against my slit. He pivots, pushing it between my swollen lips, rubbing his tip so close to my entrance I'll cry if he's not in me in the next twenty seconds.

His hand comes up, cups my cheek, and his eyes drink in my torture. "There are two nights I'll always remember, Robbi. One was when I took your cherry all those years ago. The other's tonight, when we start fucking like we're meant to."

"Please," I whisper again, the only word I'm able to form in my fuck-me-or-fuck-you state.

"You're on the pill or something?" he asks, a question he really should have brought up earlier.

I nod. "Good girl," he says. It's a phrase Miles says a lot throughout the film during the bondage scenes, but it's all too fitting here.

His hips fall back, and then they come forward, colliding with mine. It's not a moan coming out of me when he's *finally* in.

More like a whimper running on pure adrenaline, years of deprivation obliterated in one thrust.

Luke fucks into me with a manic energy. It's a friction I've missed, nasty and real, his hips pummeling mine so hard every time my butt slams into the wall.

It's sex, no holds barred. My legs shift open wider. His hands wander, lower down my sides, until his fingers dig into my ass so hard it's bound to leave bruises.

I do my fair share of damage, too. My fingernails scratch,

raking his arms, needling the wild ink stamped on him like a warning.

Consider every last warning ignored, now that we're skin-on-skin. His eyes drill into mine, and I meet his gaze, holding my eyes open when pleasure tries to force them shut.

"Harder," I pant. Yes, I'm aware I'm asking for fire, but it's been so cold for so fucking long, I don't even care.

Luke brings one hand up, grabbing me by the throat. He holds it there gently, just like our very first night, a reminder he's always been savior and destroyer in equal measure.

It takes my pussy several minutes just to get used to accommodating his big cock again. It's been *years* since a man stretched me like this. But my cunt opens willingly, more every time he thrusts his passion to the hilt, taking the hot pink flesh that's always been his, and his alone.

Fucking other men after him did nothing except teach me disappointment. Now, my master is back. The man who's always owned my body, down to the chemical level.

This isn't Ali running her lines, spitting make believe phrases like master, sir, or please. It's me, Robin, and everything we're doing is real.

The walls shake when he picks up speed, bringing his hips into me faster. He's grunting when his forehead touches mine, warm with a sheen of sweat. We're fucking eye-to-eye, and if the friction sending my pussy into flames doesn't send me over the edge alone, his look does.

"Come for me, babe," he says, his eyes growing brighter

blue with every word. "Come. Need you to remember what it's like to be sore."

I'm drowning in his dense blue gaze when my eyes start rolling, and then I'm seeing nothing but stars. My pussy hugs his bare cock so tight I think I'm going to pass out. Orgasm carries me to heaven, and he fucks me straight through it.

It's a machine sculpted like a man doing the fucking, hammering his cock into me, and I'm his willing receptacle. My fingers clench his shoulders for dear life, and I realize I'm screaming halfway through it.

"Oh, Luke – fuck!"

He silences me with another kiss, growling his pleasure into my mouth. It's the only time his cock slows when I'm coming down from the bliss, trying to find my balance again, ready to take his thrusts as long as necessary before he goes crashing over with me.

"There's my little bird," he says through several thrusts. I'm in a half-moan when he pulls out of me, and I think I give him the most hateful look of my life. He smiles. "Now that you've found your wings again, I want to take you straight into the storm. Turn around, and put your hands over your head."

I don't hesitate more than a second before I obey. One O alone won't satisfy the rampant itch deep inside me. I think I'd do the unspeakable right now to have him back inside me, finishing what we've begun.

Luke takes my wrists in one hand as soon as they're over my head, holding them together in his iron grip. His cock's head flicks against my pussy lips before he shoves it in, making me gasp.

"One," he rumbles, right before his hand crashes against my ass.

I whimper, jerk, and flatten myself against the wall. It's sudden, unexpected, and stings like hell. But damn if it doesn't make my pussy burn hotter when he pins me down, grinding his cock into me, blowing warm breath against my neck to complete the full body burn he's intent on bringing.

"What the hell was that?" I ask, while I can still get it out, before pleasure makes it impossible.

"I had your sweet little ass owned on the set. Now I want it off the clock, Robbi. I want it for real. Want to fuck and spank you so hard the last five years without me are nothing but a bad memory."

He's a bastard, using a bastard's logic. An irrational spark runs through my blood when I wonder how many times I'll come while his palm cracks across my ass.

Yes, I'm a slut for his crude, threatening style.

I was his virgin once, wasn't I? Hard to believe I'm becoming his willing whore, one violent O at a time.

I'm ready now, I tell myself. *Do your worst, Lucus Shaw.*

Sex can't fix everything that went haywire. I'm not even sure it's fixing it now, even though I'm enjoying the hell out of having him inside me, his abs crashing into my ass, every merciless thrust carrying me a little closer to completion, closer to him giving it up.

"Two." It comes out between his teeth in an angry rush. His palm crashes down across my right cheek, and he wastes no time moving to the left, tanning both with the same sharp force. "Three! How you holding up, baby girl? You high on it yet?"

High? I don't know where the fuck I am. I'm leaving my body and then some, drifting into a new kind of ecstasy at a frightening pace. My hips just know they need more. So they tilt back into him while I push my hands against the wall.

"God. Don't. Stop." I whisper the three words I manage to get out, wondering if he can hear them.

The wall shakes more with our thrusts, harder because I'm leaning into it. These cheap dividers thrown up by the studio really are crap. I have a flash of the embarrassment we'll never live down if the entire thing caves in while we're naked like this.

But when he brings the fourth strike down on my ass, I don't care if our sex gets broadcast to the entire world. "Shit, yes!"

I'm screaming. I'm on the verge. Blood roars so thick and hot through my ears I don't even hear it when he yells out *four!*

"With me this time," I whimper, closing my eyes as his cock slows its thrusts to a delicious grind. "Please, Luke. With me."

"I've never seen a woman jonesing so hard for my come. You'd better not be fucking around," he says, fisting my hair into a ponytail, pulling it tight so my ear comes to his lips. "I'm coming soon, Robbi, whenever you give me another O. If you think I was playing back there on the set, pretending I wanted to give Ali a baby, think again. One of these days, I *will* knock you up, and you'll beg for it."

My ovaries blaze so numb with heat I can't feel them anymore. "Please!" I'm begging, and it's far more crazed than anything Pierce or Isabella Frieze ever wrote for *Bare.*

I'm not going to get more specific. I'll let him read the notes in my plea when I start to chant it, until he fucks me so hard I can't.

"Please, please, please, Luke. Please."

My ass shifts into him, my pussy more desperate by the second, eager to wring every drop of magma hot seed from his balls. The asshole never gives up control.

He slows his strokes, just enough to bring me to the edge, leaving my legs a shaking mess. I'm too deep in the zone to even squeak another plea.

"Robbi?" He pulls my face to his by the hair, breathing heavy. "Before we come together, there's something you forgot."

I remember just as his palm sweeps over my ass, shattering the calm on both cheeks. *Five.*

Five strokes of lightning for five years apart.

And then a dozen thrusts, his cock digging into me so hard it lifts me up, slams me into the wall, and carries me to paradise.

Coming! Sweet surrender, down to my soul. Every part of me comes swiftly, comes hard, comes apart on his take-no-prisoners thrusts.

My pussy takes every stroke he gives, coiling tighter around his length harder every time, leaving me breathless.

Muscles turn to stone, spasm, and find their delicious release. The fierce blows he delivered hurt at the time, but now they've brought me something else.

A warmth surrounds me. It's like my whole body glows as I sink in scalding ecstasy, lost in him, this time, never coming back.

I'm not alone in my rapture. A second later, Luke tenses, throws himself into me one more time, and holds his cock deep in my twitching walls as he swells. "Fucking hell! Yeah, baby, yeah."

Yeah. Every syllable comes with a sharper intensity. He's been holding it as long as me, for five hellish years, and now it's coming out.

He holds me down, jerks my hair in his fist, grunting as he comes ropes into me. This is what it's like to be filled with fire, another first for a girl who's never had a man without a condom before.

Call me addicted. My mouth hangs open in a lonely, shaking O while the same rough pleasure courses through us.

We're joined. Fused. Slaves to the flesh, the seed, the lightning rending our muscles to steel.

I don't know when the fever breaks. Probably after him because his grip eventually loosens. I have just enough energy to turn around, falling forward into his arms.

His lips brush mine with a sweeter, softer power like a fire down to its embers, always threatening to start again. His hands kiss my skin while his lips are busy, reaching to my backside. He rubs my ass, gentle as Miles Black in the aftercare scenes from the script, but there's nothing movie-like about it.

This is real life. This is real love. This is the man I've missed, coming home, telling me with more than just words he isn't ever leaving again.

"Love you, Robbi. Never stopped once in all these years."

I press my face to his chest, looking up, loving the soft mischief in his eyes when they're calmer, but no less intense. "I love you, too. Were you serious about what you said in the moment? About knocking me up?"

He smiles. "Someday, little bird. We've got our whole lives ahead, now that everything's right with the world."

Is it?

Mom's furious expression runs through my mind. I'll catch hell if, and when, she finds out there's more between Luke and me than work. Especially when I swore up and down it was just professional.

"What's wrong? Talk to me." He runs his thumb gently along my cheek, reading me with a keen insight nobody else will ever have.

"There are still some things I have to take care of before it's smooth sailing. Nothing that can't be fixed with time." I stop to lean on my toes, planting another kiss on his lips. "We're on the right path, Luke, thanks to you."

"Good. Glad you're following my lead again because I think it's past time we got the hell out of here."

He's right. I don't have to listen hard to hear the production crew walking past, laughing and chattering among themselves as another day on the set wraps up, one more reminder how thin these walls can be.

"Your place, or mine?" I say, gathering my clothes.

"Mine. Got it a little while longer before we're done with Chicago and they want us back in L.A. for wrap up. I'd like us to give the bed in the place I'm staying a work out it'll remember."

Yes, sir. I'm humming to myself as I wash up, fix my regular makeup, and walk out with him. It isn't a perfect look by any means, but it's enough to hide the sex crazed mess we'd become just minutes ago.

We're in the parking lot, heading to our cars, when I decide to take his arm. He walks me to my vehicle and makes sure I'm inside it with a smile on my face before he heads for his.

It's been an eternity since I felt right. Now, I finally do.

If the rest of the world will just stay out of our way, we'll find our shortcut through the ugliness, the hurt, the turmoil that's drowned out our happiness for far too long.

No, it won't be easy. But as long as I'm sharing Luke's bed, his arm, and his patented smirk, we'll make it across the finish line to the future we deserve, baby fever and all.

X: Spent (Luke)

My eyes are so bloodshot from the sleepless nights I need the makeup people to work their finest magic the rest of the week. Every last bit of extra effort is worth it.

My baby's back, and we haven't lost a spare hour making up for all the sex we've missed. I fuck her late into the morning, catching a few hours of sleep in between the next round.

In my bed, in the shower, in front of the glass overlooking the balcony that's got a direct view of my brother's tower. Hell, even on the kitchen counter. I'd take her outside, too, if I didn't have to risk Hayds or his girl seeing us with the telescope I know he keeps at his penthouse for the skyline view. He'd give me shit forever.

At work, I'm shooting the scenes where the Senator's goons catch me off guard, throw a hood over my head, and push me into his private plane. Harkness leans over me, giving his best evil villain sneer as he says Bluhd's catch phrase. "You really should've taken the fucking bribe, Mr. Black. You could've walked away with a lot of loot, without risking anything. Now, you've lost it all: your fortune, your girl, and yes, your own life. Congratulations. This time tomorrow, you'll be the world's biggest missing person's case, and Allison will be a mere footnote next to your name. Enjoy your flight." His boot lands in my ribs. If it wasn't for the stunt safety built-in, it would hurt.

I let out my best agonized scream, faking the pain. Harkness laughs, slamming the heavy metal door in my face.

All is silent until I hear Pierce bellow through his megaphone, calling us to wrap up. "Marvelous, gentleman. That's our third take today, and I think we've got our suspense. Let's call it a day before we shoot Luke's Houdini escape scene back in L.A. I want to allow plenty of time to pack our crap up and start saying our goodbyes to Chicago. We won't be back here unless there's a damned good reason to be."

Everybody bursts into applause. I'd join them, if my hands weren't cuffed behind my back. There's laughter next to me; a low, distinguished chuckle from a man old enough to be my father.

Harkness opens the door, reaching in to help me out of my hood. He extends a hand before the production crew descends on us for clean up. "You're a Godsend, Aaron," I tell him, as soon as I'm free.

"Just don't tell my agent, or she'll want an extra piece of my hide next time I'm up for negotiations." He smiles. I walk with him off the set while the crew swarms in like bees on flowers.

"Don't know how you do it. If I last half as long as you

in this biz, still doing films into my sixties, I'll sacrifice a chicken to the Hollywood gods."

"My good man, you've got a longer career than me ahead. You have one distinct advantage – you're bringing passion. I'm sorry to say I lost my creative spark years ago. Now, it's all about the money. If I were half as rich as what I've heard about your family, I'd have retired ages ago. I'm sad to say ten acres in Beverly Hills and a summer home outside London don't pay for themselves."

I laugh, surprised the veteran actor is letting me into so much of his world. "You're a hell of a talent, regardless. If you're just here for the money, you could've fooled me."

"There are things far more important in this world than chasing the next dollars. Fame isn't worth much either." He looks up, slowing with me when we're approaching our dressing rooms. "I've seen how you look at Ms. Plomb off set, if I may be frank."

Frank? Is this guy for real? I'm not used to his old world manners. Smiling, I nod. "You may."

"Coming from a man who made his mistakes when he was your age, please consider giving the girl a ring if it's as serious as it seems. These romances on the set have a terrible way of ending with a whimper over the slightest misunderstanding if there's nothing in place to bind them. If you want her for keeps, I suggest making your move."

"Uh, thanks for the advice." Whatever else I signed up for with this erotic thriller crap, I never thought I'd be getting input about my love life from a multiple Oscar winner. "If you ever need a lead on a new agent or any other help, I'm open. Just say the word."

"Agents are a lot like regrets, I'm afraid. Once you're wed to a halfway competent one, they're usually there forever." He smiles knowingly.

I smile back, pretending I know what he's talking about. My phone goes off in my pocket just then, and I grab it, wondering if it's Robbi calling about our plans tonight. She teased me yesterday evening about her trip to the lingerie store downtown. Two can play at surprises, though. My woman has no clue what I've got in store for her as soon as Pierce turns the lights out here tonight.

When I see Jim's name on my screen, I frown. "Speaking of agents…here's mine. It's been good talking, Aaron. Thanks for your wisdom."

"Likewise." Harkness retreats to his room with a parting smile and a wink.

Stepping into my own room, I kick the door shut and hold the phone up to my ear. "What's going on, Jim?"

"Five alarm fire! There's some lady who needs to talk to you, and she's more pissed than a bull in Red Square. I almost called security."

"Shit, slow down. What lady?"

"Says her name's Ericka. At first, I thought she was an overzealous Frieze fan trying to chase down the man who's playing her dream boat. But she's after you, Luke Shaw. Told me she's hanging onto a mountain of dirt that's going on social media if you don't get in touch with her. I'm worried, my man. After we saw what happened with your brother, Hayden, when that crazy broad came after him, we really don't need a repeat. I've seen how this crap in the press works – the wrong hashtag at the right time could torpedo your career!"

Ericka Plomb? I'm thoroughly fucked, if that's the case. It has to be about Robin. I'm silent, unsure how to respond for the next few seconds.

"What do you want me to say?" he's still talking, panicked as ever. "I take it you know what she's talking about? Christ. Do we *need* a lawyer for this?"

"Take a couple breaths," I say, maintaining control. It'll take more than dumb threats from Robbi's mom to rile me up. "I know this lady. She used to do business with my dad. I'll handle it. Let me talk to her. Did she leave a number?"

"Yeah, let me see…" He rattles it off, and I take the digits down on my contacts.

"Take care of this, Luke. Seriously. Cool her heels, or we're going to have problems. Anything falling through at this point due to bad press means they could even start cutting us out, clawing back money!"

Oh, the tragedy. I'm more worried about a wet blanket on the fire I've re-kindled with Robbi more than anything else. Not even this damned movie or my career matters when it's stacked against us.

"I'll talk it out with her, Jim. It's not as scary as it sounds, trust me."

"I'm going to. And keep me updated, will ya?"

"Sure, sure. I'll let you know when our fire's out." I end the call.

I'm pressing my fist against the wall, wondering if

anyone will notice a fresh hole punched through it before they strip our rooms down and pack everything up for the trip to L.A.

Fuck the rage. There's no time.

I send a text to the number he gave me, telling her we need to talk.

Ericka sends a one word reply: WHEN?

I name the time and place. My room here at the studio, tomorrow morning, bright and early. Ideally before we do one last promo shoot for a couple magazines before the flight west. Early, before Robbi shows up, and has to wonder why I'm hanging out with her mom.

I'm in my car when the reply comes back, telling me we're on. My jaw tightens. There's too much at stake, but there's no mystery about what I have to do.

I think about what Harkness said an hour ago, *give the girl a ring.* That's the plan, and it's been in the back of my mind all week.

I still have the rock I meant to give her that day before the drama ripped her away from me. It's moved to a new box, but the ring itself hasn't changed since the day I first set my eyes on staking my claim forever.

It's in my pocket now. It's coming out the first night off we have when we're home. I don't care if I'm risking anything less than a resounding *yes.* I'm not waiting one more year, much less five, to have it on her finger.

Nothing's getting in the way of that. Not the past, not the present, and most definitely not her mom bringing daggers meant for my side.

I played it coy with Robbi the first night we fucked in this room, before I brought her to my sheets. *Someday,* I said, when she asked me if I was serious about the baby thing.

If only she knew *someday* means *soon* in my world. I can't stop hallucinating whenever we fuck, every time I stare into her eyes, pumping my fire into her. *Can't.*

It's my ring I see on her naked finger when she brushes the stubble on my cheek, her pale grey eyes melting into mine. It's my kid stretching her belly when she rides me, those sweet, suckable tits I intend to see bobbing every time she throws her head back, coming on my cock with a breathless moan.

It's our whole future I see rolled out like a red carpet, infinitely more meaningful and important than anything Hollywood can ever give us.

I'll find out what Ericka wants, and settle. Whatever happened before, she's not taking her away from me again.

* * * *

Later, we're on the rooftop at the condo I'm renting, the essentials packed up for our return trip tomorrow. The Chicago darkness hangs around us like dense silk, the city's lights peaking through in pinhole clarity. A few rare stars hang above, so bright they shine through the light pollution.

"One more thing," she says from the nook of my arm, turning her face to mine. "No more secrets, Luke. Never."

Shit. Does the meeting tomorrow with her mother count?

Deep in my lying gut, I know it does.

But there's no salvaging us if I let Ericka turn it all to shit. If the outcome is what I expect, the icy understanding I'll give my everything to get, then Robbi doesn't need to know. There's no point in worrying her over what isn't coming down because I won't let it.

I answer her with my silent lips. I kiss her, harder than I intend. Her lips come into it, tasting me and the wine that's still on my lips, the bottle we've shared half-depleted. Must be the nerves I didn't know were there a minute ago, or the gravity tugging at my gut, hiding an elephant I have to face alone. "Now, let's see your surprise."

Her face lights up. "Only if yours comes first."

"Fine," I say, rolling my eyes as I help her up. "Promise me you'll give it a chance, without freaking out."

My serious glare shines straight through her. After several seconds, she cracks a smile, laughing. "Wow. It's going to be good, isn't it?"

"You have no idea." Grabbing her hand, we walk to the elevator. Soon, we're back inside, and I'm leading her to the bedroom.

I wait for her gasp when I turn on the light. Predictable, but damn if it doesn't bring a smile to my face, and instant heat to my dick.

"Oh my God. We're *dead* if the studio finds out!" She turns to me, flattening her hands against my chest, wide eyed and searching.

"They're on loan, don't worry. I slipped the guy managing the props a couple hundred this afternoon. Told him I'd have them back tomorrow, safe and sound." Tugging on her hand, I lead her toward the sweet display waiting on the bed. "You know this stuff's imported from France? Some freak who makes it custom, and earns plenty doing it, casting sex supplies in gold and platinum."

I pick up the handcuffs. They're heavy, solid gold, and I've only seen them once in her little hands. "Ever been fucked like a million dollars? That's about how much you'll be worth, once it's on you."

Robbi resists when I grab her, but it isn't serious. She's all smiles as I pinch the zipper on her back, slide it down, and push her dress to the floor. My cock jerks when I see what she's been hiding underneath it.

"Didn't know they made lingerie with targets." Fuck, it's cheesy, but the red and orange color scheme focused around her nipples, her pussy, her ass turns me on like a candle. It's a WWII era aviator's icons, bright circular rings focused around her best parts on a black canvass.

"You're the one with the fly boy fantasies, always prowling around in this thing." She tugs on my jacket. A growl slips out my mouth as I let it roll off my shoulders, smothering her lips with a kiss. "Whatever. You know you like it."

"I do. Just not enough to keep it on for long." I reach for the leather flogger, thumbing the diamonds set in the platinum handle. "On your knees, beautiful."

Her ass gets a quick pat as she turns, stares up at me, and obeys. I don't have to ask her to get to work. Her hands go for my zipper, tug out my cock, and engulf me in her tongue.

Heaven. Who knew I'd find it in such lush, eager lips?

"Slow down," I warn, when she shoves her little tongue underneath my swollen head, moaning when my pre-come pulses into her mouth. "The night's young, and we're going to savor it, little bird. Can't leave Chicago without making everything right."

I'm serious. This was where it all began, years ago, the love and the tragedy between us. There's even a chance we'll settle here again, if California becomes too tedious one day. I'm not letting bad memories obstruct a fresh start. Making new ones, good ones, ensures they won't.

I control the flogger like a sorcerer testing his spell, dragging it along her throat, her soft shoulders, down the snowy space between her tits. Christ, those tits.

They wobble, calling to me, irresistible as the very first day I had them. She moans, pushing her sweet vibration across my cock, feeding the fire in my balls.

My free hand goes to her gold locks, twines them around my fingers, and pulls. She loves it. Her eyes show me how much when they roll back in her head, losing themselves in the same pleasure crawling up my cock.

She sucks harder. Faster.

My girl's grown up, learned a couple things about how to suck cock since I left her behind years ago. It makes me jealous I wasn't the one to teach her, but that ends now. Moving the flogger up her neck, stopping it under her chin, I fold it into her skin until she looks up from the pressure, her little hand fisting the base of my dick.

"Warm up's over. Get on the bed, and spread your legs.

Don't move unless I say." I watch her crawl away, breath rising. She's trying so hard not to show how turned on she is, and failing miserably.

The sleek blue blindfold is the first thing I grab so I can smile without breaking the mood. It's Egyptian cotton with enough stitches to make a sultan jealous. She purses her lips as I tighten it around her head, before moving to her legs.

Thank God the studio ordered extras. I use one pair of gold handcuffs to hook each foot to the posts, after I take down her target practice panties with my teeth, stopping to relish the slick spot she's left all over them.

"That fucking wet for me, and you didn't think I'd notice?" I tease her, bringing the flogger up her bare leg, loving how her thighs ripple. "Why didn't you tell me how much I turned you on?"

"I like surprises, sir. Especially when they're for you."

Sir. It should make me laugh because I've heard her say it often as Ali. Instead, my cock throbs like a rocket fueling up, aching to fuck her like any bastard worthy of the title should.

"No more tonight, babe. You tell me when you're coming – or else." I give her bare pussy a gentle whack with the leather implement in my hand.

She cries out, her sweet red lips going wide, moaning her surprise and delight. I'm wishing I had one of those blindfolds myself. Too much time watching her naked body bound up and writhing might be dangerous, like looking at the sun. Staring too long threatens to make me shoot off before I'm good and ready to put my seed in her again.

Talk about a tragedy. The fuck if we're having it.

I move over the bed, reach between her legs, and tease her swollen lips with two stiff fingers. "Luke, yes!" She rocks her hips into me.

I slow my strokes and study her. She wants it bad, but her body doesn't *need* it yet.

Patience is a virtue I can teach her. I circle my thumb around her clit a few more times before I pick myself up, walk over to the chair next to the little marble table in the corner, and pour myself a glass of wine.

"What was that?" she asks, lifting her head, straining because I've cut her lust short. "Luke?"

"We're taking a breather. Good time for another surprise while I take a load off."

"Um, what? What the hell are you –" She stops moving when she hears me get on my feet, twirling the glass of wine in my hand.

I smile, taking a good long sip. It's not just the high end bondage gear I've snatched from the studio that's sponsoring our surprises tonight. I reach into the small black bag next to my gear, and pull out the silver bullet I've chosen.

It took a long time to find one with just the right speed. Robbi's tits bob beautifully when I'm next to her, running the cool, smooth surface around her inner thighs.

"Put it in. Please," she whines, sucking her lower lip with her teeth.

"Be careful what you wish for, babe. You don't know what it is I'm holding." I stare into where her eyes should be through the blindfold, wishing I could see them. Too bad it's so much more fun leaving her in the dark.

She gasps much louder than she would with her eyes uncloaked when I turn the little bullet on, and push it deep inside her. The tiny remote fob attached to my key chain will do the rest. I walk back into the corner, taking another pull from my wine, watching her transformation.

Her skin goes red with pleasure in under a minute. Sweat drips off her, adrenaline distilled into sweet droplets. Every time she breathes, she says my name, hate and desire clashing on her lips. Every time I draw another breath, I smell her sweet cunt, spilling its scent into the room while it leaks cream all over the sheet underneath her.

"Okay, this isn't funny anymore! Turn it up, you bastard," she says, her voice trembling a little more with every word. "Asshole! Please!"

"Hm. Not very respectful tonight, are we?" I stroke my chin, wondering if I should give her another few minutes before I drop the bomb. Nah, it'll be more fun to tell her sooner. "I'm afraid the way it's vibrating inside you now is as high as it goes. They don't call it a speeding tease for nothing, little bird. It's meant to give you a lift, not carry you all the way to the sun."

She's squirming in her restraints. Her knees buckle, lips popping wide open, and I watch muscles ripple at random as the craving overtakes her.

It's not like a one way torture either. My cock won't stop hammering in my pants, pulsing so hard it hurts every time I remember I can end this now. Just walk over, rip that thing out of her, drop my pants, and push inside her.

But it's our last night in Chicago. We're here to make memories, damn it. And the human body is wired to find its most unforgettable release when it's been denied.

She's moaning. Turning over as far as she can in her cuffs. The sex fever I've lit near her womb with the little bullet must be insufferable.

Orgasm denial? Fuck, it's so much more. I've chiseled away a piece of her soul, holding it, while I feel my own burn away every brutal second I'm not inside her.

"Safe word!" she screams, as soon as I'm next to her, gently running my fingertips over her brow. "We're too kinky to have one, but I'm telling you, I've had it. No more, Lucus Shaw. I need you."

There isn't a man on the planet who could say no. I reach between her legs, pull out the little bead, and listen to her latest gasp like wind rolling through my ears, smooth and seductive.

It has the desired effect.

I want to kiss. I want to touch. I want to fuck, and nothing's going to stop me. But first, I lift the remnants of my wine glass to her lips, helping tip her head while she swallows. "Good?"

"It's...Jesus. I've never tasted anything so delicious," she says.

"Your senses are heightened. All of them. That's what this trick does, something I learned at an underground club in Portland a couple years back. Try my kiss next, babe."

When our lips touch, there's always a delicious push and

pull. Except this time, two seconds in, she comes back with a moan, sinking her teeth into my lip so hard it almost draws blood.

"Sorry!" she whimpers, shaking her head when I break the kiss and pull away. "I'm not sure what came over me. Too intense. I had to, Luke, or I thought I'd never get another chance. I'm not sure what you've done to me."

"I do," I say, slipping off my clothes, letting my eyes drink in her panting, desperate body one last time before I plunge in. Her whole face trembles when she feels the bed sink beneath my weight as I make my way between her legs. "Whatever you do, keep breathing, or I *will* have to smack you harder than I'd like. It's like a drug when you come the first time this way, Robbi, and there are side effects. Just keep breathing, baby. Even when I fuck an O so hard into you, you're thrown out of your body, don't stop. Remember who owns this now."

My cock rubs against her pussy while I'm growling my words, steadily up and down, three long strokes before I push in. She screams when I take her. Senseless, raw lust given a voice. And I'm training it to sing each time my hips plow into her, stretching her tight cunt around my length, taunting something raw and primal deep within me.

"Luke!" My name is the only thing she can say. It's never sounded as sexy as it does tonight.

Fire churns in my balls. I realize this isn't the last time I'll have made her my willing slave. It's going to be like this on our honeymoon, and the night I decide to get her pregnant. I'll wind her up so fucking hard she snaps when her pussy takes my come, squeezes it out of my dick like it's the missing key to her survival.

It damned well might be. I don't know how the hell I ever lived without her mouth on mine, even when she's biting into me, matching my growls with her feminine thunder through the tango of our lips.

What happens there moves through the rest of our bodies, too. It's a horizontal dance, a fuck first invented sometime in the stone age, raw and real and unapologetic.

I don't feel sorry when her skin flushes so red it has to burn the first time I bring her over. Good thing the restraints are doing their job, or she'd pinch her legs so tight around my waist they'd probably break my hips.

Robbi comes with a force indistinguishable from the current burning through me. She comes rough, she comes crazy. She comes like a woman who's finally at peace.

I'm too busy slamming myself into her to smile, but damn if it isn't happening deep down inside.

Discomfort and deprivation work magic. They're pleasure's warped twin cousins, waiting to have their fun when a skilled man unchains them to frolic. They heal the worst kind of pain, and free love from hate.

Tonight, they're burying the bitterness of the last five years in the grave originally meant for our love.

I know why I'm fucking, even as the same sharp animal instinct I always feel when my balls burn rises up, and squeezes my throat.

I fuck to excavate.

I fuck to bury.

I fuck to make her mine, make her swoon, make her regret every bitter minute we're apart, knowing we're never going back to that dark place again.

I fuck because she'll wear my ring soon, the second best gift I'll ever give her after our first born.

Yes, I fuck because I want her to come like I promised, so hard I have to slow down and bring her another sweltering kiss just to make sure she doesn't die deep in the ecstasy.

I'll never let her go. I'll never stop. I'll never, ever quit until I've secured the forever that was always meant to be with this beautiful spitfire.

My hips pummel straight through her second O on my cock. It's even harder than the first. I fist her hair, pull her face to mine, and dig my teeth into her sweet lip until I see her chest starting to rise and fall again.

She's lost in the ecstasy. Mumbling, moaning, and incoherent. So driven over the edge some men wouldn't find it sexy, but fuck, I do.

I love this insanity because I made it. And I'm a psycho for our love, the destiny I feel written in our flesh.

My best friend, my former enemy, my woman, my little bird.

I can't hold back anymore. Snarling, I reach behind her head and rip off the blindfold, touching my forehead to hers when we lock eyes. "Babe, pinch this dick as tight as you can. I'm coming."

"Oh, yes. Yes!" Her soft blue eyes roll when the realization sets in, deepening the scarlet flush on her cheeks. "Give it, Luke. Give it fucking all."

I do. Grunting, fucking, crashing into her so frantically my hips nearly bruise, I let the fuse raging in my balls hit the charge.

"Fuck!"

Sweet fuck, help me. I'm coming harder than I ever have in my life when it boils out of me.

Balls pumping, electricity flowing through the base of my spine, hitting my brain in love-lust waves so intense I don't know if I've died and gone to heaven. Or maybe it's hell, with this fire, blazing jets pouring out of me, into her steaming pussy.

One more kiss, and I've entered Valhalla. We lock lips for a long time coming down from our high. I keep my cock in her long after it's stopped twitching, holding in my seed.

My caveman instinct is in control, and it wants her flooded. Bred. Owned.

"Love you, little bird. Wherever we go next, whatever we do, whoever we pretend to be on the screen, love never changes."

"Never?" She smiles, staring into my eyes. "Even if you find out I'm not half as much a freak in the bedroom?"

"Okay, you can stop playing coy," I say, smiling. "You loved it, and so did I. We've got twelve more hours before we have to book it to the airport after the promo shoot. Plenty of time to come to terms with everything I do to you, and learn how to tell me how much you like it."

My thumb trails her cheek. She stares into my eyes, and even if she didn't say anything, I'd know by the way her chest rises and falls, by her pale eyes lighting up like a moon coming off an eclipse.

"I did say no secrets, didn't I?"

I smile, trying not to think about the early morning meeting I'm due to have with her mom. "You did. So, tell me, are you a spankaholic, or is it the orgasm denial that gets you hotter?"

* * * *

Heaven always demands its price in hell. I wake up with a few small bruises and a fresh ache in my hips, and I think I've gotten off easy. Every last sting in my bones is worth it. I leave Robbi to sleep in while I shower and throw black coffee down my throat. She'll meet me at the studio later for our last team meet before L.A.

I've already packed up last night's toys, and left a note for the condo's landlord about where to ship it after I'm gone.

She'll see herself out and drop her rental car off before she joins me at the studio. I head there alone, into my dressing room, and wait as planned, trying to keep a lid on my doubts.

Ericka is predictably late. I'm starting to wonder if she'll show at all, or if the delay is a fucked up negotiating tactic when I finally hear her little fist on my door.

"It's me," she says, as coolly as if I've been expecting the devil himself.

I open up slowly, and come face-to-face with the woman who took five years off my life, stealing my girl away. "Have a seat," I say, reaching into the small fridge in the corner for a couple waters.

She shakes her head, refusing it, and I settle in across from her while I pop the cap. It sickens me how much she looks like Robbi. Roughly how I imagine my beautiful bird would look after being pummeled by bad choices for thirty years, soaked in guilt, and run over by life itself.

"Look, I know why you're here," I begin, breaking the icy silence. "You're afraid I'm going to hurt Robbi, and I get why. What happened between you and my old man years ago wasn't exactly kosher. He stuck his nose where it didn't belong, got between you and your family, and did wrong. If he wasn't dead, I'd invite you to lay into him one more time."

"I visited the tomb," she cuts in, a smile pulling her lips up at their corners. "Amazing what money like yours can buy, isn't it?"

"Uh, it came out of his estate. My brothers and his wife at the time did the arrangements. I gave the okay, wasn't as involved as they were, so I wouldn't know."

"Such a shame. You always were the one who had it hardest, weren't you? The servants said he wasn't quite the monster he became when your older brothers were home. Have you even seen his grave?"

"Not since the funeral." What the fuck is she getting at?

"You should. It's beautiful, the gold and stone and onyx. Especially his name, chiseled into the plaque that'll probably last forever. I love the way it caught my spit when no one else was looking."

Anger cracks through my expression, before I regain control a second later. She's trying to get to me. I can't let her.

"What do you want, Ericka?"

Her eyes darken, and she leans forward in her seat, clasping her hands. "I want you to leave my daughter alone, Luke. Finish your little movie, and then never talk to her again. Believe it or not, I'm doing you a favor. Don't piss on my kindness, or you'll regret it."

"I'm not going anywhere. We're involved, Ericka, and that's not going to change." I don't flinch at her vague threats. The bitch doesn't blink. We stare, while I decide the only option left is nuclear. "I'm sorry you don't like me. I'm sorry my dad got under your skin, did some fucked up things, and got in the middle of a family that was going to pieces, without his interference or not. Did you know I got your husband in rehab years ago? You abandoned him the day you stormed out with Robbi in tears. I called the ambulance to take him in because no one else would. I tried to fix your mistakes, just like I'm doing now."

"Watch your mouth, boy."

"Watch yours, before you say something you'll regret to your future son-in-law." I let myself smile when I see the horror deepen in her eyes. "That's right. Soon as we're in L.A., I'm asking Robbi to marry me, just like I planned to years ago, before you got in the way. It's happening, like it or not, and you won't talk me down. All that's left is my very *strong* suggestion we hash this out, and come to an understanding, but we don't have to. It's your choice. I'm taking her to the altar either way."

"You want an understanding?" Her face tenses. She needs several seconds to collect herself, but she recovers without throwing a fit. *For now, anyway.*

"I do," I say, giving her a serious answer. "We don't have to be enemies. If you can't put the past behind us enough to give me a chance, then I'm asking you to tolerate it. Don't get in the way. Let your little girl be happy, Ericka. She hasn't been, all these years, ever since the shit came down between our families. I'm giving her the chance we always deserved."

"Christ, you Shaws are all the same. You're really blind, aren't you? Thinking this is some kind of talk, a negotiation?"

"Isn't it? Tell me what you want." I lift the water bottle to my lips, keeping her in suspense while I take a nice long pull. "Is it an apology? Money? I'm more than willing to dole out both. I'll do it sincerely, if it'll stop you derailing us."

"No. You're staying the *hell* away from my Robin. No deal, no discussion, no kombuya. I've come too far to deal with her finding out the truth."

I sit up straighter than before. "What truth? You're talking about the arrangement you had with my dad?"

She narrows her eyes. "You think it was easy, living with a goddamned alcoholic? Danny didn't go down the drain because he found out I was having an affair with an asshole. He circled it for years. I can't tell you how many times I forced him to his meetings, brought him into counseling, watched him start hitting the bottle again two days after he swore he'd had his last drink. I couldn't change him, or fix us. All I could do was hide it from my little girl, minimize the damage."

Damn it. Her look of hate aimed at me may be ice, but

I think there's actually a beating heart under it. There's nothing worse than realizing the demon in front of me may be human after all. "I'm sorry. My father was a selfish fool. If he had any sense, any morals, he wouldn't have gotten involved, knowing what was going down between you and your –"

"My husband was a self-destructive prick!" She stands, catches herself, and then sits down again, rage boiling to the surface on her face before fading just as quickly. "Fine, you want the truth?" she sniffs, haughtily, a nasty smile appearing.

"I want anything that'll make you come to terms with me and Robbi."

"That isn't happening. But because you've pretended to be so nice, I'll let you in on a little secret – your father never blackmailed me like I said. If he had, you'd better believe I would've come after him. I didn't give up the cleaning business for law just to let the world walk over me."

Fuck. I never thought being right could feel like a punch to the gut. I'm still listening, distracting myself with a sip of water, trying not to retch over everything she hid, destroying my woman with her lies.

"Your father was a bastard in the end. He had his fun, dropped me for a younger girl, and sent me on my merry way with enough severance pay to send Robin to acting school. He even offered to pay for Danny's treatment. Maybe I'd have taken him up on it, if the drunken idiot hadn't stumbled on the notes your father wrote."

"Notes?" So much for not being sick to my stomach.

"That's right. They were lovely when we had our fling. He put on a nice romantic act. Had me fooled, thinking we might have a future. I should've known girls like me don't belong with men like him. Rags to riches, maid uniforms to wedding gowns? All bullshit. Whatever you want with my daughter, I know you're stringing her along." She raises her hand before I can say anything. "No, don't apologize. I don't want to hear it. It's in your nature, just like making sure she avoids the same mistake is in mine."

She's wrong, dead wrong, but I still don't know what this is all about. Why the rancor? The demands?

"I don't understand. If there was no arrangement, no blackmail, then why the lie? Why persist?" I'm trying my damnedest not to look at her with total disgust, show her a shred of understanding for the failing marriage with a drunk that made her this way. "Are you really so proud, you can't tell your daughter the truth?"

"Bravo! And everybody says Hollywood is dumb." She starts clapping. Her sarcasm shows me what it's like to be a bull with bright red rippling in front of its face. "I thought the world of Frank Shaw, before he threw me away, if you want to know the reality. Hurt like hell when he did, but knowing what Robin would think if I told her, if I came clean about the affair and her screwed up father...she's a fragile girl, Luke. You have to know that. Sensitive, innocent, worth protecting from the sick taint you Shaws leave over everything."

"She's stronger than you think. Wouldn't be marrying her if she were the sheltered weakling you think she is. Shit, she's not seventeen, cleaning my family's house anymore. She's a grown woman, acting her heart out in a multi-million dollar film." I'm glaring. I still can't figure this out, and the sinking sensation in my gut tells me we won't resolve shit here today. "Why tell me anything if you're not here to figure this out?"

"Oh, I'm *going* to figure it out, Luke. Since I know you're too damned stubborn to do it the easy way, we'll do it my way instead."

That part where something so insane happens your life starts flashing before your eyes? For the next sixty seconds, I'm living it.

First, Ericka reaches into her purse. I hear a plastic bag popping open, and she brings a handful of something I can't see to her mouth. Her jaws work violently, chewing a mess. Then she stands up, reaches past me to my desk, and grabs the big glass paperweight off it.

"I'm sorry it has to go down this way. You look just like your father, you know. I'm sure those good looks and rich connections will help you into a comfy prison cell." She's slurring her words around the red crap drooling down her chin from the corners of her lips.

I don't realize it's fake blood until she brings the paperweight up, smashing herself hard in the face. She slides out of her chair, stunned. Or maybe exaggerating because she's got the strength to hurl the orb against the wall so hard it shatters.

"What the fuck are you doing!" It's not a question.

I'm reaching for her, pulling on the back of her dress

more violently than I should. It rips as she struggles out of my grasp. She turns the doorknob and hobbles to her feet, walking down the hall stooped over, heading into the studio.

I'm fucking frozen.

I contemplate doing a dozen things. I want to chase her down, throw her to the floor, and stop her before she finishes whatever the hell she's attempting. But I'm so stunned I hang back for too long.

She's halfway down the hall before I rush after her, get in front of her, and hold up my hands. It doesn't do anything to slow her down. She's smiling through the thick red mess drooling onto her blouse.

Christ. The woman could give a zombie a run with the way she looks, or at least an extra from an action flick.

The evil grin melts away when I hear the door opening behind me. I have just enough time to turn around, and see the crowd coming in, before I hear the voice that shoots a hole clean through my heart.

"Mom?!" Robbi runs forward, her eyes huge as she looks past me, reaching her mother just in time, before Ericka collapses.

"Oh my God! What's the meaning of this?" Another voice, and it couldn't be more shocked and appalled. Isabella Frieze grabs Ericka's other arm when Robbi isn't strong enough to help her up alone, and the crazy bitch goes face first into the author's white sweater.

"He...he hurt me. My jaw. I think it's...broken..."

How does a man describe a chaos so huge and

unexpected it chews up his life and shits it out in front of him in all of five minutes?

By the time I'm no longer paralyzed, roaring my denial, two heavy security guards are on me, slamming my face into the floor. The handcuffs they clap on my wrists aren't the kind of kinky surprises I still had in store for us. Neither is Robbi wailing, and I'm not sure who's louder.

Her, or Ms. Frieze. The author won't stop shrieking at the top of her lungs, ever since Ericka peeled her face off the poor woman's shirt, and she saw the blood. What she thinks is fucking blood, and isn't.

"My Miles!" she keeps saying, over and over and over again. "Why, why, why?"

Pierce, the press people with him, and the rest of the production crew won't even look at me. There's no time for denial, self-defense, or escape.

I underestimated Ericka, and I'm paying for it with everything I care about. The soulless freak lays against the wall, holding her face with her eyes closed, stifling a smile in her palm as she watches me getting ushered away. Robbi keeps whispering in her ear between sobs, probably something about the paramedics coming soon.

She looks up once before I'm out the door, meeting my eyes for what I'm sure will be the last time. *I trusted you. I loved you. I lost my fucking mind.*

It's too much. I can only close my eyes as I'm thrown into a squad car and driven through the old Chicago streets lining the warehouse district where the studio is closing up shop. By the time everything is moved back to L.A., even if they have to find a new Miles, I know I'll be wearing orange and a number for a name tag.

I'm fucked, and for once it isn't my own fault.

XI: Over, Done, Forgotten (Robin)

Life as I know it is over.

Destroyed.

Forgotten.

I'm dragged down into a numb, gut wrenching haze so thick I spend my evenings dialing crisis hotlines. I always hang up as soon as someone answers.

I don't have the courage to tell anyone else I loved a violent psychopath. Not even enough courage to admit that deep down, a part of me still might.

Mom's condo feels like a tomb after the place the studio gave me, not to mention the nights I spent in Luke's luxurious splendor. Future accommodations given to the actors are up in the air, as is everything else with the movie while they desperately try to salvage the horrific PR damage inflicted by 'Mr. Black Hearted.'

That's what the press is calling him, ever since it lit up social media. Honestly, they aren't wrong.

Ever since we came face-to-face again after our long absence, I tried not to trust him. I feared the worst, but the absolute darkest places my mind went when assessing the risk a second chance with Lucus Shaw could bring never went *here.*

I sleep in my old guest bed, the one that used to be mine alone. Colder than I've ever been.

The only silver lining is, it hasn't taken mom long to recover. Somehow, the wound was worse than it looked, and the reconstructive jaw surgery they talked about hasn't been necessary. Her bruise is a little better every day, fading after a week, and it doesn't take much dental work to repair her two cracked teeth.

"One day at a time, sweetie," she says, as if I have another choice. "You'll get through this. Learn to forget him. The more you dwell on the past, the more it'll control you."

Wise words, if she lived by them herself. She hasn't shut up about how awful Frank Shaw was to her all these years. I think the only reason she doesn't discuss what happened with Luke is because she doesn't want to make me feel worse than I do.

Whatever, she's oddly supportive, when it should be the other way around. She goes about her life like nothing happened, staying strong for me. She'll probably have TMJ issues forever, but it seems she's decided I'm the one who's suffered more. I guess Luke told her about his plans to propose before their talk got heated, and he decided to smash her face in.

I don't know if he meant to.

I don't fucking care.

It's incredible what a bullet I dodged, escaping him

before he decided to do something just as awful to me.

It isn't easy counting my lucky breaks, of course. I'm too eaten up with regret, shame, and disbelief that shouldn't even be there after what he did, after what I saw with my own crying eyes.

His brothers finally stopped calling this week. I told Hayden and Grant to fuck off, or else I'd seek a restraining order. Apparently, they listened. And no, I don't care what they want.

There's no fix for this except what I should've done years ago – write Luke out of my life. Forget him. Move on.

I'm not interested in excuses, or second guessing, or therapy. I want to finish re-shooting my scenes with his replacement, collect the royalties, and move far, far away.

Japan sounds good, or maybe New Zealand. Some distant island where *Bare* won't be the main American export for the next year. There has to be a magical place on this planet where I won't have to re-live this lie disguised as love, and where every day I survive a nervous breakdown feels like a major accomplishment.

* * * *

One Month Later

Time's up. There's none left to cry, or reflect, or grieve because I don't let myself do it.

I ignore the headlines and the buzz on social media about the film. The studio wants me to finish my last scenes with Harkness first, before they find a proper replacement for Luke. I'm happy to comply.

I give my best tearful speech as Ali, pleading with the Senator for mercy. I'm supposed to make him show his weakness, giving Miles the opportunity he needs to save us by strangling the villain with his own handcuffs. Harkness gives an incredible performance with the stunt actor they've hired to stand in for Miles.

His fencing skills are truly a lost art. I thought the sword scene at the end sounded dumb the first time I saw it in the script, but that was before I saw what a living legend could do with his fancy footwork and heroic slinging.

"Truly a shame about your man," he tells me one day, squeezing my shoulder, his wise old eyes crinkling at the corners.

"Thanks. It's not your problem."

"Hang in there, lovely lady. These things have a funny way of working themselves out."

I give him a fake smile. Older and wiser doesn't mean a thing when his advice is insane.

There's no happy ending here. No third chance, now that our second one is blown. Not after he savaged my mother, tearing my heart out in front of me.

Bebe calls me several times a week when I'm not on the set. She's in a mad rush to protect my mental state, hoping I won't breakdown and walk, causing her to lose an already tenuous commission.

I swear up and down that work is all I care about. It's a huge lie, of course, but since when were the comforting ones the most sinful?

Sweet distractions. Thank God for them.

They're a small relief from the nuclear surprise I'm doing my best not to acknowledge.

It doesn't hit me until I'm at mom's place again, alone during the nights, a sheet pulled up to my neck while I fight not to let my mind wander. She's taken several days off to go to a conference upstate, leaving me alone.

There's only one place my brain goes, and it isn't good.

Hell, will anything ever be good again after the pregnancy test last week confirmed my worst fears?

I'll never know how or why my birth control failed. It must've been our last night together, before the world came down the next day. He dialed my baby fever up to ten, or maybe I just missed a pill or two I really shouldn't have in all the commotion that started as soon as he went to prison.

No, I haven't been to a doctor yet.

Hell no, I haven't told mom.

For now, it's my secret, and it's the most bittersweet excuse to hide from the world when I'm not in front of a camera. It's also great motivation to get on with planning my life after the movie in earnest.

I *need* to leave Chicago, and never come back. Anywhere, far from the wealthy, evil reach of the Shaws will do.

This isn't about running from a big, fat mistake anymore. It's about keeping my baby safe, keeping it innocent, and most of all, making sure it never learns the truth about its father, Lucus Shaw.

They say a woman can't erase a man who's made his mark down to her DNA. Obviously, they're wrong.

They haven't felt the hate in my heart.

They haven't felt my pain.

They haven't figured out that with enough anger and hurt, a woman can do anything. That includes extracting the venom, erasing the good times and the bad, learning to forget the man who came to me camouflaged in love over and over, only to jam the dagger of truth he was hiding deep in my side.

No more. I'm pulling it out, however much it hurts, and then I'm walking away. One agonizing step at a time, I will leave Luke behind.

XII: Rewind (Luke)

Pushups keep a man sane when he's wearing orange.

I used to watch bad prison movies growing up, and always laughed at the lengths guys would go to get their time lifting weights in the glorified recess pits outside. Now, it's not so funny, and I'm about one more week away from siding with the creepy guys wearing motorcycle club tattoos if it means a permit to pump iron.

Actually, I have these guys to thank for nobody else fucking with me yet. Hayds told me they're on notice, men from an affiliate of the fearsome Grizzlies MC, who he used to do deals with cage fighting downtown. If anyone gives me trouble, they're bound to get a broken nose.

It's not much consolation when I'm stuck like a pig waiting to be slaughtered. Pushups, on the other hand…they're practically a divine kiss.

I work myself until I can't in my tiny cell. Grunting, sweating, muscles giving out after a couple hundred body lifts. The exertion sends the precious hellfire through my veins that lets me momentarily forget the blinding need to choke Ericka Plomb with my bare hands.

My brothers promised I wouldn't last a week. It's been at least five, and I'm starting to lose track of time.

For all our wealth and connections, they underestimated the power of a movie star in a popular film committing a horrific crime. Hell, I'm starting to believe it myself every time one of those bikers slips me a tabloid in the cafeteria, or shows me the latest Twitter printouts they've smuggled in.

BARE NAKED SHAME! LUCUS SHAW HEADING FOR SERIOUS TIME IN THE SLAMMER!

The headlines screamed it high and low for about a week, each more insufferable than the last. Then King Silas saved his wife and royal baby from a shipwreck overseas, and my dirty deed receded into background noise as the people moved onto happier diversions in the news.

I've thought long and hard about how to get her back. It's all I think about whenever exercise hasn't stunned my brain quiet.

Prison makes me miss a lot of things, but nothing compares to her.

I'll give up my fortune, my fame, even my pilot's license if it means having her know I didn't lay a finger on her insane mother. There's no obvious way to prove my innocence, except for one.

I'm collapsed on the floor when I hear a warden's boots shuffling toward me on the cement floor. The lock to my cell door buzzes, and the tall, wiry man I've seen before stands in the doorway. "You have visitors. Let's go."

It's a minute's walk down the hall, past the other cells,

toward the small room they give the prisoners as their only contact with visitors from the outside world. Most of the bastards in their cells have stopped leering, scared off by the MC protection I've got thanks to Hayds. A few of them, though, know exactly who I am.

They stare through the openings in their cells. The brave ones curse, spit, tell me I'll be left alone in the shower one of these days, and then they'll give my 'rich boy ass' payback in spades for beating an innocent woman.

The noise fades when we're through the security checkpoint. I stand still while he opens the door, wondering why Hayds bothers to see me when he can't do a damned thing.

"Thirty minutes," the warden says.

I nod, and step inside. This time, my billionaire brother isn't alone. There's another silhouette towering over him, familiar scruff on his face, wearing a thousand dollar Oxford shirt with the top two buttons undone.

"Fly Right, what the hell have you gotten yourself into?" Grant stands up when I lean in for a brotherly hug.

"Can't believe you came." If he's here at all, it's good news.

We share a quick embrace before Hayden slaps our shoulders, his stern look reminding us why we're really together. "Grant's people ran the tapes," he says.

"Shit." I thought I'd be ready for this, receiving my one ticket out of here, and back to Robbi. But my heart tells another story, pounding like a war drum, threatening to rupture if this doesn't go how I hope. "And?"

Grant smiles, the blue eyes we share twinkling above his beard. "And Wall Street's a place where a man can buy anything, for the right price. Lucky for you, I called in a few favors with the data firm I told you about. They owed me big after the money I poured into their company last year. You wouldn't believe how fast the bastards came knocking when they thought I had another seven figures waiting for them."

"Come on, Grant, let's get to the point. We've only got half an hour." Hayds reaches into his pocket, pulls out a small black box, and lays it on the table.

I raise an eyebrow. "Really, bro? The nineties called, and they want their voice recorder back."

"It's this, or our word of mouth. The guards don't let us bring phones. Hell, I had to bribe them four figures just to keep them from confiscating this thing. Here, have a listen." He pushes the big white play button in the middle.

The room falls silent while I hold my breath, hands clenched underneath the table in a silent prayer. It's audio from dad's library five years ago. When I hear my old man's voice, I tense, knowing what's coming next will make or break everything.

"Why so much overtime, Ms. Plomb? This library doesn't even have a speck of dust. If I didn't know better, I'd say you were trying to get my attention with your work ethic more than that short, fuckable skirt."

Laughter fills the silence after his words. A woman's. "Oh, Mr. Shaw, I've heard what they say about you. Stop with this Ms. Plomb stuff. Must you be so formal, or is it just because you haven't had to call me Ericka yet when I'm on my knees?"

Dad growls. All three of us try very hard not to imagine what the fuck is happening on that tape. I doubt my brothers brought barf bags.

"Well, Ericka, you're a married woman. I heard about your husband's discipline problems in accounting when I decided to check into your family."

"Oh, Danny's a damned idiot. I wouldn't be here flirting if I was getting what I need at home." She inhales sharply, and there's a sound like a zipper coming undone. "Forget him, Mr. Shaw. If I'm not worried about him finding out, there's no reason you need to be."

"Who said I was worried? Cute, really, thinking you're the first gal with a ring on her finger I've ever had. We'll do this, and we'll do it dirty, but you'll follow three simple rules." Inwardly, I'm groaning. He sounds like he's cutting a business deal, not seducing the woman who's brought me nothing but misery.

"Just three? I can handle a lot more than that, Mr. Shaw. A whole *hell* of a lot more."

"Fuck," he grunts, lust heavy in his tone, regaining his composure a second later. "First rule is, this only happens in our off hours, usually late, and always in private. You don't call me, I'll call you, whenever I'm ready. Second, no money. I don't pay for sex or make favors. If that's what you're looking for, then you can pull up your dress and walk the fuck out. Anything from me that's not part of your regular salary is a gift, or extra hours on your pay stub to fool anybody getting nosy. I'm nobody's sugar daddy. I can go downtown any night and have my pick, Ericka. Never forget it."

"I'm a lucky woman, aren't I?" she coos, sarcasm and genuine worship smearing her words. "What's the last?"

"No drama. I don't do scorned women or pissed off husbands when I fuck married pussy. It's your responsibility to keep your feelings in check, and make sure nobody finds out about us. If you'd like, I'll help send your husband and daughter places where they won't worry why you're not home most nights."

"Oh, my. Whole nights, you said?"

There's a long pause, and a smacking sound that can only be a kiss. My stomach turns.

"If you keep me interested, then yes. Your body is already doing a damned fine job at it. Oh, and one more thing." I hear a rustling sound, fabric snapping, a woman gasping as she goes down hard on a desk. "Call me Frank."

Grant punches the old recorder with his fist. "You've heard the relevant part. The rest, you really don't want to hear."

"Thanks," I say. "I'm glad you got your friends at the data recovery place to do your dirty work. Don't think we'd ever be able to sit through hours of this. Tell me there's video as well?"

Hayden leans forward, his hands folded. "Fortunately and unfortunately, there is. Where do you think we recovered the audio from?"

"Christ." My hand is almost shaking as I bring it up,

wiping the sweat from my face. My brothers are just as drenched, the hot lamp hanging over us glowing like a second sun. "You're sure this is the first time they ever fucked? You're certain?"

"Brother, the guy who fed me this knows I would've busted his balls if he left anything out," Grant says. "I came all the way from New York and swore off a camping trip in Maine for this. If I wasted my time, I'd wring necks, and he knows it."

"You have to get in touch with Robbi. Show her," I say, guiding my fists slowly to the table.

"Yeah, that's a problem. She threatened us with a restraining order over the calls a few weeks ago," Hayden tells me. "There's also nothing damning on this tape that'll prove Ericka lied about what happened in your dressing room. Will it make your girl second guess what went down five years ago? Probably. Will it get you off the hook with her, and the rest of the world?"

"No." I admit it. My heart sinks into my stomach. Much as I hate it, he's right. She mixed her blood too well with the fake crap when she punched herself in the mouth. Even the lab tests we ordered came back inconclusive.

"Tell us how to reach her," Grant says, his shoulders bowing up. "You know her best. There's got to be something we can say, or do, to get her attention, and make her listen."

"I don't know how many lies Ericka's told her since the morning it went to shit. She'll walk away pissed off and confused unless she hears it from the horse's mouth."

"A confession?" Grant's eyebrows go up. "Luke, stop talking crazy. There's no way we're getting jack out of the crazy, lying witch unless you're asking us to break the law."

"Obviously not. Won't do the family any good if we all wind up behind bars." I look at Hayden, sadness filling my eyes. "Especially when Hayds has a daughter on the way."

I'm happy for him, but damn if I'm not jealous. Every minute he's not in this place, working and playing as a free man, a woman he loves at his side with his kid in her belly....he's living my dream.

Same one I chased that landed me here. Same one costing me my sanity every dark minute I ponder letting go, cutting some kind of plea deal, and leaving Robbi to a life without me a second time.

No.

Fuck no.

"Get them in a room together," I say. "We're Shaws, for God's sake. Richer than royalty put together, and smart enough to make our own fame and fortune. Figuring out how to get a woman and her daughter together for a sit down with the video ought to be easy."

My two older brothers share a look. When they turn back to me, they both nod.

"Whatever it takes to get you out of here," Hayds tells me.

"Any ideas?" Grant asks, leaning back in his chair.

I smile, a gesture that's alien after tension ruled my face for so long. "I have a few. Listen closely..."

* * * *

One Week Later

In five minutes, it's going down.

I've tracked the time religiously, heard what few updates I can get through my brother's biker buddies, and I know it's scheduled for nine, at a small hotel next to the studio. My brothers roped in my agent, Jim, to fake the studio's invite.

He wasn't real keen at first, but when he realized he could make up a decent chunk of his lost commission from my role on *Bare* falling through, he jumped.

The guards are shuffling us into the cafeteria for another late morning breakfast. If Hayden and Grant can't fix this, there's a strong chance I'll spend many more years here, stuck, living like a shadow.

It's not half as mortifying as losing her twice. I need Robbi back, and I need to carry out what I started. I need it down to my bones.

The ring on her finger, the kid I'll give her, the life we're supposed to share until we're nothing but dust in the wind…it's out of my hands. It's fucking infuriating.

I did all I could, wracking my brain to help them find the tapes, and then giving them an idea how they could get Ericka and Robbi in the same place to drop the bomb.

What happens next is up to fate.

The hopes, the prayers, the love I remember bring me no peace. There's no making any.

I'll never breathe well again unless Ericka gets exposed as the monstrous fraud she is.

XIII: Tumbling Down (Robin)

I don't understand why the small conference room is almost empty, or why they brought us here. Fishing into my purse for the phone, I read the email again, eyeballing the extra chairs, coffee, and cups waiting on the table.

Special guest, 9:00 a.m. We'll be discussing how to move the film forward with a new Miles Black, plus some surprising news.

It's such a brief note, and it doesn't sound much like one Emmie would send out, the lead assistant who does the scheduling for Pierce and crew. I'm still standing when I hear the door open behind me, five minutes earlier than I expect, knowing how many late stragglers come into these meetings.

I do a turn, and my jaw hits the floor.

It's Hayden Shaw. Plus another man it takes me several seconds to recognize, until I remember the old photos in the house, and the two times he visited near the holidays. Grant, the eldest, in all his high end lumbersexual glory, wealth and ruggedness colliding in a way that's almost as handsome as Luke's hard edge.

As handsome as he *used* to be, I mean. I hate him now, I have to keep telling myself. Almost as much as the two persistent idiots taking up the same space in this room.

"Robin, have a seat. Please. We need to talk." He goes to the head of the table and pulls out a chair.

"Holy shit, no. I'm *out* of here." I turn, and start heading for the door, but Grant steps in front of it, blocking the entire frame with his huge body.

"Cooperate, and this won't take long. We're just waiting for one more person to get this show going," Grant says.

Sit the fuck down, his expression says. I march back limply toward the chair Hayden holds out for me, wondering how fast I can humor them before I get a chance to call the police.

I'm not even in the seat ten seconds when the door opens again. Grant steps out of the way, making way for the woman who stops dead in her tracks when she's several feet in, a bewildered look on her face.

"Mom?!" We're both deer in the headlights. "Okay, what the hell is going on here?"

"Please have a seat, Mrs. Plomb. I'm afraid this isn't quite the reception the email promised for your firm's clients, but you're sworn to the truth as an attorney. Cooperate, and I promise, you just might keep your license."

"Hell no." Mom makes a dead run for the door, and runs smack into the big man's chest. He isn't moving.

"Hayden, the tape," Grant says. "Get it going *now.*"

"You're going to step away and let my daughter and I out of here this instant, you wretched man, or I'll see to it personally you're both sharing a cell with your freak of a brother!"

Hayden isn't listening. He pulls out his phone, taps a few keys, and the slim TV mounted to the ceiling corner flickers to life. The low res, grainy footage isn't easy on my eyes at first, but I can hear the audio much better.

"Why so much overtime, Ms. Plomb? This library doesn't even have a speck of dust..." the older man in the distinguished suit on screen can't be anyone except the dead senior Shaw. And the woman next to him, sitting on his desk with her eyelashes fluttering and her legs crossed, is my mother, five years younger.

The entire world comes to a stop. Everything except the insane, disgusting scene unfolding on the screen, ending in their wretched kiss as he hikes up her skirt, bends her over, and shoves himself inside her.

Very willingly. Without a shred of sadness, fear, or disgust in mom's eyes.

"Off. For fuck's sake, turn it off!" Her voice comes out hoarse, a whisper rubbed raw by a truth I'm afraid to call out. "Robbi..."

She turns away from Grant, walks toward me, and reaches out. I get over my fear. I throw myself back against the wall so hard it hurts when the chair slams into it, before I'm on my feet, a pointed finger in her face.

"Don't. All those years, pretending you were some innocent victim, bribed and blackmailed to do things with him against your will..." I can't go on. The bitter lump in my throat chokes me.

It's like watching an older, corrupted version of myself in a demented mirror as the tears start rolling down her cheeks, hotter and angrier than mine. "This isn't what it looks like, I swear!"

"Ericka, stop," Hayden says, icy anger creeping into his voice. "Have a seat. Tell your daughter the truth. That was the first time you ever slept with my dad. First of many. We've gone through the rest of the footage during the time you worked there. Always shows you two prowling around the house like a couple horny teenagers. Not one time did you ever tell him to stop. He was drunk and crude plenty, sure, but did he force anything? Video says no. You never talked money, either, except when he gave you an extra bonus."

"Lies," mom says, hiding her face in her palms, shaking her head violently. "Awful, awful lies! Why the hell are you doing this?"

"We want Luke set free, and the record cleared. You can do that with a statement to the judge," Grant says, growling his words. "We don't give a shit about shaming you over the stupid affair you had with our old man, and then lying about it. We want the truth. This was the only way you'd even think about telling Robbi what happened that day."

Breathe, I tell myself. Right now, it's a chore. *If you can't do it for you, do it for the baby.*

"You're holding me here then as your prisoner?" My mother snaps. "God. You Shaws are stupider than I even thought. Robin, come on, help me get out of here. We're leaving this place and marching straight to the nearest police station. We're going to tell them exactly what kind of sick games you're –"

"No, shut up!" I'm in her face, my finger stabbing at her chest, blood running so hot it's hard to form words. "Mom, just shut up."

"Robin, I…" She's silent. Lost for words. No longer wounded, but deflated.

"As for you two," I look past her to Grant, and then Hayden. "Please. Step outside. Let me talk to her alone. I'll deal with this."

The two strong brothers share a look. After a second, Hayden walks toward his bearded sibling, and they head for the door. "We'll be right outside," he says.

I wait to hear the door click shut. Then I let my anger loose on the psycho standing in front of me, pouring betrayal out my eyes, and into hers. "You lied to me. You sent him to jail over *nothing.*"

"Honey, no! You saw what he did to me with your own eyes. They've got you confused. You're doubting it because of this stupid five year old footage they probably had pieced together by a video editor?"

She can't stop. I don't know if it's a sickness or just pure evil.

"You're still doing it," I say, my own disbelief straining my throat. I can't comprehend why she's like this. "What kind of person are you? What the hell is wrong with you?"

The light in her dark eyes becomes a pinprick. "I'm the victim, and nobody cares. Do you really think I had it easy, living with your father while he pickled his brain drinking?

It didn't magically start as soon as we got jobs with Mr. Shaw. It was going on a long time, and I hid it. I became a human shield to protect you."

My stomach gurgles. I can't even look at her, so I turn away, pacing the room, trying to find the right combination of words to touch her basic humanity, if she has any.

"I never asked you for anything," I say, meeting her angry eyes. "After everything that happened, after everything you *told* me about the Shaws, I had to claw back every piece of my life. I thought I finally had weeks ago, when we were happy. He clicked back into my life like the missing piece. Now, I see what I've really been missing – the truth. Everything that never made sense about what happened to us."

"Robin –" The way she says my name tells me another lie is coming, and it's probably a doozy.

"No! You're not leaving this room until I find out what really happened with Luke. I *knew* he wasn't a violent man." I'm in her face again, whispering demands. "Please. Just tell me the truth. I want to hear it from you."

"I couldn't let him take you. Couldn't let him use you, throw you away, turn you against me after he told you about his father and I." She breaks eye contact, looking at the floor, and I wonder if she's feeling shame for the first time in her life. "Yes, I set him up. I hit myself in the face. Chewed fake blood to make it look worse than it really was."

I thought I was ready. Hearing this…this lunacy rips open a whole new chasm in my heart. I stagger back, catch myself against the table, and try my damnedest not to cry.

It's impossible. I'm shaking my head again when I look at her, trying to process what will never make sense. "Why, mom, why?"

"Because I can't, and I won't, let you think I'm a monster. I made mistakes, and maybe I did some underhanded things. But I did them all for you, Robin. I wanted better for you so you'd never, ever have to play with dirty, wretched men like Frank Shaw just to get ahead. I wanted you to succeed so you'd never be tempted by their power like I was, so you'd never have a miserable marriage driving you into a devil's arms. I wanted him to stay the hell *away* from you, and I decided to make it happen. I did wrong, but I did it for a good reason. I won't apologize for anything except hurting you."

"Apology?" I look up, wrinkling my nose. The sour taste in my mouth won't go away. "You really think that's what I'm asking for?"

Her eyes stare, dumb and blank. So much for the humanity, the shame, or any basic understanding of just how wicked she's been.

"Mom, you're going to do exactly what Hayden and Grant said. We're going to sit down at this table, and you're going to write a statement. I want a second one for the studio and the press, too. What you've done...there is no forgiveness. I won't even think about it until we've cleared his name."

"Cleared him? And throw away everything I've worked for?" She turns her head up, crazier than ever. "Robin, no. I'll go to jail before I get out of the way, and let that wicked man hurt you."

"I'm not asking, mom. You're *going* to sit down and write it out, and then we're going to find you a shrink. You put the love of my life in jail over your own fucking ego. I'm not some fragile angel, and you're no martyr."

"Wow." The bitch tone is back in her voice. "So, that's the thanks I get? After everything I did? You wouldn't have even gotten a second chance with that selfish, screwed up bastard if I hadn't paid your way through acting school!"

"But I did, and now I know the truth. There's no going back, mom." We share an icy look. New hurt fills my head, the realization I'm not getting anywhere, trying to reason with her.

"I guess you'll have to turn on your own mother to stop me, then." Her eyes say she isn't joking. Yes, she's really this crazy, daring me to block the door.

Time to play my last card. "You'll stop, if you ever want to see me or your future grandbaby again."

She stops mid-step, heading for the door, and whips her head around. "Grandbaby? What?"

I smile through the pain. "That's right. Luke gave me a gift before you sent him to prison. I'm several weeks pregnant. Not how we meant it to happen, but you're more insane than I already think if you believe I'm not happy about this. I'll wait with our baby while he's in jail, however long it takes. And I'll make damned sure it's a lonely wait for both of us. Whether you help or not, he'll be free one day, and you've got the rest of your life to look forward to without me or the baby if you keep going."

Walking past her, it's my turn to head for the room,

hiding my latest hot tears. I hear her behind me when she breaks.

"Robin, wait!" Mom calls after me, but I'm not stopping.

My hand is on the doorknob before she catches my shoulder, frantically pulling me backward. "You can't do this. You can't take away my family – it's all I ever cared about!"

"Then prove it by listening for once, instead of being a completely crazy, self-righteous bitch."

Game on. We stare through each other. I watch my hateful gaze sink deeper in her eyes, turning them darker.

There's no response. With a heavy sigh, I throw her hand off my shoulder, and move back to the door.

Mom whimpers, dropping to her knees, tears sliding down her cheeks. "Don't do this to me, Robbi. Don't make me choose. Please."

Her hands are clasped. Begging. It's a sight to behold, terrible and unexpected, and not what I want.

I have to free Luke. Nothing else matters.

"I can't be alone! Christ, don't you get it?" She bangs her fists on the floor. "All those years ago, the reason why I got tangled up with Frank, why I was willing to put everything on the line for you…"

She isn't making sense. I look at her, folding my arms, refusing to hide the scorn in my expression.

"Danny and his drinking destroyed me. I had you young, and married the wrong man. We never had much money. There wasn't time for friends, or parties, or trips across the country to see what little family we had. You think I'm a monster, driven by hate, but it's the loneliness, honey. You were all I ever had. I'm so, so alone in this world. Make it worse, and I'll die. Is that what you want?"

Oh, guilt trip time. Good thing I've had my fill of her bullshit.

"I want you to do what's right, instead of whining about how hard you had it. You drone on and on, blaming dad. He had his issues, yes, but he's gone. Whatever he did, he didn't force you into another man's bed. Luke told me about his father's drinking, too. I can't believe I didn't see it before. You traded a poor drunk for a rich one, and then played innocent when he didn't want you anymore. You never got over it. Frankly, you're horrible, and I'm seriously wondering if I should ever let you see us again even if you do what's right."

She lowers her face, shocked into silence, several more large tears dripping down her cheeks. "You're right, and it kills me to say it. Maybe I need this. Maybe I need to be cut off, locked away, kept from your beautiful baby so I don't corrupt it."

"It isn't like that," I say, right before I realize she's playing me again. Trying to make me feel like the guilty one. My teeth sink into my lower lip.

I'm not sure why I'm still wasting my time. I need to go, get with the Shaws waiting outside, and figure out how we're going to free Luke without her help.

"I don't know what to do, baby," she whimpers. "I don't know, but I *can't* be alone. Please. I'll see a doctor, and work through this, if it gives me a second chance."

Second chances. She hits an ache deep in my gut, the very thing that brought me here because I found one with Luke. I still haven't lost it, if I can bring him back to me.

"Not good enough," I say, glaring. "Work with me, mom. Swallow your pride. Confess. Then we'll see about finding you some help. There's a lot for us to work through, but you don't have to ruin the rest of your life."

The next pause is agonizing. This time, I swear I'm leaving if her next words are more woe-is-me crap.

"Okay!" she sputters at last, pounding her fists on the floor, the redness on her face deepening in defeat. "Okay, damn you."

She lets out one of the most painful moans I've ever heard when I open the door. But I'm not leaving her. I stick my head out and see the brothers stand up straight, pulling themselves off the wall they were leaning on.

"Ten more minutes. I'll have something that should get Luke out of there by tonight."

* * * *

"Oh my God. No matter how many times you hear truth is stranger than fiction, it never sinks in until you see this stuff." Bebe can't believe her eyes.

Honestly, neither can I.

I'm sitting in her office, the very same place I started, checking my phone every few minutes for a message from Grant or Hayden.

The judge should've seen mom's confession by now. She's standing by at the police station, ready to surrender, assuming Luke wants to press charges, as is his right.

"I know, I wouldn't have believed it myself if I hadn't heard it with my own ears," I say.

"You poor, poor thing." Bebe cocks her head, sympathy glowing on her face. Then her eyes go wide. "Wait. This doesn't mean you're backing out just when they're getting the movie back on track?"

I sigh. Everybody cares about their own piece, especially my agent, who does nothing except blur the line between ambition and greed.

"No, that's not what I'm getting at. I *do* want the film back on track. I want to know if there's a way to get the studio to agree to bring Luke back as Miles?"

"Oh." Her relief that I'm staying on board melts when she realizes what I'm asking, and does a double take. "Ohhh! Well, obviously, I have no direct control over that, you understand? It'd be messy, assuming he's released soon. *Very* messy, considering the bad press."

"That's why mom's other statement is going out to the public. Hayden already sent it to his friends in the media. I'll do whatever it takes to clear his name. Freedom isn't enough if he walks out of prison without his reputation."

"If you'd like to speak on his behalf, I can reach out to the studio's marketing team, and clear it through them. Once they're updated on the new developments, of course."

"Bebe, they'd better. If they think I'll leave him hanging out to dry in front of the world, they don't know me. That's the one thing that'll make me walk."

"Now, now! Let's not be hasty." She throws her hands

up in a panic. "I'll send a message to Pierce's assistant about it right now, if it's really bothering you that much."

It is. I'm not leaving until I hear he's released. And I'll never sleep totally easy unless it's all fixed.

Us, the film, his reputation. Everything my mother's self-absorbed lies destroyed.

"Tell him I want to sit down and talk if he isn't sure. PR issues aside, he knows damned well Luke is the best Miles there is. I won't have the same chemistry with the replacement. Don't care how hot he is. He isn't the man I love."

"All right, I'll do my best. If this goes off like you're hoping, I may want to revisit compensation in future contracts, you understand." She turns her nose up, dismayed by the risk I'm asking us to shoulder. "You're lucky to have me, Robbi doll. Why, if it wasn't for my expertise, every muckraker and two bit blogger would've chewed you up alongside him for not joining in the ten minutes of hate aimed at Lucus Shaw over what he did."

"I'm lucky I didn't. If I'd gone on record, if I'd screamed and hollered about what he did to my mother without knowing what really happened, I'd be feeling about a thousand times worse right now." My head throbs just thinking about it. "Let's fix this. Bebe, I'm here for the long haul, as long as Luke is by my side. I'll make you millions if you help me get his job back."

"Deal." Her fingers tap quickly across the keyboard in front of her for a few more seconds. When she's done, she spins her screen around so I can see MESSAGE SENT.

"Pierce should be in touch soon. The studio has the upper hand, certainly, but they're not used to two badass bitches who know how to drive a hard bargain."

That gets a tiny smile because it's true. They could easily give us the finger, tell us they're going with the veteran actor they have lined up to replace him, and then find someone to replace me, too, if I decide to walk.

Yes, I'm fully aware it's career suicide if I do.

If love makes a woman do crazy things, then a second chance at putting her heart back together must make her a certified lunatic.

My phone vibrates with a message from Hayden while Bebe and I are walking to our cars.

> **Hayden:** He's out. Going to get him cleaned up and dressed at my place. Here's the address.

I copy the place listed in the next message. It's the imposing glass tower downtown, where he lives with Penny, making their lives above several dozen businesses paying prime commercial rent.

I'm racing down the city streets, my eyes giving up new hot tears above my crooked smile.

This love is me. Indistinguishably, indisputably, irrevocably.

Through all the pain, the heartache, and the confusion, I've always been his. I know it's true because the past few weeks were hell, a grim throwback to our first break five years ago.

I'm not whole without him. With God as my witness, I swear I'll find the other piece of myself, and this time super glue it in place with the world's most passionate kiss. Nothing will ever knock it loose again.

Together, we've seen heaven and hell.

We made a baby on nothing more than love and raw desire.

We've lived the divide: friends, enemies, and lovers. The last one is what we're meant to be, where we're meant to stay, and the sooner his lips are on mine, the quicker the world rights itself again.

This isn't just about the right thing, or making sure we're in a place to live the best and worst of us again. Luke completes me. He's the other half of my soul, my home, and about a thousand other sappy, indescribable things I used to laugh at.

Notice I'm not snickering at love cheese anymore. I'm not even doubting it. Losing him twice taught me how real, how serious, and how special it is to find a man who gives you a reason to breathe.

I need him like I need the steady hum of my own heart. And this heart is going to make some *serious* noise, hammering its glorious rhythm, as soon as I'm home again in his arms.

XIV: Shut Up and Kiss Me (Luke)

I never knew how amazing a hot shower could be. Prison taught me a lot of things, but one lesson I doubt I'll ever forget is how incredible it feels to let the suds and steam roll down all six feet plus of me without having to worry about what freak is sneaking up behind me to do harm.

My brother's place is another world after weeks in the slammer. Shit, I even stop a few seconds to admire the lions, jaguars, and tiger art he has everywhere, paintings and statues immortalizing his spirit animal, if there is such a thing.

Mine is with me in ink, and it's never meant more.

I take my time drying the falcon stamped on my chest. Today, it's a free bird, and every damned inch of me is grateful to be soaring with it.

I slip into the fresh change of clothes the studio sent over in a box. Adjusting my cufflinks, I let myself think about her since the first time I shed my neon orange suit and left a life I'm eager to forget.

I owe her big.

This was Robbi, and my brothers. Sure, I came up with

the plan to set me free, but if it wasn't for them following through, I wouldn't be standing here today.

"It's time," I whisper to myself, thumbing the little box in purple leather nestled in my pocket.

Losing five years away from her the first time was pure hell.

Losing six more weeks, knowing she thought I was a demon, taught me hell has dark corners I hadn't begun to imagine.

The box is what's going to make sure she's never taken from me again. It was right where I left it at the studio. It's the only possession I cared about when they dragged me behind bars. Thought about it more than my plane getting impounded. Whoever packed up my dressing room and gave it to my brother for safe keeping never even saw it, thank God.

This ring has been my secret, my longing, my unrealized dream for too fucking long.

No more. It's the key to everything. It's the reset button, the deed to her heart, the promise I never gave up, even when I thought I'd suffer alone without her until somebody got through Hayden's biker buddies, and snuffed out my life.

It's what I've always wanted, what I've always needed. Second only to the baby I swore I'd put inside her one fine day.

It's the next fifty years, or maybe longer. Every day I've got left on this rock drawing breath, and every day I'm privileged just to taste her lips.

"Ms. Plomb is here and waiting in the front sitting room, Master Luke." Hayden's valet, Reed, knocks gently on the bathroom door. "Shall I bring a bottle of wine up from the cellar?"

"Hold the drinks," I say, brushing back a few stray hairs on my head before I pop the door and walk out. "When we're ready, I'll let you know. Tell Hayds and his girl I'd like a little privacy, too."

"Certainly." He gives me a respectful nod, and then I'm on my way, heading down the marble halls of my brother's condo, more like a museum than a proper living place.

Hayd's style has always been grand and proper. It will clash. The reunion I have planned is a lot more rough and tumble.

I stop at the entryway and stare a minute later. She's on her phone, and doesn't see me for a few blissful seconds.

Blissful because I get to drink her in like a fine wine.

There's the long blonde hair I missed. The grey eyes I remember lighting my fire, the only flame I had most prison nights. There's her bottom lip tucked into her mouth, begging to be bit, sucked, and tasted. Everything I imagined and missed when I wanted to stay sane, or just drive myself crazier, thinking I'd probably rot in my cell without ever having again.

"Ahem." I clear my throat. She looks up, startled.

"Luke!" I wait until she's on her feet before I'm on her.

Then she's in my arms, and our lips are all over the damned place.

Nothing ever tasted as good as she does now. Our loss,

our longing, and our fresh new hope sinks through me, marinating my soul.

Yeah, I know that sounds like some flowery crap. The kind a man says when he's smitten. Overwhelmed.

Fuck it, *I am.* I press her up against the colorful rocks in the mantle that dominates the room, drinking my fill with every kiss. I missed this like the beat of my own heart as a free man, and I tell her with my mouth.

"It's been too long," she whispers, after a good minute, as soon as I let her come up for air. "I'm so sorry, Luke. I never should've let you go. If only I'd questioned her sooner..."

Her eyes shut painfully. I let her have a moment, running her little palm on my face, feeling the smoothness after I shaved away the angry scruff prison left me. Tears dance wild in her eyes when she opens them, sorrow and regret competing for the upper hand.

Doesn't she get it yet? We've had our hurt. There's no time for more.

"Enough, babe." I catch her wrist in my grip, pressing my fingers into her soft skin. "You didn't know. You did right. If it wasn't for you and my brothers, I wouldn't be in front of you today, turning the rest of this fucked up world upright."

She tilts her head, smiling, resting her eyes in forgiveness before she speaks. "I'm not finished yet. Not until you're back in the film, playing my Miles. Social media's eating up our story, at least. Check it out. You're a hero."

She holds up her phone with a grin. My face fills the

screen of an online gossip rag in a Facebook post, a headline screaming over the image in red caps: HE'S FREE! HOLLYWOOD HEARTHROB WANTS TO PLAY MILES BLACK AGAIN, AND YOU WON'T BELIEVE WHY!

I snort, and push her hand away. "What if I wanted to say fuck the movie, and do something better with my life?"

Her face goes pale. I let it for a few seconds before I bust a smile. "It really has been forever, hasn't it? You've clearly forgotten my sense of humor, little bird."

"Ass!" She punches me playfully in the arm. I grab her around the waist, spin her around, and bring her back into the center of the room, behind the big sofa. I'll need the extra clearance around us for the next part.

"I'd be lost without you, and you know it. I'll read it later. Right now, I'm a lot more interested in giving those chattering bastards something else to add to their story."

"Oh, yeah?" She wiggles her eyebrows, bracing for another gag on my end.

I've never been more serious. I stuff my hand into my pocket, fish out the tiny leather box, and drop to my knees. Grabbing her hand, I give her a look that obliterates the past, and shows her the future shining in my eyes.

"Robbi, when I was cooped up in there for the shit I didn't do, I promised myself one thing if I got out. Swore I'd bring a clean slate, and I wouldn't wait a minute longer than I had to. This is it." I suppress a smile as I see the awe in her eyes, mustering my focus for the most important part. "This is no ordinary ring. I had it five years ago, meant to put it on your finger then, before everything went to hell. That didn't happen, and I kept it. This ring came with me like a friend on the battlefield. I had it all these years, knowing deep down I'd find its rightful place, and I'm thinking the day has finally come. Marry me, Robbi. Don't leave us lost another day."

My thumb opens the box. Her jaw drops, and for a second I'm ready to grab her, stop her from falling over in disbelief. The diamond catches the light on the chandelier above, glancing like the stars I used to see at night when it was clear, my hands at my jet's controls.

I want my stars back someday, when I've got the time for my plane. Not a thousandth as much as I want – *no, fucking need* – her to say yes.

"Luke..." My name comes out in a strained whisper. Those tears she's been holding back since I stepped into the room break loose, heavy and hot, sliding down her cheeks to the floor. "I can't."

"Can't?" I repeat it dumbly, rage and humiliation churning in my veins. "Why the fuck not?"

Slowly, she gets on her knees, clasping my hand with the ring box in both of hers. They're small, fragile, and one more inch of her I want to own forever. If she's saying no over some hangup behind us, or because some small part of her still thinks I'm a risk, then fuck. Talk about a miscalculation I'll never live down.

My ears bristle when she smiles through her tears, opening her lips to speak. "Because I'd be crazy if I said yes before I told you the news."

"News? What the hell do you mean?"

"I'm ready to be your wife. I just hope you're ready to be a father."

"Father?" I'm honestly confused. My eyes wander down to her belly while the bewildered rock in my head tries to sort itself out.

She pauses, familiar red heat flushing her cheeks. It takes me a minute, but when it clicks, it's like half a bottle of good booze hitting my brain at once.

Oh. Shit.

Is it possible for a man to see his two biggest dreams granted in one day? I can't believe I'm this lucky, after everything else that's happened. Fuck, I have to be sure.

"Jesus, Robbi. Are you telling me you're pregnant?"

She can't even speak. Her little head nods, brisk and nervous, another tear leaving her right eye and blazing a trail down her skin like a comet through the sky.

"Little bird, I'll be the best husband, father, and man you ever laid eyes on. You just made me the happiest one on this rock. No more delays. No mother of my child is going another hour without wearing my ring."

I hold back the need in my lips to be on hers while I rip the ring from its box and slide it onto her finger. It's an elegant fit. Beautiful thanks to its design, but it truly shines because it's *her.*

I know she's at a loss for words when she's trembling, overcome by everything happening around us. Hell, so am I, but when has that ever stopped me from anything?

My mouth moves on hers like it's the end of the world.

Honestly, it is, and the world we're about to make will be perfection compared to the dreadful fucking tragedy we're leaving at light speed.

Laughing, we go down hard, rolling on the floor. I pin her under me, pushing my tongue into her mouth, cradling her face in one hand. My lips do the talking hers can't.

She's anything but quiet. I taste her adoration every time her little tongue submits to mine. I savor the best and the worst of us, everything we've had on this mad, mad journey.

It's the little bird who used to clean my old man's house, the grown up star playing Ali who hated me, and the woman I lusted for more times than a man legally should. It's her, it's love itself, and it's the credo I'm living by every last day of my life.

"It's like a dream," she whispers, still lost in the moment when I pull away.

"Babe, it's better. Dreams can turn shitty without any warning. We've done those parts already, and I swear, they're done. We'll have our issues and we'll face what every parent does bringing junior up right. But fuck if I'll ever let you doubt us again. The entire world's done plenty of that for several lifetimes. Time for us to show we're solid. Nothing's *ever* coming between us again while I still have a pulse."

I can't keep my lips off her. They search and destroy every last tear left on her face, drying her sweet skin with the heat of my love.

My wife, my first born! I still can't believe it. I'll need about a thousand more kisses before it sinks in.

She's going to pieces, but I ought to be the one breaking down in gratitude.

If she doesn't know it, she's given me the world. I run my hand down her side, move it over her lower belly, and smile, touching my forehead to hers. Never ceases to amaze me how much heat that spot returns, enough to warm the darkest winter in my heart.

And with this ring on her hand and my baby growing in her, summer is here. Permanent, clear, and fucking beautiful.

* * * *

Two Months Later

"By the power vested in me by the great state of California, you may now –"

I don't even wait for the priest to finish. Shit, I've been waiting a whole lifetime to hear the words, *kiss the bride*, and take the woman who's just promised me forever with the hardest kiss my lips can muster.

It's a gorgeous day. Sunlight streams in through the rustic cathedral, adding warmth to the ceremony. The cheers, grins, and ball busting shouts from my brothers do the rest.

I catch a glimpse of Hayden and Penny through the crowd when I pull my lips off Robbi. He points at me and winks, one arm around his smiling wife. She's getting bigger every time I see her. Won't be long before their baby comes.

That'll be my Robbi in a few more months, I tell myself, a prideful smirk tugging at my lips. *Who cares about the timing? I wouldn't change a thing.*

We've kept the pregnancy part to ourselves. Family and friends will know soon, and she'll get one hell of a baby shower in the coming months.

The priest clears his throat and gives us a friendly nod. We've missed our cue to head down the aisle and out to the limo. Grabbing Robbi's hand, I lead her through the cheering throngs.

Grant reaches through the pews and slaps my shoulder. "Easy with the lady, brother. You're looking so damned sharp I think you'll cut her to pieces today."

He isn't kidding.

I haven't willingly donned a tux like this since I finished playing Miles Black. Jet black jacket, charcoal trousers, and a black bow tie with a splash of cherry red in the middle. It's a fitting ensemble for the color she's added to the dull palate I used to call my life.

There's no time to stop, so I squeeze his hand one more time, shouting over my shoulder while we're moving. "She's a lucky woman, and she knows it. Cuts and all."

"Please!" Robbi rolls her eyes, laughing for the hundredth time today. "I should've known this wedding stuff would go to your head."

"Damned right," I say, gently guiding her down the steps to the long black limo waiting for us below, a driver with sleek shades over his eyes holding the door open. "And you didn't let me finish, babe. You have to be a lucky woman to marry the luckiest man on earth."

"Nice save, ass," she whispers, digging her little fist into my arm.

It is. It's also nice to know I'm never going to get tired of riling this woman up, even when I'm eighty and grey.

We climb into the car together, taking one last glimpse at the crowd pushing their way out the cathedral to watch us depart. We haven't had this kind of attention since we showed up at our movie's premier. This is a lot more personal.

We barely touch the champagne or the non-alcoholic cider I had stocked for Robbi on our ride to the reception hall we've rented out for the evening. Our lips hunger for something else. As soon as the privacy visor between us and the driver goes up, I've got her pinned down under me, stamping my lips down her tender throat, heading for her cleavage.

Her taste goes to my head. Dick raging, I want to be inside her, lashing her tit with my tongue while I drag my pubic bone across her clit.

Shame the place is only twenty minutes away. Not enough time to shake these clothes, and bring her off on every inch of my cock the way I'd like.

Too bad. We'll have a proper honeymoon soon.

A little patience goes a long way. Tonight will be magical, no doubt. I'll take my sweet time blowing her mind for the first time as my wife.

* * * *

"Don't go, Miles, baby, don't go!" A tearful Robbi gushes fear with every word as Ali on the huge screen hanging over the reception room.

The scene flashes to me. I smile, watching myself say the lines through my fake pain, a hand over my gut to stop the hemorrhaging from the bullet wound. "I'm not going anywhere, love. Tell the reaper to save his debt for another day. Funny...after everything we've been through, you're still doubting us. You think I'd leave you to someone else's hand spanking you like mad? Think I'd ever let you raise our kid alone?"

"Oh, Miles!" She grins, and there it is. The kiss, while we're scratched and bruised, remnants of Senator Bluhd's compound going up in smoke behind us, the kids we saved from his trafficking ring clinging to her dress. "I love you."

"Oh, Miles?" Robbi nudges me in the side, whispering her line a lot more playfully here, just as the sirens sound on the screen, heralding the fade to credits. "She's coming. Let me know if you aren't ready for this."

I stiffen when I see Ericka walking our way. I haven't seen the crazy bitch who tried to put me behind bars since the day she busted her jaw in my dressing room. Supposedly, she's been under heavy treatment. They've put her on some stuff to straighten her brain out, and hours of talk therapy are chiseling her into a decent human being again.

Still, my guard doesn't go down easy. "Ericka," I say with a nod.

"Beautiful wedding, Luke. I'm not just saying it either. It's probably the first one I've ever been to feeling...normal, I guess. I'd forgotten how to enjoy a day like this without other feelings getting in the way. I'm happy for you two. Really."

Really? I have no choice but to believe her, and give her a second chance.

I thank her, before she turns her attention to Robbi. "Oh, honey, how are you holding up? It isn't too much, is it?"

I ignore the sour taste in my mouth. It's a twisted irony she's the only one who knows about our baby at this stage, and the news was a threat to make her bend.

"Mom, it's fine. I've had more energy today than I think I've had since our last day on the set."

"It certainly looks like the film lived up to expectations," Ericka says, her eyes drifting to the huge screen.

As Miles, I'm kissing my way down my woman's shoulder, loving each other as husband and wife one more time in the shower, before everything fades out one last time. Robbi's mother looks back at me, her eyes distinctly different from the crazy rage look I know to watch for.

"I simply love the passion. It's the same on the screen as well as off it. We've had our differences, Luke, but whatever I thought before, I'm grateful my daughter found someone who loves her. I don't think any man could ever adore her half as much as you."

I study her eyes before I speak. Her gaze is weirdly placid now. Honest, in a way it wasn't before. Whatever they're doing in therapy, it must be working.

"Past is behind us now," I say, taking Robbi's hand and bringing the back to my lips for a brief kiss. "Finding her again was our second chance. If it's taught me anything, it's that people deserve another shot. We want you to be involved in our life, and in our baby's, Ericka. Now, go and enjoy yourself."

I mean what I said, even if there's a leery edge in my gut. We'll be keeping her on a short leash until her treatment proves itself solid awhile longer. Still, I'm glad I took the high road, rather than bringing down the hammer and throwing her in prison, which I easily could've done after I'd gotten out.

She smiles at me, leans over the table, and gives her daughter a peck on the forehead. The warmth in Robbi's face tells me I did the right thing.

The sun, the moon, and the stars around us were chaos before. I set them right, and all it took was a little blood, sweat, and a piece of my ego. My ears prick up when she leans further, whispering something to my girl I have to strain to hear.

"I know we're not supposed to dwell on the past, but I wish your father were here to see you today. He loved you, whatever his problems. Somewhere, he's happy, looking down and seeing you're loved."

Robbi nods solemnly when she pulls away. The tears can't be far behind, but she's on her guard like me. She won't be letting it down before we've rebuilt trust with the woman in front of us.

"Well, I'd better go. I've never been one to pass up a good Bloody Mary, and it looks like the bartender here knows a thing or two about serving a full meal with the drink."

We share a smile. There are a lot of people walking

around with the thick red drinks, about a dozen large chunks of olives, pickles, and cheeses speared in a neat line sticking out of their glasses.

"Have one for me," Robbi says. "I need our guests to get their money's worth with the drinks since I can't."

Holding hands, her fingers tighten around mine as we watch her mom turn with a smile, and head back to her table. "You're really not mad? Not even a little bit?"

"I'm a forgiving man when I need to be," I say, reaching for her brow with my free hand, sweeping a loose lock of golden hair over her ear. Damn, whatever they've done with her hair, it's immaculate today. It'll be so much more fun to mess up later. "I meant what I said about the past. It's behind us, babe. Everything that happened with you, with me, with our fucked up families. We've got each other, and we're forging a new family. That's what matters most. What happened before is only relevant because it's a great guide for what not to do."

Nodding, she stares into my eyes. I've never seen her baby blues a happier shade. "Keep going, hubby. You're just so perfect I think I'll do something extra special for you tonight."

I can't help but smirk while my cock jerks, loving the tease in her eyes. "Like, Ali and Miles special, or Robbi and Luke?"

"That depends. Which one is naughtier?"

I've had enough. I won't wait longer than one more limo ride to find out. She laughs while I pick her up, carry her through the tables while a few last people wish us well, and out to the driver waiting for our departure.

On the way, we see Grant in the lobby, barking orders into his phone. My high strung, money grubbing brother never takes a day off when his phone rings. I wonder how many millions he's just made when he punches a button on the screen, sees us, and waves, running over before we're in the car.

"Brother, shit. Glad I caught up to you. Forgot to give you this thing I've been carrying around since I got here for the big day." He reaches into his pocket, fumbles out something that looks like a small jewelry box, and plants it in my palm. "Go ahead, check it out."

Robbi and I both stop and stare at the small golden pin inside, a different gem in each of its four corners. It takes me several seconds to realize where I've seen it before.

"Holy shit. Why me?" I whisper, trying to stop my hands from trembling. I'm holding the tiny eagle pin my mother used to wear in her old photos, the very one she went down with in the Alaskan bush, one of the few things they recovered from the crash site.

Grant shrugs. "I remember dad saying this used to be with her all the time when she'd fly. Hayden found it in dad's old office, before the estate was sold. We talked it over and thought it'd make more sense with you, seeing how you're the fly boy in the family. You need the extra luck more than we do."

"Thanks, bro. Seriously." My hand clenches it, and I press it against my chest.

Back in the cathedral, when I watched my beautiful wife

coming down the aisle, I wished like hell there was some way mom could've seen this. Turns out, she's found a way to be here after all, and it's a much more solid presence than the old letters stuffed in my box at home.

I haven't looked at them in years. Stopped about the time I grew out of writing passive-aggressive songs, about the time I loved, lost, and found my way back to Robbi again.

"Luke? What is it?" she asks, probably for the second or third time.

"Something that belonged to my mom. You know I'm not the sensitive type, but damn if it doesn't make this day extra special." I have to stop there.

Grant slaps me on the shoulder, a big grin peaking through his thick beard. "Please, get the fuck out of here and enjoy your honeymoon. We'll catch up over drinks next time I'm in from New York."

"Whatever," I tease. "You're just eager to get back to hashing out another billion with some jackoff trader on Wall Street."

His smile fades and his eyes shift back and forth. "I'm actually, uh, hiring a new assistant. Real pain in the ass finding a good woman."

Robbi and I look at each other, and I raise an eyebrow. "A good what?"

"Good help, brother," he says, smiling through his correction. "Don't you listen? Must be all this newlywed excitement!"

"Whatever, bro, enjoy the spread here and then have a

safe trip home." I bring Robbi out the revolving door, leaving him to his mysterious love life.

We're waiting for the driver to pull around and get us when I feel her hand in my pocket. She lifts up the small black box, takes out mom's old pin, and slips the clasp through the sleek white layers of her wedding dress before closing it.

"Perfect fit," she says, taking my hand, and laying it against her cheek. "I wish I'd met her," she says.

"Doesn't matter. Long as this baby turns out to be the first of many, she'll live on. It all will, the good and the bad, past and present, the best and worst of our families. Finally one."

I don't think about how strange it sounds until it's out of my mouth. But the way she kisses me just before the car comes tells me it isn't so odd.

What better goal can a man and woman have than spinning tragedy into gold? We've done plenty of that already. There's a lot more coming, just as soon as I've given her a wedding night she'll never forget.

* * * *

We're in the spacious suite, we're naked, and I'm staring in stunned silence at my wedding present.

"Where – no, fucking *where* – on God's green earth did that beauty come from?" I'm staring down at the little bird stamped on her ass, sitting on a twig spreading out along her hip, musical notes coming from its mouth in the shape of hearts.

The inscription circling it in a crest would almost bring a tear to my eye if I wasn't drunk on lust, seeing my name on her bare, fuckable ass for the very first time.

LUKE'S FOREVER. THROUGH LOVE, THROUGH LOSS, WE ENDURE.

"Had it done last week. There's a reason I've been pretending to save my energy for the honeymoon." She sticks the tip of her tongue out at me as I turn her around, and I bury it in my kiss.

I knew she'd been holding out on me for a good reason. We never had a week long dry spell for sex since we sorted out our issues. Sure, the pregnancy and impending wedding stress could've put her under the weather, but the lust and excitement in her eyes never disappeared once when we went to bed.

Moving my hands to her ass, I cup her cheeks, and squeeze, swallowing the satisfied moan leaving her mouth with another sultry kiss.

"Your only mistake was waiting a whole week to fuck. Babe, everything we've pent up is coming out big time tonight. I'd be a damned fool if I didn't take full advantage of the sweet new target you've given me." My palm cracks across her ass cheek. Hard.

She shakes with a whimper on impact, writhing in my arms. Even the skin I haven't spanked feels ten degrees hotter when I run my fingers up her back, slow and sensual.

I want to bring her the same delicious torture she's given me. I'll have her pussy soaking wet before I bury every inch inside her. "Let's see what it looks like from the air," I say.

My hands go to her shoulders, helping put her on her knees.

She knows what to do. I watch the flicker in her grey-blue eyes dancing as she takes me into her mouth. My big cock looks like art once her lips hug it. I stare, admiring the tattoo as she crouches, bubbling her ass up, giving me a wonderful view.

Looks good. Looks right. Looks like it's made to be there, my name inscribed on her sexy skin from now until kingdom come.

"Yeah, fuck, yeah." Groaning encouragement, I hook my fingers through her hair, wind several locks around my fingers, and pull.

Nice and steady, baby girl. Keep fucking going.

Love when she explores, but I love to lead her, too. I help her mouth up and down my cock, growing harder by the minute, oozing its slickness onto her tongue. She moans when she tastes my pre-come, and I fuck her face faster, quelling the burning sensation in my balls when I remember how good it'll be to blow when I'm in her, balls deep.

Fuck, it isn't easy.

My new wife looks hot as sin. Her beauty matches the room. It's lined in old world red where the gaping mirrors end. Sinful, seductive romance all around us.

My eyes move mirror to mirror, taking in my cock in her mouth from every angle. I stop, tilting her face when she slows to rest her jaw, urging her to share the view. "Look, little bird. See how happy you've made me, taking my dick with my name inked on your skin? Our hearts matched before. Now, we can say the same about our flesh."

I'm not joking. It gives me a rough, almost giddy pleasure seeing the design on her butt. It's not just the primal signal, having my name stamped there, but the fact she chose a tiny robin for a bird. It's no match for the falcon tattooed on my chest, but we've grown beyond primal and prey.

Together, we've earned our wings.

Together, we're taking off. Soaring. Free.

Her mouth moves slowly, taking me in like she can't believe it herself, never once breaking eye contact unless I tell her.

She's taken to her training so well. I'm smiling when I think how she could barely stand to look at me when we first started fucking again. It's taken months to fuck the shy, scared little girl out of her, and now I've got a woman taking as much of me as she can fit into her mouth.

And what a beautiful woman, perfection sculpted in soft curves, golden hair, and gemstone eyes. Everything I always wanted to love, to cherish, and to ravage.

Everything that matters, and so much more.

"Okay," I growl a minute later. My balls steam hotter beneath her fingertips, warning me they're about to give it up if I let her continue.

There'll be another load for that. Right now, I'm not wasting a damn drop while my wife's freshly married pussy hasn't been mounted, fucked, and owned by her husband.

"Kiss me with those dirty lips, and then get ready to spread your legs." I help her up, never taking my hand from her hair. It helps when I pull her in for a kiss, tasting my salt and sex all over her.

She's still so sweet behind it, especially when she moans. The more we do it, the less I'm able to tell where she ends, and I begin.

Tonight, it's harder than ever. Doesn't stop me from sinking my teeth into her bottom lip, making her moan louder, taking her sweet, wicked energy down my throat.

I take her sexy purrs like a demon in rut. My cock glides against her belly, still leaking on her skin, aching to be in her.

"Chair, babe," I say, walking her to the black leather seat in the corner. It's tall, sleek as a shark, and like something from a Medieval documentary.

Grabbing her ankles, I swing her legs open as soon as her ass hits the chair. Then my tongue is on her, winding up her calf, licking a steady, kissing trail to her thigh. That's where I stop until I feel her shake.

I flick my free hand against her pussy, testing her raw little clit.

It's swollen, and she's sopping fucking wet. My taste buds prickle, hungry to taste her.

Hungrier still to make my wife come on my mouth for the first time. It's like she's a virgin all over again, and I'm just as excited to fill her blank slate.

Before I move in for the kill, I hold her thighs with my hands, waiting for her eyes to open so they see mine drilling in. "Lay back, breathe, and don't you dare shut your legs."

She nods frantically, her nipples pulsing red like small berries on her breasts.

As I roll my tongue across her hot cunt for the first time,

I'm amazed at how many firsts there will be with this woman.

I thought I had it all when I took her cherry, all those years ago.

Thought I'd conquered the world when I took her again, against the rickety wall in my dressing room, fucking her to Jupiter and back as my cock had the only pussy that would ever tame it.

Then there was the sex when I got out of jail. I came so hard my heartbeat burned in my eyes, biting into her shoulder, slamming into her from behind while I had my hand between her legs, frigging the clit I'm all over now until she screamed herself hoarse.

I should stop thinking I've figured out a damned thing about us.

Honestly, it's better than it's ever been because the energy isn't predicable. My mouth moves up and down her pussy, grinding into her when her hips squirm, my tongue lashing her clit. It comes down wet, focused, and raw, summoning the same energy I first used spanking her ass as Miles.

He wishes he had half of this. Everybody's favorite billionaire bad boy can go fuck himself while I'm devouring her cunt, fucking my tongue in and out of her, shoving my face so far up in her every growl I make reverberates in her belly.

"Oh, Luke. Oh, yes!" She pauses, just enough to draw her breath, coming to the edge. I slow down to tease her, waiting for the magic word I'll never get sick of hearing. "Please."

There.

In a flash of tongue and teeth, she's screaming. I tilt my head, never taking my tongue off her clit, making room to shove two stiff fingers inside her. I find the second best target on her body after the new tattoo.

Know I've hit pay dirt when her screams go ragged, breathless, and hot cream gushes out of her.

She wasn't a born squirter. I made her one. Perhaps my finest accomplishment, playing her body like a fiddle, knowing I can break her down however I want on command.

The whimpers don't stop for a good sixty seconds. When they're finally over, I back off her sweet pussy, giving the soaked mess between her legs one last kiss.

She's ruined when I stand up. I pick her up, haul her over to the bed in my arms, and lay her against my chest, cradling her head in my palm. I can't stop kissing through the minutes where I let her rest.

Fire moves up my spine and pools in my balls, a slow building wave screaming *fuck her.*

I will, but not yet.

My forehead touches hers, steaming with excitement, urging her to open those eyes I love. "You know that kiss made me fall in love, right? Seeing you come for me drags me deeper under the spell. I'm a cursed man, little bird, and I'm happy."

"Love you," she whispers, breaking a smile.

We kiss through the entire spectrum.

Slow and sweet. Soft and hard. Vicious, rough, relentless.

The stubble on my chin grazes her throat, and her pussy rubs my cock, already aching to be filled.

"No more teasing, Luke. Please. *Please.*"

"Say it a few more times, and I just might come inside you."

"Ohhh." I don't let up, burying my teeth in her neck, palming her breast with my hand.

I take my time warming her up good and proper, plucking her nipples soft with my teeth, my tongue, my lips forming a perfect ring around them. I'd be content listening to her moan for me forever, but the insistent urge in my balls hounding me to fuck my wife won't be satisfied until I do it.

The head of my cock rubs deeper in her pussy folds every time her hips grind into me. She's trying to get me in her before I'm ready, the little minx. I hold back, giving her tit one more suck, flicking the very tip of my canines into her tender flesh – a little trick that always sends her into another world.

"Roll the fuck over," I say, as soon as I'm ready. "I want to see my name when I go off in your married pussy."

"Sure, hubby."

Hubby? Fuck.

I'm starting to like that word more than sir, as sappy as it sounds. Coming from anybody else, it would be, but because it's my wife, it's lightning.

Taking my cock by the base, I watch her get on all fours, offering her ass to me. There's barely enough time to give it a whack before I'm in her.

We fuck like there's no tomorrow.

Truth is, there hasn't been enough yesterday. We're *still* making up for lost time every time our bodies collide, fucking through the pain that's kept us apart for too long. There'll never be enough. Not even when we're celebrating our tenth wedding anniversary, working on our sixth kid.

Yeah, okay, let's not get ahead of ourselves.

For once, I listen to my better instincts. It's not a chore to shut up the chatter and enjoy the moment, thrusting into my beautiful wife good and hard, love and lust colliding in every thrust.

She sweats.

She moans.

She begs.

Somewhere between those desperate breaths, before I slam her ass against my pubic bone and come, I hear the love I see in her tattoo.

"There's my girl. Come, Robbi. Come like you fucking mean it." My hips go wilder than my words, hammering into hers, swinging my balls on her clit each time our bodies mesh.

Hot? My testicles are screaming fucking meteors, about to become magma.

I rail her through one O into the next. She's so turned on, it doesn't take long. Normally, I'd take pride bringing her off in something like one unbroken, beautiful chain of release.

But frankly, I'm too crazed with the seed burning to my core to stop for anything.

Need to get it out.

Need to fill her sweet cunt.

Need to finish loving her in this animal language words will never be a decent substitute for.

My hand cracks across her ass before I can't hold it anymore.

Once. Twice. Three fucking times.

"Fuck, coming!" I shout, trying to hold my eyes open, catching one last glimpse of my name on her delectable ass before my vision goes black and red and white.

My balls lurch, burn, spit hot jets into her. They don't care if she's been bred once, claimed at a biological level. Every time I give it up deep inside her cements the bond between us, turns me crazier, and makes me see new stars.

This time, they're bright and hot and beautiful.

Every single one of them says, *I didn't know I could love you this fucking much.*

XV: This Time, Forever (Robin)

One Year Later

I'm living the Hollywood life I always dreamed, but it's not why I'm smiling.

It isn't the sweet southern California air billowing in from the coast, wrapping around our mansion, tucked in the exclusive foothills just up the coast from L.A.

It isn't watching Hayden, Penny, and their little daughter, Abby, rolling in the grass with our new French bulldog, Theodore.

It isn't even watching the love of my life bicker with Grant at the giant grill over whose rub on the meat will do a better job at making our taste buds pop.

It's him. The little man in my arms, Zane, his tiny eyelids falling shut while I cradle his head, covering his familiar blue eyes.

It's quiet moments like these, surrounded by family, when I think how different it could've been.

Where the hell would I be if I hadn't taken a second chance?

If I'd walked away when things were at their bleakest?

If I hadn't gotten over him the first time my mother lied to me?

If we hadn't gone through love and hate and hell itself to claim paradise?

It's here.

Here. It's a time and a space so beautiful it makes me tear up when I open my heart and let the reality sink in.

Everything we've done side by side. The new contracts we've signed, the autographs and pictures we've doled out together to Frieze's fanatics around the world, the day my water broke up in the sky, and he brought us down to Portland in an emergency landing so I could deliver the gorgeous little boy snoozing on my shoulder.

Life is hectic with a baby, a career, and a man who never lets up. It makes me appreciate the slow, special days like this one, when I can sit back and marvel at the smirking, handsome angel who's delivered my forever happiness.

"Brother, you'll ruin half a cow if you douse that shit in your barbecue. Take it from the man who wined and dined the finest chefs in the world last month when they entrusted me with their hedge funds. Less is more. It's – shit." Grant pauses, curses, and grabs for his phone. "I've got to take this. Don't wreck the meat."

Luke is still bristling when I come up behind him, resting my cheek on his shoulder. He turns, his frustration evaporating, love and light in his eyes when he sees me holding his son. "Amazing how he's able to sleep through the commotion. Some people have it lucky."

"Some. Do you need help? He took off abruptly." I nod toward Grant, now a distant speck on the horizon, heading toward the cliffs, his hands animated.

"Probably that chick he was strung up on months ago. I don't ask about his love life, and he doesn't tell me. Any woman who wants to work themselves in between his million dollar deals and trips to Maine is welcome to that craziness." Growling, he slathers more barbecue on the meat, defying his brother's advice. "These are ours. We'll split the beef fifty-fifty, and let everybody decide their favorite recipe."

"Hey, hey," I say, quelling the fury flexing in his muscles with a kiss on his neck. "Aren't you glad *this* is our problem now? Remember when we had more to worry about? I was just thinking about everything before Zane."

For a second, he looks at me intently, his eyes narrowed. Then the tension on his face melts, blooming into a smile. "Shit. You're right, babe. I'd rather be arguing over spices with my brother than flying all over hell without any purpose, or spending my nights behind bars because a crazy woman lied."

"Shhh," I whisper softly. "Mom will be here anytime."

"Fair enough," he says, his eyes continuing to soften. "She's made a lot of progress. I'm honestly not even worried about her staying in the other wing of the house anymore."

"She's better," I agree, cradling Zane tighter in my arms.

The human capacity to forgive is incredible. Mom came dangerously close to shattering it for me and Luke both, but we persevered. We expanded our second chance to mercy for her, and so far, so good.

She'll never be normal, the doctors say. Not without a lot of therapy and oversight. But the meds and months of counseling have taught her to keep the worst of herself in check, and she's also learned how to handle her own trauma left over from a rocky childhood bleeding into a bad marriage.

"Bebe called this morning. She says we'll make a lot of money if we follow up with the trip to Redding next week for the wine branding."

"What the hell do I know about wine?" Luke snorts, moving the fresh meat to a rack and firing up the flame. It's rare to see him cook, but it's sexy when it happens. "Never gave much thought to picking out a vintage with my name on it. If we're going up there, I ought to let Hayds' biker buddies have a say."

I laugh. "Hard to believe they'd be the wine drinking type. Seriously, it's good money, *and* a getaway. This *Bare* wine could really take off with our following."

"I'm in for the experience, babe. Hell, I'm always in it for you," he says, doing a slow turn, a smear of barbecue sauce on his chef's apron.

Watching him cook is almost as unusual as seeing him in the tight grey t-shirt underneath the apron. A delicious tingle pulses between my legs. A wicked part of me wants to forget about our little family gathering, take him upstairs, and help him get 'changed' for the next half hour.

But little Zane stirs in my arms, cooing as he reaches for my face with his hands. *Obligations*, I remind myself, rolling my eyes.

I wouldn't trade them for anything. "It's time for his

nap. I'll hand him off to Maisy before the food is ready. Mom will keep him plenty active with whatever new toy she's brought as soon as she's here."

"Wait," he says, grabbing me by the shoulder before I can move away.

He never forgets the kiss.

Never.

It's warm, tender, and just a little bit mischievous. It puts an extra power in my step and gives me hope for spending more quality time together later. After he's done with me, he plants a quick peck on Zane's forehead, who opens his eyes and smiles at his daddy.

I'm the one grinning on the way back to my house. It's like a drug, this love. I vow I'll never take any kiss he gives for granted. I hand the baby boy off to our head housekeeper, Maisy, and then head back to the grill to help him.

Things go much more smoothly prepping the food with Grant sidetracked. It's amazing how the pieces fall into place after breaking up the everlasting dick measuring contest between the billionaire brothers.

Soon, we've got ourselves a huge spread of ribs, veggies, sausages, and about ten different kinds of pie. The caramel apple cheesecake is my signature dish, something I charmed the instructors with in acting school plenty of times. I work with Penny and a few of our other housekeeping staff to wrap things up while the brothers set the huge picnic table.

It doesn't get any better than this.

* * * *

An hour later, we're gathered around the table, a feast heaped on serving plates in front of us. Luke sits at the head of the table while I'm on his right side with Zane. Mom sits across from us, truly smiling to be in our space. Even little Theodore takes a break from barking and chasing butterflies to rest at my feet. The puppy drools into the grass, nuzzling his face into the earth, a living symbol of how happy and content I'm feeling inside.

Our guests are hungrily loading up their plates. Hayden pours himself a fresh glass of wine before he goes for the meat, locking eyes with Grant in a tribal challenge over the pile between them.

"Hayden!" Penny slaps her husband's wrist when he tries to throw an extra sausage on his plate, already stacked higher than even his big appetite should allow. Grant chuckles, and it makes me smile. I think all three Shaw brothers are trying to prove their masculinity by being the biggest carnivore.

The constant chatter building around the table comes to a stop when Luke stands, cuts in, and dings his scotch glass loudly with his spoon.

"It's not really our tradition to make grand speeches or say grace, but I wanted to do both, in our own special way, since everybody I care about is at this table. Whatever's brought us here today puts a smile on my face. I'm not afraid to hide it. Say it's God, or fate, or whatever you believe, but I think it's our mother, sometimes."

He pauses. I reach for his hand, twining my fingers with his, holding it there as I study everybody's faces. Mom watches in respectful silence, same as Penny. Hayden and Grant stare with their eyes a little wider, heads tilted very slightly, surprised and wondering where this is going.

Honestly, so am I. This isn't like him.

"Going on thirty years ago, isn't it? The crash happened this month, as a matter of fact. The years that came after, I thought our lives were over. I mourned a woman I never really knew, blamed her absence for all the mistakes our old man made in his later years. The drinking, the womanizing, bad business, Kayla." He's careful with his words, talking about his father's mistakes, eyeballing my mother. So far, she's undisturbed, thankfully. "I only saw the bad when I lived loss. Couldn't forgive because the world itself was so damned merciless every time I tried to make good on things I wanted. Today, it's different, and everybody around this table is the reason why."

Smiling, Penny nods, lowering her lips to Abby's forehead. My fussy niece doesn't appreciate the eerie silence, or the kiss, and shouts in the sing-song way babies do when they're bored or frustrated.

"Grant, Hayden, you pulled me through some tough times. Penny, you were my brother's rock when he was mine, and I'll never forget it. Ericka..." He waits for her full attention, or maybe he needs a few extra seconds to get his words just right. "You're family. We'd be living our lives with a bigger, darker hole behind us if I'd turned my back on you. I'm glad every day I didn't. Zane deserves a grandparent, and he's got one in you. And you, little bird..."

Oh, God. His fingers pinch tighter to mine, so hard it drains the blood from my knuckles. I tighten the hold right back.

"You've been the perfect wife. You never gave up when we had our issues. Every day, you give me reasons most men can only dream about to wake the hell up and make my life count. Yeah, it helps that you're drop dead gorgeous, but that's not what I'm getting at. I say it often, and it's still not enough, so here it is again. I love you, Robbi. You're the first, last, and best love I'll ever have. We've done right by our second chance. We'll keep on doing it, too, no matter how rich, how famous, or how tough the future will be."

I don't wait for the applause or compliments from the others. With Zane in my arms, I rise to end his speech with a kiss, my hand never leaving his.

Without him, I'd be nothing. I think I'm still just beginning to realize how good it feels to be complete.

We take our sweet time locking lips, not caring who watches, or how cold the food might be getting.

It's animal attraction. Loving gratitude. Baby fever. Marital bliss.

It's feelings running through my blood I know instinctively, but can't put into words, because everything about this man speaks to me on a higher level. I don't need poetry when our eyes and skin carry our song so well.

Deep down, I know exactly what we are when his fingers hook through mine, his mouth covers my lips, and we melt into each other with our little boy between us, perched between our hearts.

Today, we're inseparable.
Tomorrow, we're better.
Forever, we're man and wife.

Thanks!

Want more Nicole Snow? Sign up for my newsletter to hear about new releases, subscriber only goodies, and other fun stuff!

JOIN THE NICOLE SNOW NEWSLETTER! - http://eepurl.com/HwFW1

Thank you so much for buying this book. I hope my romances will brighten your mornings and darken your evenings with total pleasure. Sensuality makes everything more vivid, doesn't it?

If you liked this book, please consider leaving a review and checking out my other erotic romance tales.

Got a comment on my work? Email me at nicolesnowerotica@gmail.com. I love hearing from my fans!

Kisses,
Nicole Snow

More Intense Romance by Nicole Snow

FIGHT FOR HER HEART

BIG BAD DARE: TATTOOS AND SUBMISSION

MERCILESS LOVE: A DARK ROMANCE

LOVE SCARS: BAD BOY'S BRIDE

RECKLESSLY HIS: A BAD BOY MAFIA ROMANCE

STEPBROTHER CHARMING:
A BILLIONAIRE BAD BOY ROMANCE

STEPBROTHER UNSEALED:
A BAD BOY MILITARY ROMANCE

PRINCE WITH BENEFITS:
A BILLIONAIRE ROYAL ROMANCE

MARRY ME AGAIN:
A BILLIONAIRE SECOND CHANCE ROMANCE

Prairie Devils MC Books

OUTLAW KIND OF LOVE

NOMAD KIND OF LOVE

SAVAGE KIND OF LOVE

WICKED KIND OF LOVE

BITTER KIND OF LOVE

Grizzlies MC Books

OUTLAW'S KISS

OUTLAW'S OBSESSION

OUTLAW'S BRIDE

OUTLAW'S VOW

Deadly Pistols MC Books

NEVER LOVE AN OUTLAW

NEVER KISS AN OUTLAW

NEVER HAVE AN OUTLAW'S BABY

NEVER WED AN OUTLAW

Baby Fever Books

BABY FEVER BRIDE

SEXY SAMPLES:
BABY FEVER BRIDE

I: Tick-Tock (Penny)

It's only ten o'clock in the morning, and I'm completely boned.

No, not in the way I want to be. There's nothing handsome, alpha, or inked about the middle aged doctor rattling off my lab results, and they're not pretty.

I'm sitting in his office, trying to listen to what he's saying, before I ask if there's been a horrible screw up.

Wishful thinking. Dr. Potter, a thin balding man who can't stop giving me the most sympathetic look in the world, doesn't make mistakes.

"Just to confirm, we ran your blood test three times before reporting the results to the CDC, as required under Federal law. There's no mistaking it." He holds a finger up, as if he's read my mind. "I'm sincerely sorry to deliver the bad news, Ms. Silvers. The fever and sweats you've been complaining about should have already diminished. They won't be back. As for the long-term consequences –"

He stops when I choke up. *Long-term...that's really what he wants to call it?*

He's just told me my blood test came back positive for the fucking Zeno virus. I'm never going to be a mom.

Not unless I get pregnant next month, which seems about as likely as the wiry old doctor ripping off his face and revealing an Adonis underneath. One who'll wink at me and volunteer to be a donor.

Yeah, nobody's that lucky. And if there's anything I'm sure about today, it's my luck running out.

It's my fault for taking that humanitarian trip to Cuba, where one bad mosquito bite was waiting to change my life forever. I can feel the spot under my elbow where the hot red welt used to be. Biting my lip, I reach down and scratch it, even though there's nothing there anymore.

Hot blood races through my cheeks. I'm shaking. Sixty seconds away from breaking down.

Another embarrassment I don't need while I'm glued to this chair, unable to put as many miles as I can between myself and this hellish consultation.

"Ms. Silvers, please...it's going to be all right," he says in his best dad voice, reaching over, pressing a reassuring hand down on my shoulder. It's not helping. "If you'll allow me, I'd like to review the positives in your situation: infertility is the only clinically known side effect of Zeno syndrome. You won't suffer anything more dire. Plus everything I've read in the journals lately sounds promising. They're working on a treatment. There's a real chance Zeno induced infertility may be reversible with good time, if the research pays off."

If? Until now, I've held in the tears. Now, they're coming, wet and ugly and full of angst.

"Easy for you to say!" I sputter. "I never should've taken that trip. I wouldn't have even thought about it if I'd known it meant giving up my chances to ever be a mom. God, if

I'd just stuck to Miami for the beaches, gave myself a normal getaway like most people…"

"No. You can't beat yourself up. Besides, Zeno has been working its way into our coastal communities, Ms. Silvers. The CDC report on my desk says as much. A hundred cases in Florida this week alone." He's still rubbing my shoulder, as if the most boring, detached man in the world can comfort me. "Listen, if you'd like, we can explore what the university has to offer in terms of egg preservation. There's no guarantees, of course, but it's entirely possible –"

"That *what?*" My voice shakes. "I'll magically find a way to pay a bunch of quacks to stab me with needles, and then pay them ten times more to keep my unborn children in test tubes? I'm a secretary for a third rate company, Doctor. I make fifteen bucks an hour. You might as well tell me I'm about to meet Mr. Right when I walk out this door, have him propose tomorrow, and knock me up by next Friday."

Potter looks nervously at the wall. His hand drifts off me. Well, at least I'm not the only one here who's embarrassed, not that it's much satisfaction.

He clears his throat, and folds his hands, leaning toward me over the desk. It takes me a second to realize he's eyeing the medical degree on the wall behind me. Okay, maybe I regret throwing the quack word around in front of him. I'm sure he'll forgive me.

"You do have eighteen months before the full effects of Zeno in your reproductive system make the odds of conceiving virtually zero."

A year and a half. Lovely.

Not even enough time to build up a serious relationship from coffee dates or – God forbid – Tinder. Much less rest assured I've really met the one, the man I want to have a baby with.

And that's assuming I'd have better prospects than the usual idiots I've met before. Like the boy a couple weeks ago, who showed up late to our dinner at an overpriced French place, bearing gifts. Gifts, in this case, being the cheap purple dildo he buried in a bouquet of plastic roses.

It takes real talent to embarrass a girl in public, plus insult her intelligence in one go.

I'm shaking my head, pushing away date nights I wish I could forget, holding in the verbal sting I want to unleash on the entire world, using the doctor as a proxy.

But it isn't his fault, or his problem. Dr. Potter isn't here to listen to my disasters in dating, or fix my non-existent sex life.

He's a general practitioner, not a psychologist, and having an incurable tropical disease means he can't even help with that.

I want to leave. But there's another horrible question on the tip of my tongue. "So, does this virus affect anything else downstairs? Like my chances of enjoying...you know."

As if sex should even be on the radar. I've been celibate for so long it shouldn't matter, twenty-three years. Maybe the disease will give me one more reason to keep my V-card.

Dr. Oblivious takes a few seconds to get what I mean. Then his eyebrows shift up. "Uh, no, not at all. You're free to involve yourself with any partner using the usual precautions.

There's no risk of human-to-human transmission, Ms. Silvers. Your partners can't catch the disease unless they walk through the wrong mosquito-infested areas at the wrong time, just as you did, and the odds of that happening are exceedingly low."

Low. Yeah, just like me.

Lucky, lucky me, with my dead love life, boring job, and distant family. Add shattered dreams to the list.

There's nothing to celebrate here. The only place I ever beat the odds was contracting a rare Caribbean virus, destroying my future without even knowing it at first bite.

Why couldn't it have been the lottery instead?

I need to get out of here. I just want to go back to work, punch in my last few hours, and then go home and pull the blanket over my head.

When I'm in my cocoon, I can pretend I never ignored all the half-assed CDC warnings to have a great time in an amazing country that's just opened up to Americans again. I can pretend my junk hasn't just been trashed by a thumb-sized vampire bite, that I'm going to get my shit together, and be an amazing wife and mother whenever the right boy comes along and proves to me he's a man. I can pretend I still have time, more than eighteen months before the sword falls, obliterating the future I always imagined.

And I can pretend the holidays aren't coming, that I won't cry over the dinner table when mom taps my foot with her cane, and asks me why the hell I haven't found myself a boyfriend yet.

"Ms. Silvers?"

"Jesus, just call me Penny, Doctor! That's what everybody

else says," I tell him, giving into the sarcasm pulling me deep into the black pit in my gut. "I read you loud and clear. I get how screwed I am. There's nothing you can do for me, right? Can we be done?"

He doesn't say anything, just turns his face to the small tablet in his hands, and begins scrawling a sloppy signature with his finger. A second later, he hits a button, and the device prints out a tiny prescription slip, which he tears off and hands to me.

"This will make you feel better in the interim," he says. "Simple pain relievers, on the off chance your fever returns. Until then, it should help minimize your discomfort from our talk today. While your viral load is dropping to acceptable levels, it could be lower. Please be sure to rest, and drink plenty of water."

If only guzzling water like a desert explorer would flush it all out of my system. I'd drink Lake Michigan dry. It's visible outside his window, behind the Chicago skyline, rippling in grey and gloomy November shadows.

"Thanks," I mutter, crinkling the paper in my fist as the doctor stands, ushering me out the door.

If I were him, I'd be relieved to see the last of me, too. I'm sure I'm about to become the latest statistic in a medical journal, one more faceless person tracked by the outbreak that's been making inroads in the country thanks to people like me. I should be grateful tropical mosquitoes are the only way it spreads, and so far they haven't found any in the Midwest that can carry it.

At least I won't have to worry about infecting anybody

else. Small comfort when I'm out the door, heading for the train so I can get across town, back to the office. Frankly, no one else deserves to have this curse inflicted on them if they can avoid it.

But I'm not thinking about them, the lucky ones. I'm being selfish, focusing on myself, and quietly hating every healthy woman in America who will never have to worry about their biological clock going up in a fireball.

* * * *

The worst day of my life gets predictably worse.

By afternoon, my right heel comes apart. I'm distracted, lost in my own head, mourning the babies I'll never hold in my arms because there's not enough time to make them happen. I don't see the small break in the marble floor that trips me, threatens to send me crashing down face first, or worse.

It's a small miracle I catch myself against the banister overlooking the twenty second floor of the Shaw Glass Tower where I work. I just wanted some fresh air and people watching, staring down at the ants in the lobby, anything to take my mind off the bad news, not to mention the mountain of work I still have left for today's clients at Franklin, Harrison, and Hitch.

Spinning, I grip the banister tightly, catching myself before I go over it. I'm crushed by the news about my childless future, but I'm not suicidal.

The pivot turns the small fissure cutting through my heel into a break. I see the end snap off, and go rolling across the floor, coming to a stop against the wall. I swear, walk over, and throw it into my pocket. At least I'm able to hide the damage for the rest of the afternoon, screening calls for the firm, stuffing envelopes, and responding to last minute requests when Mr. Franklin himself walks up and bangs his fist on my desk.

I'm so distracted, I've lost track of time.

"Hey, you're twenty minutes past quitting time. Go home and get some rest, Penny." My normally gruff boss flashes me a softer look, before he turns around and heads back into his office. "Looks like you need it."

Ugh. Finding out I'm Zeno positive is the last thing I need. The second to last is sympathy from a sixty year old partner, especially one whose manners typically match his bulldog appearance. If Mr. Franklin sees how worn down I am, then I must *really* look like hell.

I gather my things and shut down my computer, dropping a few last envelopes in the mail on the way out. I'm careful heading out onto the windy streets, wrapping my coat tight against the late autumn chill.

I can't wait to get home, curl up on the couch with my cat, Murphy, and watch something that will put Zeno and the babies I'll never have far, far away. Then it hits me that the overfed little lion I call my pet will probably be the *only* baby I ever have.

I'm wiping my eyes, waiting for the train, trying to hide the hurt. My luck doesn't improve when the doors slide open. Of course, it's more crowded than usual for rush hour.

I'm so angry on the way in, I only catch a glimpse of the man in the corner, but I feel his eyes. They're on me, hard and searching, glued to my back until the inevitable chill courses up my spine. I tuck myself deeper in the standing crowd, gripping the steel pole, hiding from his gaze.

I don't notice him again until he's right behind me. He wastes no time. His fingers graze the back of my coat, just above my butt.

I've always been creeped out by the pervs I've run into in the city's transit system, but they've never *scared* me like this man.

I'm also pissed. I spin around and shoot him a death glare, lashing out with my fear.

"What the fuck do you think you're doing?" I turn my nose up. I'm not sorry about it when I see him.

He's probably twice my age. Unshaven. Liquor rolls off his breath when he cracks a half-toothless grin. My hand forms a fist that wants to wipe it off his disgusting face.

"Thought you looked lonely, baby. It's a full house here today. Come a little closer. Let's be friends. You're cold, and I've got all the fucking warmth you're ever gonna need."

His hand reaches for my wrist. Now, I'm really worried.

Run of the mill pervs aren't this persistent. I don't have time to think, or enough space to punch, kick, or scream. I'm stunned by his aggressive, pawing hands. He catches me around the waist, and pulls me against a tiny open space in the wall, away from the steel pole I'd been hanging onto for my life.

Shit. I don't know what to do. I need to make up my mind *fast.*

This man could be the city's next serial killer for all I know. He's already eyeballing the door, like he's ready to drag me off, into the unknown, threatening to make my crap day so much worse.

Two choices: I can either kick, bite, and scratch with everything I've got, or I can scream bloody murder and hope one of the fellow sardines packed into this metal box will actually help me.

"What'sa matter, baby? You a fighter? My boys like that," he rumbles, studying my eyes, drunker than I thought. "Don't fret. Don't move. Just listen. Stick with me just a little while longer, girlie, and I'll help you find your way to the perfect –"

"Love! I've been looking all over for you," another male voice interrupts.

An arm crashes into the bastard whispering weird threats in my ear a second later, knocking him through the crowd. Several people curse and grumble. My perv is gone, replaced by the handsomest six and a half feet of masculinity I've ever seen packed into a suit, a tie, and a long dark jacket.

Eyes as bright and blue as oceans engulf me, set in a determined face with a jaw that looks like it could break fists. Mr. Strange and Sexy replaces the creeper's hand on my wrist with his own, and leads me through the crowd, leaning into my ear with his lips.

"Play along. I caught him eyeing you the second you stepped on," he whispers. "Follow me. We've got to put some space between us and that man."

Tingles rush up my back. There's certainty in his voice,

like he knows a lot more than I do, and none of it's good. He lays his free hand gently on my back, and doesn't take it off until he has me settled in the only free seat in this car. He stands next to me, hanging onto the pole. He's smiling down at me with his strong jaw and brash blue eyes, utterly unaffected by the restless crowd around us as the train jerks away from its latest stop and resumes its journey.

I don't know whether to breathe, or start sweating all over again. There's no time to decide. I'm paralyzed an instant later, when I hear the familiar slurred voice ring out behind my hero.

"What's your problem, buddy? Butting in like you've got some business with her? Don't think you got any goddamn clue who you're dealing with, and you don't wanna find out." His voice drops another octave with every sentence, evil and furious.

Oh, no. I grip the stranger's hand tighter, begging with my eyes. *Please. Don't let go.*

I'll handle this. That's what his eyes say to mine, before he turns to face the perv, speaks a few words, and pats a spot on his hip barely covered by the end of his jacket.

My heart won't stop pounding. I'm afraid because the creeper keeps coming, growling words in the stranger's face, so persistent on a train this crowded.

Who *are* we dealing with? I don't want to find out. I just want him gone.

An announcement comes through the speaker and a couple next to us squeeze by, laughing loudly. I can't hear a thing between the two men. My savior says something, and it must be big, because the older man's eyes go wide. Creeper does a quick turn, barreling through several people toward the door, who give him dirty looks the whole way.

We don't say anything until the train slows at its next stop. His suit feels so soft beneath my fingertips. The sheer quality hits me through my frightened haze.

I have about sixty seconds to wonder what a man like him is doing here, when he looks like he could easily have his own driver.

His suit has more stitches than the ones the partners at the firm wear, and they're millionaires. The man underneath is even better. He's seductively tall, built, and refined. Strength and sophistication brought together in one Adonis. My eyes go to his like magnets when he looks at me again, and he gives me a reassuring nod.

"He's gone."

I look down, heat flushing my cheeks, ashamed of the sudden attraction I'm fighting. I should just be glad for his kindness, and get ready to go. "Good thing you were here. I didn't like the way he moved on me. Did you really tell him you had a..."

I stop myself, look around, and whisper the last word low underneath my breath. "A gun?"

The stranger smiles. He reaches into his pocket, plucks out a fancy new phone in a leather case that looks like it's lined with honest-to-God platinum trim. Smiling, he holds it up, and taps the screen.

"Worse. I've got a reputation. The man was probably mafia, just so you know. It's satisfying when they run like the bitches they are."

"Mafia?!" I say it too loudly, and I feel several eyes on me. I'm covering my mouth as more red shame brushes my cheeks.

Strange and Sexy looks up, freezing my eyes in his stark blue stare. "You were about ten seconds from having a syringe stabbed in your thigh so you could be dragged off to the highest bidder. I told him he'd back the hell off my wife, or he'd be seeing the sheriff with a few broken bones. Didn't have to say much to make him believe me. He took off as soon as I said my name."

Mafia? Sheriff? His name?

Who the hell am I dealing with? I'm reeling so hard, I can't force the question out.

It's just as well. He's looking at his phone, firing off a text message to someone, which dings a second later.

"Is that your wife?" I ask. "The real one, I mean?"

He smirks, looking up over his phone. "I'm blissfully unmarried. Not looking to settle down anytime soon, as a matter of fact. I'm a very busy man."

Yes, of course he is. His jackass streak is starting to show through his five thousand dollar suit. I don't know whether to be relieved or irked he hasn't suggested I owe him yet for helping me out with some lewd remark.

Then again, if he's really as rich and powerful as he looks, he probably has his pick of high class women lined up each and every night. I hate that I'm wearing my cheapest work dress, grey and black, boring as the office itself. Plus the stupid bandage from my blood test at the clinic is still stuck to my arm.

"What do you do?" I ask, wondering if I'll regret making this small talk.

"Real estate. I'm on my way to a board meeting in the 'burbs right now. Can't beat the train for cutting through rush hour." He ignores me again, tapping away at his phone.

I have to clear my throat before he looks up again, bathing me in those bright blue eyes. "Funny, you look like you're a few years older than me, but it seems like you can't put that thing down. What's so important? Hot Tinder match?"

I've pegged him in his late twenties, at least. His eyes meet mine, more amused than before, and his kissable lips turn up at my challenge. "Business, love. I'm not done until around midnight most days, but this makes it easier. Thank God for technology, right? There's plenty of time over my late night snack to talk to the next girl I'm going to bang."

Eye roll time. I remember he's saved my life, though, and hold my sarcasm in check.

"It must get exhausting," I say, letting my eyes sweep down his massive chest.

Sweet Jesus, that body. It looks like he could hold up his Tinder dates along with half the world on his washboard frame, without breaking a sweat.

My mind goes places it shouldn't. Places off limits. I'm forced to imagine planting my hands on his tree trunk chest, underneath his princely exterior, and riding the patronizing smirk off his lips with everything my hips are worth.

"You get used to it," he says, narrowing his eyes. He

holds out his phone. "Here, I'll let you hold this. Now, tell me all about what was on your mind when you almost wound up a missing person."

The fun is over. Today's rotten news comes bounding back. I'm biting my tongue, hating he noticed how distracted I was.

Hating it even more that I have to think about the most tragic day of my life. Somehow, a future without kids and a broken heel doesn't seem half bad when I think about the terrible things that could've happened if the perv had done what Strange and Sexy warned me about.

"You know, it looks like you're a fan of keeping your business to yourself. I think I'll do the same." It comes out more harsh than it should.

"Wow. I didn't mean to pry into your business if it's going to upset you," he says, holding his hands up. "All right. Quick, let's play twenty questions on safe mode before our stops. Mine's coming up in about five minutes. Let's keep the focus on me."

I don't want to ask him anything. I want to be done, but his firm, mysterious smile has a strange way of disarming me. Sighing, I fidget with his phone in my hands, my finger tracing its cool metal edge.

Holy shit, I think it really might be platinum. I look up, gazing into his eyes, wondering if I'm dealing with the President's nephew, or something.

"You said that man was mafia. How can you possibly know?"

"Told you I'm in real estate, city and 'burbs. Cockroaches

are everywhere. Tough negotiators. Boys who hide their dirty money in legit businesses. It'd freak you out to know how far old money, blood, and crime gets you in my industry." The look on his face says he's completely serious. "Don't worry. I'm not a criminal myself. These hands are squeaky clean."

He holds them up again so I can see. They're refined, but thick and strong, just like the rest of him. Heat flares between my legs when I think about what they'd feel like all over me. After everything that's happened today, it's wrong on so many levels I can't even count them.

"And where do those hands go when they're not stuck to your phone?" I ask, digging my teeth gently into my lower lip, hoping he won't see.

Fine. If I'm going to lose my head to this silly crush, I might as well go all the way.

He doesn't answer right away. His smile grows wider, and he leans down, reaching above my ear. He pushes a loose lock of hair away so there's nothing blocking his whisper. "These hands are explorers, love. They've been places. Everywhere that makes desperate, redheaded angels like yourself scream."

Holy hell.

"Desperate?" I'm taken aback, breathlessly forcing it out, failing miserably to hide my reaction. "What gives you *that* idea?"

He isn't wrong, but I can't fathom why. No man can read my mind. Or did I also put on a sticker that reads 'VIRGIN' in screaming neon caps sometime today? Like, sometime in between colliding with this sexy freak, and finding out any sex I have is probably going to be emotionally and biologically empty, despite waiting my whole life for the right package?

"You want me, love. You want it bad when you've just pulled yourself out of some seriously fucked up shit. If I wasn't on my way to a board meeting, for real, I'd get us a ride at the next stop, bring you back to my penthouse, and eat your pussy until that other heel you're wearing snaps like a twig."

Oh.

Fuck.

I don't realize my eyes are closed until his hand slowly winds down my neck. When they're open, I'm looking into raw temptation. A man with a face and body offering to take away all my heinous problems for one night.

A man who won't disappoint. I know in every word, every glance, and every breath he delivers.

My fingers tighten on the strange phone still in my hands. "Should we swap numbers?"

"It's only proper when I've saved my damsel in distress, obviously."

His arrogance doesn't put me off frantically digging through my purse, searching for mine. I don't trust that he isn't instantly going to delete anything I put into my phone the instant he's off this train.

I don't know this man. He could be toying with me. I've heard the way the partners talk about women when they think their doors are closed. The rich, boisterous, bragging talk involving their latest conquests – especially the poor, clueless girls half their ages, totally in the dark about getting fucked behind their wives' backs.

I realize I'm not thinking right now. I'm going to follow through on trading digits, but I need to mull this over. I'm looking for a happy distraction from my problems – not another big fat mistake. Not even a big, dark, and muscular one.

"You mentioned your name…" I say, ripping open my purse and pushing my phone into his hands with the contacts screen open.

"It's Hayden." He types quickly, staring at the screen.

My lips purse. It's a fitting name, powerful and seductive. I'm amazed there's no lock screen on his phone, allowing me to go straight for the contacts.

"Oh, shit," he mouths, handing my phone back to me. We share a look, and realize a second later the train is stopped. People bolt down the aisle, brushing past us.

"You've got my number. Sorry, love, I really have to run." Before I can stop him, he reaches for the little black object laying on top of everything else in my purse.

As luck would have it, the one that isn't his phone.

Nope. He's got my personal diary.

"Hey!" I stand up, wobbling on my busted heel, panic crashing over me before I rush after.

There are too many people talking for him to hear me. He's already stuffed my little black notebook into his pocket, thinking it's his phone. And I'm left holding the speedy bastard's unit in what feels like a ten thousand dollar case.

He's gone.

I've just bought myself another problem. I'm gritting my teeth as I stumble around the seat, struggling to pick everything up I can reach, making sure I don't lose his phone.

I want to kick myself for jumping at the only good thing that's happened to me today, and causing more grief.

But kicking or jumping anything is out of the question. Not until I get myself another pair of shoes.

GET *BABY FEVER BRIDE*
AT YOUR FAVORITE RETAILER!

Printed in Great Britain
by Amazon

61240567R00181